Ms. DENALI

NOT YOUR TYPICAL TEACHER

C. M. CONNEY

Published by
Ace Lyon Books
July
2018

Published by
Ace Lyon Books
Acelyonbooks.com
First Edition
Cover Design by S. M. Savoy
C. M. Conney Ms. Denali
ISBN 978-1-947122-12-3
ISBN: eBook 978-1-947122-14-7
ISBN: 978-1-947122-33-8

Books by C. M. Conney

The Real Deal

Take the Shot

Moon Caught

The Enemy at Home

CONTENTS

Ms. DENALI

NOT YOUR TYPICAL TEACHER

ONE

No One is Perfect

Dim light from the hallway filtered into Denali's bedroom from the opening door.

"Iggy?" she called as she sat, pulling the blue comforter to her chest.

"Nali, I had a bad dream," Iggy answered in a soft, scared voice.

Denali turned on the bedside lamp and patted the bed beside her. The little girl climbed on, dragging a frayed pink blanket embroidered with a white rabbit.

"Want to tell me about it?" Denali tucked her sister close to her side and smoothed the unruly curls of tight, black hair.

Anxious, dark-brown eyes met bright blue ones. The two sisters looked nothing alike.

"Can I stay with you?"

"Sure." Denali glanced at the bedside clock. "Want

me to wake you when I go to the gym?"

Iggy nodded, sticking her thumb in her mouth and laying her blanket against her cheek. Denali rubbed her sister's back until she fell asleep, then settled Iggy beside her in the twin-size bed. Another empty bed laid across the room from her. She'd shared this room with her sister Meteora since childhood. Now a doctor at Washington General, Meteora no longer lived at home.

Denali hadn't stayed in this room in years except for brief visits over the summer. At twelve she'd gone away to college in Boston, living with her oldest brother, Tianzi, and his wife, Clare. Meteora had attended Boston University while Denali attended MIT.

At sixteen, Denali had moved into a small apartment within easy biking distance of the two campuses with her sister and two other girls.

When she'd received her second doctorate at eighteen, her parents had bought her a houseboat where she lived alone while working and taking classes on both campuses.

Denali shifted in the small bed, wondering why she didn't take over one of the bigger upstairs rooms. *It wasn't worth the bother*, she reminded herself. She'd only be here until spring.

Her sister Olympia had asked her to teach for one school year at her private school. Denali was sure her mother was behind that request, wanting Denali home to judge her social growth herself. Denali was aware her entire family thought she was too isolated. Her father called her weekly, asking anxiously about her social life, of which she had none.

"They don't understand," Denali whispered to the sleeping five-year-old.

Unlike the rest of her siblings, who enjoyed the hustle and bustle of a large household, Denali favored the peace and quiet of her home at sea. While she loved her family, she preferred to socialize with them one-on-one or in small groups.

And she missed her friends at school and even her coworkers, some of whom, despite their brilliance, couldn't seem to grasp the concept of secret project and drove her nuts with their pestering to be included in her work.

Reminded, she promised herself to send a note to Jerome, explaining her code wasn't ready to be seen yet, but as soon as she and Mary worked out the kinks, he'd be the first person she asked to test it. Hopefully, that would satisfy him and he'd stop bugging poor Mary.

Her door creaked open again, and her father peeked in. "Want me to take her?" Her father, Gui, asked in a thick Chinese accent that did nothing to hide his concern.

"No, let her stay. I told her she can come to the gym with me. She said she had a bad dream."

Gui entered the room and kissed Denali's forehead before sitting on the edge of the bed. "Your mom and I are a bit worried. She won't tell either of us about the dreams. Olympia says we shouldn't fret, but you know your mother."

Denali winced. She did indeed. Her mother found it a personal affront if her children didn't come to her immediately to air their hopes and fears. A firm believer in 'talk' therapy, Hester Rubinstein-Wong found it hard to accept that all her children didn't care to speak of their problems and worries.

"Olympia would know. Iggy probably doesn't have the words to express her dreams anyway, she's only five." Denali kissed the small girl's forehead. One of the nicer things about living home was getting to know her younger siblings better.

"I'm so glad you decided to work with Olympia. Your mother worries you isolate yourself too much. Not just from your family, but everyone." Gui took her hand. "Friendships and lovers are what make this world wonderful. Your mom and I don't want you to miss out."

Denali blushed and stared down at their clasped hands. "I'm busy, Da. And I have friends."

"Take more time to play. Visit with family and travel. See the world and form your own opinions." Gui hesitated. "Don't let your mother's and my work keep you from friendships with all kinds of people."

"It doesn't, Da. Just most people are so… stupid."

Gui laughed and ran a gnarled hand over her hair. "You, my beautiful child, have a mind anyone would envy, but you limit yourself if you lock yourself away."

Denali snorted. "I'm hardly locked away."

Gui sighed. "The company of children is good and necessary for growth, but it can't replace the companionship of a mate."

"Da, I'm twenty, not fifty…."

"I worry that you're too— exacting in your standards. No one is perfect."

"I haven't met anyone yet who interests me that way. The boys I meet are, well, boys. Some are brilliant, but generally the smart ones get out of breath climbing stairs. I want a real person."

Gui winced. "I understand what you're saying, but sometimes— "

"No, Da, I'm not going to settle. And yes, you and Mom influence me. But what's wrong with waiting for a smart, kind, strong man? One who can provide for a family both emotionally and financially?"

Gui nodded and rose. He kissed both girls and paused at the door. "You're right. I want that for you too." He switched to Mandarin. "Be happy, my beautiful mountain."

"Good night, beloved father," Denali replied in the same language.

*　　*　　*

At five-thirty she woke Iggy and dressed in a sweatsuit. She took a moment to braid her long auburn hair and pull Iggy's thick curls into a tight ponytail.

The house remained quiet above them. The bedroom above hers used to be Olympia's room. Now Iggy occupied it. Their parents shared a suite of rooms on the third floor, and woe betide any child who woke them early. That's why Denali preferred this first-floor room even though it had no private bathroom and only a small closet.

The kitchen around the corner more than made up for the lack of storage space. With its large door opening onto the stone patio it provided a quiet entrance and exit. Both she and Meteora had loved to run, going out together in the middle of the night to run downtown without fear of being seen, jumping and climbing over obstacles in their path, cutting straight across the landscape.

"Hungry?" she asked her sister, gesturing to the bowl of fruit on the counter.

Without waiting for the reply, she handed Iggy a banana and took one for herself. Wilma Collins, the housekeeper, would have breakfast on the table by six-thirty. Breakfast was served until nine a.m. Lunch from twelve to two, and dinner always at seven.

Mrs. Collins had been with the family Denali's entire life and kept everyone's favorite snacks on hand. Treated as a beloved aunt, she was a member of the family.

Gui thought they should hire a younger helper, but Hester didn't want to insult Wilma. Hester compromised by hiring another full-time maid, one who could also do shopping, errands, kitchen chores and oversee the part-time staff and left Wilma in charge of her. Caring for the nine people who lived in the house was no small job.

And cleaning it was an impossible task, Denali thought in amusement as she nudged aside a wire contraption she was certain Simon had made to the side of the wide steps beside the door that led downstairs to the family's gym.

Built deep into the ground, the exterior resembled a garage with fake doors and long narrow windows around the roof line. Denali hesitated beside the locked door leading to the family's indoor firing range, but with Iggy along it wasn't a good idea. Besides, it was too early. Despite the soundproofing, gunfire would be sure to wake and annoy her parents. She could practice later when she got home from school.

She opened the door leading to the four thousand square feet of space containing state-of-the-art gym equipment. Well-worn oak steps led down into the large room. Nets dangled from the thirty-five-foot ceiling, covering a third of the room ten feet from the floor. Hester had just added a trapeze bar for Iaia and Simon. Denali hadn't tried it yet, but it looked fun.

Beneath the nets, a boxing ring sat in the corner beside a wooden hot tub. Mirrors lined the end wall with a ballet bar bolted to it before a scuffed wooden floor. Right in the center of the room, a set of parallel bars sat beside uneven bars. Blue mats covered the entire floor. Two balance beams, one six inches from the ground, the other regulation height, stood to the left of the door. Beside them, a four-foot swath of rings at varying heights dangled from the ceiling, going the entire length of the room.

Denali loved the rings, racing the length of the room and back was one of her favorite exercises.

To the right of the door, standard exercise equipment sat in even rows, everything from treadmills to rowing machines. A row of lockers bordered the entrance to the room, which smelled faintly of chlorine. An indoor, Olympic-sized swimming pool was separated from the gym by another set of wide stairs. Two full bathrooms and a steam room flanked those stairs.

"Show me what you're learning, Iggy."

The little girl ran to a locker and slipped on ballet shoes. Denali grabbed an old pair from her locker and tied them on.

"First, we stretch." Iggy began doing stretches.

Denali copied her. A smile lit her face as she remembered doing this same thing with her oldest sister, Olympia. Back then, she'd thought Olympia the most beautiful graceful girl and strove to emulate her.

She still thought her sister was beautiful. Beautiful and brilliant although less graceful than she had been. Her sister was three months pregnant and had given up most of the sports that had earned her the nickname Olympia. Thirty-nine and pregnant for the first time, she was taking it easy.

Iggy stared with wide, eager eyes as Denali showed her rolls on the mat.

"Tuck your chin and commit to the roll. It's important to have total control of your body."

"Weak body — weak mind," Iggy said.

Her mother's words said in Iggy's childish voice cracked Denali up.

"Exactly. To become a homo superior requires discipline." Denali tapped Iggy's forehead. "What's up here will guide your actions, maintain clear thought for right action."

"Isn't she a little young for that lecture?" her brother Zane asked.

"Zane!" Iggy ran to him and grabbed his legs.

He grinned and swung her into his arms.

"When did you get home?" Denali asked as she kissed his cheek.

Zane and her brother Lee were her closest age siblings. The three had been inseparable until she'd gone to live with her brother Tianzi. Angry she'd left him behind; Zane hadn't spoken to her for a year. He'd gotten over it, but they were never as close as they once were.

"Yesterday while you were out running. I went straight to bed, figured I find you here bright and early."

"Want to run with me later?" Denali asked eagerly. He and Lee were free runners too, and it was always more fun to run with others. Meteora was always too busy, and Denali suspected she couldn't keep up anymore.

"Sure," Zane said as Iggy asked, "Can I come?"

"Sorry, squirt, big kids only. Your little legs can't keep up with us yet." Zane squatted beside her.

Tears filled Iggy's eyes. "I'll never have a little brother. I'll always be the baby."

"That's not true. You won't have a baby brother, but you'll have a baby niece or nephew, and that's just as good." Zane scooped Iggy into his arms and hugged her.

"You'll have lots and lots of nieces and nephews," Denali said, resting her hand against Iggy's back.

"But they won't live here with me. No one will share my room or be my best friend." Crying now, she hid her face against Zane's shoulder. Denali exchanged dismayed glances with her brother.

"Iggy, you'll always have us. We're your family forever. And you have Bee like I have Lee. She's only two years older," Denali said.

"Bee likes Sensei better," Iggy said sulkily.

Denali took Iggy from Zane and placed her on the ground. She squatted before her and took her chin in her hand. "How we live and who we love makes us who we are. I want you to think about two questions that we'll talk about later. First, why do you think Bee prefers Sensei's company? and second, is it worth changing your behavior so she'll prefer yours?"

Zane gave Denali an exasperated glance and picked Iggy up again. "Each of us had to learn to share our brothers and sisters attention. I remember when I started school and the other kids made fun of me, saying they weren't family because we look nothing alike. I used to love that I looked like Dad. It'll be harder for you because you don't resemble either of our parents, but it makes no difference. You're as much my sister as Denali or Anya or Bee. Skin color or age has nothing to do with it."

"I want to go to school with Lympia and Nali."

Denali ruffled Iggy's hair. "Next year, when you turn six, but I won't be teaching then, I'm going back to school in the fall."

"Da says you're going to go to school forever."

Denali and Zane laughed.

"He's probably right. He is about most things. Da is a very smart man," Denali said.

"He says I'm very smart and it doesn't matter if the other kids don't like it."

Denali sighed and frowned. "Yeah, it sucks when they make fun of you for being smart, mostly because you realize how stupid they are for making fun of achievements to be proud of. Homo sapiens will try to make themselves feel better by making someone else feel bad. It doesn't work, but they keep trying."

Zane snorted. "While homo superiors think they're better than everyone else."

"Not 'everyone' just most people." Denali stuck her tongue out at her brother and did a backflip away, making Iggy laugh. "Bet I can still kick your as—" she glanced at Iggy and grimaced while Zane

11

laugh, and emphatically said, "butt!"

Zane chuckled and leaped forward. He kicked at her chest with his left foot while swinging a fist at her face.

She batted his foot aside with one hand, grabbed his fist, and yanked.

"So predictable, always with the fake punch," she said, then grunted in surprise as Zane rolled by using the momentum of her tug to summersault past her, kicking her in the back of the knees and knocking her to the floor.

Iggy clapped her hands. "Show me, Zane."

"When I'm done with him," Denali said as she leaped to her feet.

The two sparred for thirty minutes, then showed Iggy the simpler moves.

"Hands up, palms out," Zane corrected, adjusting Iggy's stance. "Right, now don't forget to watch the entire person, not just their hands. A little thing like you needs to be fast and avoid my grab. If I catch you, you're in trouble because I'm so much stronger."

"Where should you run?" Denali asked.

Iggy hesitated, glancing around the room.

"Nope, never hesitate or show us where you plan to go, just go. You can always change your mind mid-flight. Staying to fight a bigger assailant can be too dangerous. Do the smart thing."

"The ring," Iggy said with an air of triumph. "You're too big to fit under it."

"Very good."

"Where else?" Zane asked.

Iggy slapped his reaching hand away and raced to the obstacle course in the far corner, shrieking with laughter.

TWO

Olympus

Denali regretfully left the family in the gym and headed out to Olympus. Mornings at home were her favorite time of day, laughing and competing with her siblings and parents. Gui taught all his children self-defense. Hester encouraged it, her theory being that homo superiors instinctively sought the best possible means of protection and kept themselves physically fit.

Her mother's life's work was proving that man was undergoing an evolutionary change, one that could be hurried with modern science. She postulated that homo sapiens would be replaced by homo superior or the race would become extinct. When cornered to defend her thesis, she would reply, "Man is too populous to support large colonies of 'feral' humans. We must evolve to a more advanced, civilized species or be destroyed."

Hester's work was both ridiculed and admired, but results were hard to argue with. All of her adult children, except one, were highly-educated leaders in their fields. And she would boast she'd taught them to be that way.

That was true, Denali mused as she drove down the winding drive leading to the school where she worked. Born addicted to crack and weighing less than five pounds, Denali had been given up for adoption by her birth mother. No father was listed on her birth certificate, and the mother's name had proven to be fake as well. The nuns at Saint Anne's had christened her Delilah. Her father had named her Na Abira Leeba Rubinstein-Wong.

Hester had chosen her as she had all her children, the least likely adoption candidate, and Denali thanked God every day that she had. By the age of four, her siblings had begun calling her Denali, and the name had stuck. As tough to cross as a mountain, a bit wild, and as isolated as her namesake, she liked to think she'd mellowed and was easier to get along with now.

Anya used to tease her mercilessly about her red hair matching her fiery temper. Her hair had mellowed too, becoming darker as she aged. Now a rich auburn, she wore it in a neat bun instead of her usual sloppy ponytail.

Olympia demanded a neat, tidy appearance for

her teachers. She'd dragged Denali through six stores, picking out clothing she deemed appropriate for work.

"No jeans, sweatshirts, or sneakers," Denali murmured as she parked in the private lot of the school. No one heard her mumbled complaints as she exited the car and straightened her black pencil skirt. She nodded to the security guard monitoring the lot and waved at his partner sitting in the small booth beside the entrance.

Black town cars dropped off students in front of the school. Livered men escorted the children to the door. Dressed alike in blue pants, white shirts and blue sweaters, the students called greetings to each other or waved to their drivers.

Two hundred and twenty-six children, ages six to twelve, attended this elite, private school. Invitation only, it took more than money to be accepted. About thirty percent of the student body paid no tuition. Applicants to the school had to pass a number of tests, not of what they knew but of what they had the potential to learn. Olympia had run this school for twelve years with a success rate of ninety-six percent of students taking above age level courses before leaving the school. With a quarter of her students chosen from low income families with troubled records, it was a staggering success rate. Many of her students skipped grades. All of her students were sought after by other schools.

The high level of scholastic accomplishment was

matched by their physical fitness and a fair number of her students went on to be star athletes in high-school. Hester was thrilled with her oldest daughter. Olympia proved daily success could be taught.

Olympia joined her on the sidewalk, putting an arm around her shoulders. Still tall and graceful, the baby was only a slight thickening of her waist.

"Admiring the building?"

"Yeah," Denali said truthfully.

She'd been eyeing the cornices in the corners. Decorative, white, brick trim surrounded the windows and edges of the two-story, red brick building. The white bricks stuck out about three inches, offering more than enough of a handhold for an experienced climber. The trick was the overhang, but Denali thought she could swing up over the top of the cornice to gain the roof. She swung the bag with her gym clothes onto her other arm and guiltily cleared her throat. Her sister would kill her if she caught her climbing the building.

Olympia eyed her suspiciously.

Denali glanced away, avoiding her gaze.

"Don't fall off the roof," Olympia said, sighing heavily as she held the door for her sister. Both women nodded greetings to the two security guards on the portico.

Denali laughed and kissed her sister's cheek. "You know me so well."

Her laughing, blue-eyed gaze followed her sister into the main office beside the door. Thick, dark-brown hair caught up in a neat twist revealed Olympia's elegant neck and classic Indian profile.

"See ya at dinner," Denali called after her.

Olympia held up a hand in acknowledgment but didn't turn back.

The thing Denali missed the most when she wasn't home was family dinners. With seven sisters and eight brothers, plus their spouses and friends, dinner was always lively and interesting. She tried to get home once a month for dinner to join the family in the candle lighting ceremony her father led to honor their ancestors.

When she was younger, she'd thought it a pointless gesture because her ancestors had never acknowledged her or even knew she existed, but she'd come to appreciate the tradition for the bonding exercise it was. Someday, when she had children of her own, they'd light a candle at her house, the small flame a symbol of her large family.

Tracy Aims tugging her arm drew her from her introspection. The ten-year-old girl greeted her with a grin.

"Ms. Denali, can I take your class next term? Marcy says we won't be allowed, but Tommy says his dad said we could." Big, blue eyes gazed hopefully at Denali.

"Sorry, sweetie, but I'll be returning to school after this term. You'll have a new teacher." Denali glanced at the hand on her arm.

"Aww." Tracy removed her hand and clasped

them together, bowing slightly as a blush climbed her cheeks. "Excuse me, Miss."

Denali nodded acceptance of the apology. "I'm sure your new teacher will be just as good."

"Maybe," Tracy said, but she didn't sound convinced. "Is it true you're working here to pay off a debt?"

Denali stopped walking and faced Tracy. "I'm working here as a favor to my sister. Mr. Rand was a good teacher and sorely missed. Did Tommy tell you I had to work here?"

Tracy stared at her feet, the blush on her cheeks deepening. She took a deep breath and met Denali's eyes. "He said, his father said, that you had to work for your family to pay back the money they spent for keeping you."

"Well, that's true in a way. You know I come from a big family, right?"

She waited for the girl to nod before continuing. "In our family, when we decide to go to college, we can pay for it ourselves or join the family pact. If we join the pact, we promise to pay ten percent of what we make in the future into the family coffers. That money is used for education and medical costs. Any of us can use that money for that purpose. If you need money for something else, you can submit a request and all pact members vote."

Denali continued walking to her classroom. Tracy followed.

"I joined the pact when I was twelve. I've begun

adding money to it but nowhere near the amount I took from it. My education cost a lot of money."

"What happens if you don't pay it back?"

"Then I become a lesser person because I'll have broken my word."

"But… what if you can't afford to pay it?"

"Well, I would have options. I could ask my family to help me, or I could take out a note. Do you know what that is?"

"Like a credit card?"

"Yep, basically I'd keep track of what I owed and pay it a later date. Or, if I was really hard up for money, I could ask to be excused for a time. But that would be embarrassing. We take self-responsibility very seriously in my family. I'd rather wear thrift store clothing and eat rice then owe money."

"Miss…." Tracy said hesitantly, lowering her voice. "My mom works really hard but can't afford to send me to college. Tommy says if I take a government loan I'll be poor forever."

Denali pushed open the door to her classroom. "First, if you continue to do well in your classes, I'm sure you'll get a scholarship. Second, taking a loan isn't a bad thing if you have a plan for paying it back. Just like anything else you do — observe — plan — act. And third, money isn't a good enough reason to do a job you hate. Being poor isn't a bad thing, being financially irresponsible is."

When Denali stepped through the doorway of her classroom the students rose, placed their hands together and bowed slightly. They remained standing until she approached her desk and waved for them to resume their seats.

"Let's talk about money today and how that affects self. Having more money makes no difference at all to happiness. Money can't buy self-respect, the only true measure of a man. True happiness can only be gained by true action. A man playing guitar on the sidewalk for change because he likes too will be happier than the man who has an office job because he thinks he has too."

Denali tapped on her keyboard a moment and showed two pictures in a split screen on the large monitor behind her. The picture on the left showed a woman smiling brightly, clutching a bouquet of flowers in obvious enjoyment. A black Mercedes driven by a man with a frown on his face filled the screen to the right.

"Which person appears happier?" she pointed to Tommy.

"The lady with the flowers."

"You seem upset she seems happier than the man with the expensive car."

"It's just a picture, I bet the guy with the car is really happier."

"Why?"

"Because it's so cool."

"What makes it cool?"

"Look at it," Tommy said, and the class laughed. "I bet it goes super-fast."

"Can we agree you think the car looks good and goes fast and if you had one that would make you happy?"

Tommy grinned. "Yes."

"That car looks expensive, so for you to be happy, you need enough money to buy it, but, and this is the important part, Tommy, lots of people don't care about cars, no matter how pretty or fast. The lady in the picture probably feels for flowers what you do for cars. Having them makes her happy. Flowers can be gotten very cheaply, so for her to be happy it wouldn't cost much at all."

"Yeah, but the more money you have, the more you can buy."

Denali tapped her keyboard, and a picture of a red Lamborghini replaced the others.

"Now, that's an awesome car! I want one of those, and you can't get one without a lot of money," Tommy said enthusiastically.

"But why do you need it? If the first car made you happy, how will this car make you happier?"

Tommy frowned, then smiled. "It's faster."

"Okay." She tapped the keyboard, and another picture appeared. "This Maserati is as fast. Are you happy with one or would owning both make you happier?"

"Both," he said immediately.

Denali gazed over her interested students. "I want you all to think about this for a few days, then write me a report on what is really making Tommy happy about the car." She turned to Tommy. "If both cars look cool and go the same speed, and you can only drive one at a time, why would two make you happier? No, don't answer now, think about it. Consider that people who own no car at all are perfectly happy. Think about the rich people you know who aren't happy and why that might be so."

Denali erased the pictures and replaced them with a photo of a bank. "Let's talk about physical money. What it is and what it does."

For three hours, she spoke to the children about money, using examples from history and literature. She had them doing math problems and asked them each to find something others traded with besides the American dollar.

"Five points to everyone who has a unique answer tomorrow." She glanced at her watch. "Okay, head to the cafeteria, and good job today, guys."

Her class rose and bowed before filing from the room, talking quietly together. She headed to the teachers' lounge. Mr. Fredrick sniffed and rose, throwing his garbage in a can beside the door. Without a word, he left the room. Mr. Mitchel, another teacher, snickered.

"Sit, don't mind him. He's jealous your students are outperforming his. I think he realizes he won't pass his peer review."

"He's a good teacher," Denali said as she grabbed a yogurt from the small refrigerator. "If he could just learn to treat them all the same…" Denali trailed off.

"He is a good teacher," Mr. Mitchel agreed. "The hell of it is, is I agree with him. But at this age, it doesn't really matter. When the boys mature and are bigger and stronger, it will make a difference, but I think Olympia is right to let them compete together now."

"I can say from experience that keeping up with my brothers kept me in shape. You try harder when others seem to accomplish tasks easier. Different ages and skill levels in the same team really promote teamwork."

Mr. Mitchel rose and placed his lunch bag back into the refrigerator. "I love this school. My hope is more like it develop. These kids are going to do amazing things."

Denali nodded thoughtfully. Olympia had devised an entirely new way of teaching. The classes held children of all ages. Two teachers taught them, sometimes trading children if they thought the child would do better in a different class. They used no school books; instead, using tablets, which the teacher could access anytime.

Occasionally, a student would video-chat with her over an assignment after school hours, and a few times she'd hosted lively discussions online after hours. These kids were bright and eager to learn. It was a pleasure teaching them.

As a teacher, Denali was free to teach them any way she wished. She taught two, three- and half-hour classes a day, using nothing in a traditional format and her students excelled.

Her next class of fifteen students was six and seven-year-olds. She met them in the school's gymnasium, an almost identical replica of the gym at her home. For three hours she played games with them. Math and spelling games designed to teach without seeming to. As a child, she'd played these games with her siblings. By the age of four, she'd learned to add any number instantly by playing number tag. These kids were learning fractions the same way.

Denali blew her whistle and waved. "Samantha, you're out. One-fourth and one-fourth is one-half, not one-eighth. James, you get the ball. Give me two and one-third." She flipped the timer to one minute.

James grinned and threw the ball at Cindy who wore a number two pinned to her shirt. Denali laughed as the girl ducked and the ball hit the girl wearing the number five-eighths. Learning to think fast under pressure and plan your moves in advance was a big part of her curriculum.

Denali glanced at her watch and blew her whistle. "Take a good look around. Five points to whoever remembers who wore what number tomorrow."

Denali grabbed her gym bag from under her desk and headed to the teachers' lounge again. Twelve teachers sat around the oblong conference table with Olympia. Denali nodded in greeting but headed into the nearby restroom to change.

When she emerged in her sweatsuit, the grouped

teachers were arguing over the latest test results.

Olympia held her hand up, and they quieted. "Every year we hit this same hump. Power through it. After Christmas, the children will be more focused. Continue with our methods. Yes, we might test lower, but so what. This isn't about us, but them. We teach them how to think for themselves; we don't make them memorize by rote."

The thick wooden door closed behind Denali, cutting off her sister's words. Sometimes, she looked at this school and was saddened. It was just a drop in the bucket of the sea of young people being taught badly. Through no fault of their own teachers were overwhelmed with children, unable to supply the kind of one-on-one teaching a smaller school could. Forced by bureaucrats to meet outdated guidelines, everyone suffered.

Denali shrugged and wriggled her shoulders, throwing back her head to breathe deeply of the crisp December air. Soon it would be too cold to climb, frozen fingers and cold metal would make high climbs too dangerous, but not today. Today she'd run for a while and climb the school when the children had left for the day. It wouldn't do to give any of them ideas.

She ran full speed down the steep, shale-covered bank that bordered the freeway. About a quarter of a mile away, a culvert passed under the highway. Half a mile further on, a chain-link fence separated the road from the back of a small industrial park. With its many stairs and plantings, it was a great place to run and jump.

Her Ford Explorer sat alone in the parking lot when she returned. She waved to the night guard and ran to the back-left corner of the building and began climbing up the decorative bricks. The cornice made a perfect handhold, and she easily swung herself onto the roof.

Sunset streaked the sky in shades of orange and red as she sat with her feet dangling, enjoying the view and privacy. Movement in the woods caught her eye, and she made a mental note to tell the guard. Sometimes kids from the nearby neighborhood tried to sneak onto campus to use the playground. Olympia allowed them on campus on weekends but never after dark.

Denali stayed on the roof until true night fell and security lights lit the school and parking lot. After one last glance over the tranquil school grounds, she lowered herself from the roof, grabbing the cornice and shimmying to the wall where she used the trim like a ladder to reach the ground.

THREE

Only One Option Remained

A large shopping bag clutched in her hands, Denali glanced at her gym bag and shrugged, she could get it after school.

"Need a hand?" the security guard called as he waved a limousine through the gate.

"Nope, I got this, thanks." Denali jerked her chin in greeting, not being able to wave with her hands full.

"Snow today, no climbing for you."

Denali laughed. "I won't climb again until spring, too dangerous in the cold. I'm not crazy, you know."

The guard chuckled and slapped his gloved hands together. "You better get along inside. You'll freeze in no time without a coat."

Already shivering, Denali nodded and hurried

her step. Cold February air nipped her nose and cheeks, reddening her gloveless fingers. She should've grabbed her coat, but the school was just yards away.

* * *

Denali didn't realize anything was wrong until the alarm shrilled, cutting off abruptly. A moment later a rough, thickly accent voice barked for attention over the intercom.

"Quiet," Denali snapped, waving her hand as her students exclaimed.

Instant silence reigned in her room. She snatched her cell phone from her desk, hit record, and dialed nine-one-one.

In the background of the man speaking over the intercom two men spoke in Urdu, likely assuming nobody there could understand them. That was a false assumption. Denali spoke six middle eastern languages fluently.

"Tracy, take my phone and stay on the line," Denali said.

"Attention," A man said in clear but accented English.

Denali let his words wash over her, concentrating on the background noise. Her heart began to pound hard. Olympia would be in the office and understand them too.

"My name is Mahir Alfarsi, and I've taken control of this school in the name of Al-Jadr. Cooperate, and you won't be hurt. Open your doors. My men will escort your students to the gymnasium to better keep an eye on them. You'll be released unharmed when your media plays our manifesto unedited. We demand the release of our families and brethren held unlawfully by the United States."

Denali ran across her classroom, crouched and peered into the hallway. Five men dressed in black bulletproof vests and what she thought were armored pants carried M-16s. Black facemasks pushed up on their heads revealed their middle-eastern faces. All had long beards with headsets perched on their heads and radios Velcroed to their shoulders. Each carried a big, black duffle bag.

Across from her, Mr. Fredrick opened his door and stepped into the hallway.

"Get back in your room," one of the men barked in accented English and lifted his rifle.

Mr. Fredrick held up his hands and retreated, leaving his door open.

Denali eased her door shut. The doors to the classrooms opened in. Set back about a foot and half, the men wouldn't be able to tell until they approached which doors were open. She wasn't going to make it easy for them.

"Tommy, Brian, move my desk to the right of the doorway," she said as she ran to her desk, flung open the bottom drawer and began rifling the contents.

"Eden, bring the flag and place it in the left corner, the rest of you, carry the first two tables and lay them on their side to the left of the doorway."

While she spoke, she grabbed the wooden pointer she used on the map hanging on the back wall. The mirrored compact she took from her bottom drawer had been confiscated from a student two days ago. She broke the mirrored piece off, discarded the powder, and taped it to the end of the pole by the jagged edge.

Mahir Alfarsi continued speaking over the intercom, "Stay away from the windows. My men will fire on anyone in sight of the windows."

Denali was already peering through hers. Only ten feet from the ground, the windows could provide an escape. And they needed to escape. The men speaking in Urdu had quieted, but what she'd heard had chilled her to the bone. They had no intention of letting anyone leave peacefully. Explosives were being placed around the school as Mahir Alfarsi spoke on the intercom.

Another man dressed identically to the first five stood outside her window holding a rifle, scanning the side of the building. Behind him, the chain-link fence surrounding the ball field glittered in the sunlight. Her eyes lit on the low concrete building that housed the water pumps for the school. A distant gunshot made the kids in the room scream.

"Quiet," Denali said. "Keep a cool head to make good decisions. I want all of you to grab your coats and put them on. If you have hats and gloves put them on too, then get behind the tables in the corner and keep your heads down."

Sirens sounded in the distance, barely heard over the opening lockers and chatter as the kids donned their winter wear. The man outside keyed his radio on with his chin, then raised his rifle and fired at an upper window. The sound of breaking glass was lost in the screams of the children.

"We're okay; don't panic. Sit with your backs against the wall as tight as you can. Keep the tables in front of you."

She pushed the tables as close as she could to the children. Huddled with the others, Tracy clutched Denali's phone to her cheek. Tears streamed down her face, but her voice was calm as she described what was happening in a low voice. She kept one arm around the girl beside her who hid her face in Tracy's shoulder, her long brown hair hiding her expression.

Denali's gaze flitted across the children. All appeared terrified although only a few cried and those cried quietly. She ran back to the door and opened it, kneeling and sliding the mirror out, using it to examine the hallway. An armed man stood in the doorway of a classroom one door down. He was clean shaven with wavy brown hair and didn't resemble the original men she'd seen. He stepped back and gestured with his rifle at the children who emerged with their hands raised. Another armed man followed the children from the room. Denali withdrew the mirror and closed the door again. Ms. Holmes glanced at her door as she passed. Denali's lips tightened at the purpling bruise across her face.

'They have the keys,' Ms. Holmes mouthed.

Denali nodded she understood and opened her door. If they had the keys, locking them out and waiting for help wasn't an option. Only one option remained. She'd have to stop them. A cold sweat sprang up on her brow, and her hands began to shake. She examined the children huddled behind the tables, and her shaking stilled. These children depended on her.

Children passed her open door; most were quiet although a few sobbed. Only one, armed man followed them. He carried his rifle in both hands at chest height. A black beard covered a weathered face. Not much of his expression was visible. From what Denali saw, he looked bored or indifferent as if herding children into a bomb filled room happened every day. A black stocking cap covered his head on which a headset sat. A radio, similar to police radios, the type you could activate with your chin, sat on his shoulder. As soon as his black booted feet passed the doorway, she knelt and eased the mirror into the hallway again. The original guard spoke on his radio as he crossed the hall.

In a cultured English accent, he politely asked the teacher next door to gather the children and exit the room. The kind way he spoke filled Denali with horror. He'd slit your throat and smile.

Denali withdrew the mirror and peeked from the window again. Another man had joined the first. While she watched, they spoke a moment before the second man resumed his rounds.

"Tracy, tell them a man carrying an M-16 and grenades is on the left side of the building. Another man is patrolling, armed the same way. Both have knives on their right thighs, sidearms on their lefts, and are carrying small packs. So far, I've counted eight additional men inside, not all middle-eastern. They have the keys to the classrooms."

A bright flare of light made her jerk back as a muffled explosion rattled the glass. The man outside the window smiled and turned towards the parking lot.

Denali took the opportunity to stick her head further up and examine the far corner of the building.

"Tracy, tell them they have rocket launchers and are planting explosives inside the building."

Her words caused the children to exclaim in fear. She hurried to the corner and squatted before them. "This is scary; it's okay to be afraid. These men are lying. Don't trust them. Take any opportunity that presents itself to escape."

While she spoke, she grabbed the teacher's tablet from her desk and typed a message to all teachers, telling them that explosives were being planted. She hesitated before adding, 'I overheard them say the deaths of the capitalist's spawn will bring many to our cause. They plan on killing all the children.

The intercom crackled to life again. "I regret the necessity, but examples must be made.

Denali straightened. The vicious anticipation in his tone put the lie to his words. Whatever he planned to do, he looked forward to it.

Women screamed. A gunshot echoed through the hallway magnified by the intercom.

"Please," Mrs. Ritchie, one of the secretaries, begged. "Please, she's pregnant. There's no need."

A cold chill traveled Denali.

"Our demands must be met. We will *not* negotiate or tolerate a police presence on this property. They were warned and ignored our warnings. Kneel."

"No," Olympia said.

The calm anger in her sister's voice brought tears to Denali's eyes.

"Kneel like the dog you are."

The sound of a scuffle broke out, hard to understand over the hysterical yelling and crying of the office staff. One gunshot sounded followed by a burst from an automatic weapon.

"No!" Mrs. Ritchie screamed. "Oh, dear God, why? She was pregnant, you piece of filth." The slap of flesh-on-flesh ended suddenly as the intercom cut off.

The cold chill became a wild tremble. "Please," Denali whispered, begging God to make this not true. The heartbroken scream of Olympia from next door caused her tears to fall. Her brother Sensei called for his sister again.

"Stay there!" Denali yelled.

The children in her room had begun crying.

Denali angrily dashed the tears from her face.

Tracy sobbed on the phone, her voice laced with hysteria. "They killed Mrs. Olympia. They killed her."

Denali pushed through the children and hugged Tracy, then straightened and reached down to each of the children, giving them quick hugs. "Stay here. We're going to get through this."

On her feet once more, she repositioned the tables as closely as she could to the children. Her gaze scanned the room. The room contained nothing she could use as a weapon. She kicked off her heels, opened the top desk drawer and grabbed a pen.

Pen clutched in her sweaty palm, she placed her mirrored stick on the edge of the desk, angled so she could see if someone approached the doorway, then climbed up on the desk and pressed her back against the wall.

She hoped the flag would draw the man's eye as he entered, turning him away from the children who hid behind the tables. She didn't know how long it would take to plant the explosives. Every second that passed put her students in greater danger.

The children sat with their backs pressed against the wall, hugging their knees. The gunman would have to enter and close the door to shoot them. Through the glass of the open door, their wide, terrified eyes stared at her from their tear-stained faces. The sight hardened her resolve.

"Keep your heads down and remain quiet no matter what," she murmured as another group of children passed her open door. Either her room or Mr. Fredrick's would be next. Tense, she prepared to spring.

FOUR

She Has a Gun Now

The distant sound of gunfire filtered to her through the closed windows. Every sense hyper-alert, the booted feet approaching her door sounded preternaturally loud. The Englishman entered, speaking as he came.

"Gather your students and — " His words cut off in a choking gasp as Denali kicked out as hard as she could with her right foot, sending his head into the doorjamb.

He moaned and lifted his rifle while shaking his head. Denali was already in motion, stabbing her pen at the man's neck as she grabbed for the knife on his hip.

"Fuck," the man gasped as he grabbed the pen protruding from his neck and reached for her. Hate-filled brown eyes stared into hers from inches away.

Rough hands yanked at her hair, pulling her head back. The soft click of the releasing snap holding the knife in its sheath energized her. She let herself fall on the man, trapping his gun between their bodies as her hand came up clutching the knife.

Eyes wide with fear, the man dropped his gun and reached for her hand. Before he could stop her, she'd stabbed upward under his chin. Hot blood spurted across her face, soaking the light-blue silk shirt she wore.

The man's suddenly dead weight pushed her back. She grabbed him by the arms and hopped back onto her desk in one fluid motion. With a grunt of effort, she yanked him across the desk and let his body hit the floor.

To her surprise, his death didn't upset her. She felt nothing except savage satisfaction that he was dead and she still alive. Thoughts of her sister threatened to overwhelm her, so she pushed them from her mind.

"Quiet," she said as her students exclaimed. Their voices dizzied her. She went from crystal clear awareness to dazed disbelief.

The quiet sound of Tracy whispering on the phone distracted her. The panicked horror in the girl's voice as she repeated herself adding to the nightmarish sensation of disbelief that this was happening.

"Ms. Denali killed him. She has a gun now," Tracy said.

The fear in Tracy's voice steadied her. For the children she could be calm. Working fast, she removed the bulletproof vest from the corpse and donned it, ignoring the blood that coated it. Sweat beaded on her brow, trickling across the side of her face. Any moment the other man would arrive. She placed the gun on the desk, taking a second to glance over the doorway.

Only a few drops of blood marred the glass window of the door. More speckled the desk, but most smeared the floor behind the desk where the dead body lay.

She used the mirror to examine the hallway. Satisfied she had a few minutes, she squatted beside the corpse and used the tail of the man's black, long-sleeved shirt to wipe her face.

The pack held a bottle of water, a grenade, two protein bars, a detonator, extra ammunition and a map of the school. The headset the man had worn was loose on her.

A grimace of distaste on her face, she yanked the knife from the man's chin and wiped it on his pants. She removed the holster and tightened it as much as she could around her hips, using the knife to poke a hole in the leather.

He carried no cell phone but did have a wallet. She opened one of the lockers, stuffed the detonator inside and thoughtfully hefted the wallet.

"Tommy, examine this wallet and tell Tracy anything you learn." Denali handed the twelve-year-old the brown leather wallet.

He licked his lips and took it. His wide-eyed stare trailed her, looking both impressed and horrified.

Denali returned to the doorway, knelt, and used the small mirror to examine the hall. She grabbed the M-16 from the desk and placed the carrying strap over her left shoulder. "We're going to go next door to Mrs. Pearson's class. Line up now like we do for field trips. When I say move, I want you to run next door."

She used the mirror to examine the hallway again while her students lined up behind her. A hand rose to her ear to press the headset closer as a sudden spate of Urdu broke the silence.

"Tracy, warn the operator they plan on firing on the lead cars in the blockade momentarily. Two men armed with missile launchers on the roof have a helicopter in their sights. It's okay, honey, you're doing great," she added as the girl sobbed, wishing she had time to comfort her.

"Move." She motioned them forward with one hand.

Tracy repeated her words in a tear-soaked voice.

As the kids left the schoolroom, Denali ran across the floor, sliding in her nylons and knelt in the alcove of the doorway of Mr. Fredrick's room across from her.

"Sensei," she called softly.

"Denali?" her brother sounded terrified.

She risked a glance into the room. Mr. Fredrick had his class standing with their backs to the wall separating this classroom from Mr. Martin's. Her gaze traveled over a science experiment set on the middle table.

"Get your coats on. Now!" She returned her attention to the hallway where the last of her students were disappearing into Mrs. Pearson's room.

Sensei ran to her and threw his arms around her neck.

"Did they really kill Olympia?" he sobbed, his warm tears running down her cheek. The distress in his voice brought tears to Denali's eyes. She hugged him tightly, breathing the scent of his hair, his small weight a comfort and source of fear. She needed to get him out of this building.

"I don't know, but we need to get out of here." She straightened and turned to Mr. Fredrick. "Send a message to the other teachers and tell them to get coats on the kids. Can you use a gun?"

"What the hell do you think you're doing? You're going to escalate this. You saw what they did when the police didn't listen. Do you want them to kill another teacher or your brother?"

Denali ignored him. "Sensei, take the pistol. It has a full clip. It's exactly like Lee's. Do you remember where the safety is?"

He nodded.

Mr. Fredrick reached for the gun she handed her brother.

"Are you crazy? He's nine years old!"

Denali slapped the reaching hand away and

glared. "He's more of a man than you are. I don't have time to explain, but trust me, we aren't getting out of here alive unless we get ourselves out."

"That's crazy—"

"I can hear them." Denali tapped the headset on her ear with two fingers. "If you stay here, you're a dead man. They have it planned. Your murder will be televised, and it won't be pretty or painless. These children are in our care. We need to get the kids on this floor into Mrs. Pearson's room. I'll shoot the guard outside, and we'll lower the kids out the window. Take them behind the watershed and get them over the fence."

"Onto the highway?"

"Don't be stupid, these are rabid animals planning to kill us all," Denali practically yelled, so frustrated she wanted to hit the man. "Sensei?

"Okay, Denali, I'll tell her." The little boy grasped the gun in both hands.

She kissed his forehead. "Ask Mrs. Pearson if she can use a gun, and if she says she can, let her have it. Go to her room now!"

Mr. Fredrick's students hesitated, peering from him to her as Sensei darted across the hall.

"Let's go, class," Mr. Fredrick said through compressed lips.

"Get me an empty soda bottle and the strongest tape you have. Then go next door and tell Mr. Martin to get his class in Mr. Robbin's room. See if you can contact the others by tablet to get the kids dressed warm and ready.

Lips pressed together in a tight line, Mr. Fredrick did her bidding, handing her the requested items as if contact with her skin would poison him

"I still think you're going to get us all killed," he muttered.

"Think whatever you like."

Movement at the end of the hall caught her eye. A group of children entered the hallway from the back staircase headed to the gym. No teacher accompanied them. One of the black-clad men proceeded them. He didn't glance in her direction, too busy waving the children into the gymnasium. The man she waited for appeared and stopped to speak to him. Denali hunkered further into the doorway.

She ripped two, four-inch pieces of duct tape from the roll Mr. Fredrick handed her and laid them along the mouth of the soda can. As quickly as she could, she secured the empty soda can to the end of her gun.

Mr. Fredrick nodded thoughtfully.

She motioned him to stand behind the door and placed her mirror on the edge of the floor, angled to show the doorway of her room. Then she stepped back and waited.

FIVE

Get These Kids Out

Mr. Fredrick spoke quietly on his cell phone. Denali hoped he was calling one of the other teachers but her pounding pulse drowned his whispers. Her gaze stayed glued to the small mirror. Seconds passed with glacial slowness. Only twelve minutes had passed since her sister had been murdered. The thought hardened her resolve. Her body tensed as booted feet appeared.

She crept forward, the gun held to her shoulder. The soda bottle muffled the gunshot to a sharp poof of sound. Denali ran forward, letting the gun swing to her side by its strap and grabbed the collapsing man, using her momentum to push him into her room. She let him fall to the floor right inside the doorway and risked a quick glance up and down the hallway.

The hallway remained clear. The children and the armed man at the far end had disappeared. Most of the blood coated the inside of the doorway. Only a small streak marred the floor. She'd run through it leaving barefoot footprints. A growing pool of blood surrounded the man's head. She wiped her feet on his back one at a time.

"It's clear," she called in a low whisper.

Mr. Fredrick exited his room and ran into Mr. Martin's. She figured she had five to ten minutes before anyone noticed no new children entered the gym. She took the detonator from the man's pack and threw it into a locker. Grunting with effort, she pulled the vest off the corpse and placed it over her head for ease of transport. His gun she slung over her back. The holstered sidearm she threw over her shoulder. The man's knife she hefted in her hand, then removed her nylons and tied one tightly around her ankle, slipping the knife into the makeshift sheath. The other nylon she stuffed in her pants pocket beside the dead man's wallet.

M-16 held at the ready, Denali crossed the hallway, heading to the next room on the right. She badly wanted to look out the window and see where help lay but couldn't afford to take her eyes from the hallway.

Mr. Fredrick had gotten the kids and teacher ready. This group of six to eight-year-olds began crying when she appeared. She didn't blame them. Even without the gun, she'd be a scary sight. Drying blood pulled the skin on her face when she spoke. Blood coated the front of the stolen vest she wore, but at least the black made it hard to see. Not so her pants. Her previously off-white silk slacks showed the blood all too clearly.

"The hall is clear; go quick." She gestured to Mr. Fredrick. "Get Mr. Reed's class and take them to Mrs. Alverez's room. Mr. Martin, you go for Ms. Brooks. Damn it, I wish we could communicate better."

"I have Ms. Brooks on the line," Mr. Fredrick said.

"Great, have her classroom go to Mrs. Alverez's room too. Mr. Martin, can you use a gun?"

When he nodded assent, she handed him the gun swinging from her shoulder and removed the extra vest. "Take this. Make sure the kids know where to go."

Without asking, Mr. Martin took the holstered sidearm off her shoulder and tightened the belt around his hips. Denali glanced into the hallway, then took up a position in the doorway across the hall, waving them across. Still adjusting his weapons, Mr. Martin ran down the hallway and into the next classroom.

Three armed men appeared near the front stairs. Denali used her small mirror to observe them enter the main office. Her heart beat so hard she worried she'd pass out.

"Hurry up," she whispered to herself, staring at

the doorway Mr. Martin had entered, willing him to hurry. Any minute now someone would notice the missing men.

Mr. Reed glanced into the hall. Denali beckoned him on, covering the children running into the room behind her with the stolen M-16. She followed Mr. Reed into the classroom.

"I'm going to go next door. When I shoot the man guarding these windows, get these kids out. Mrs. Alverez, go out first, and Mr. Reed can lower the children to you. You'll have to hug the wall until everyone is outside.

"There's an armed man on the roof and a guard patrolling. I'll place covering fire on the roof. Mr. Martin will watch for the patrol. Get the kids across as quick as you can and put the cement pump house between them and the school. Tracy Aims is on the phone with the police. I'll have her warn them we're coming out and are headed to the highway. About six hundred yards up the highway, a culvert goes under the road. If there aren't police there to help you, take the kids there. It'll be a tight, dirty squeeze but better than leaving them in the open."

Denali ran to the room next door. "It's me," she called softly as she entered.

Sensei knelt on a desk in the corner with the pistol pointed at the door. She wished she had a bullet proof jacket for him. Thirty kids crowded the room, huddling against the lockers as far from the windows as they could get. She repeated the plan.

Without her having to say anything, Tracy repeated everything she said into the phone. She gave the girl an approving nod.

"Sensei, you'll need to go last and watch this door. When they hear the gunshots, they might come search the rooms." She kissed her brother's pale cheek. "I won't leave Bee or Simon here."

He nodded, his face serious.

"Tracy, ask the officer if they can give us a distraction. Just something to make the guard on our side look away."

Denali debated checking the hall again and decided it didn't matter. Either there were men there or not. She closed and locked the door, hoping it would slow them having to get the keys. Neither of the men she'd killed had carried keys on them. She took the wallet from her pocket and handed it to Tommy.

"He's dead. When you're safe, give it to the police, or if you're hiding, tell Tracy just like before." She took the cell phone from Tracy and stuffed it in the nylon from her pocket and tied the end around the girl's arm. "If you drop it, leave it. Stay with the class. Don't worry about talking to the police until you're across the fence." She gave the terrified girl a quick hug.

"Everyone, be as quiet as you can." She closed her eyes and took deep breaths envisioning the firing range. In the far-left corner of the room, she rested her gun against the windowsill and lifted her head slowly until she could peep through the window.

The gunman stood with his rifle held loosely in his hand and pointed at the ground. Police sirens sounded in the distance, and a man with a bullhorn yelled something, but he was too far for Denali to make out what he said.

The guard turned towards the noise. She slid the window up and rested her stolen M-16 on the edge, took a deep breath, sighted, and pulled.

The man's head disintegrated in a rush of blood and bone. The children in the room screamed but stopped quickly. She leaned out the window to scan both sides.

A babble of Urdu on her headset made her smile. "I am shooting to kill," she muttered.

The rifle slung to her back, she grabbed the edge of the window and dropped, landing lightly on the balls of her feet. As soon as her feet touched the ground, she swung the rifle to chest high and started forward.

Movement on the edge of the tree line caught her eye. She dropped to one knee and aimed, clutching the rifle hard in her sweaty hands. The trees were over six hundred yards away, and she wasn't sure she could hit anything that far. Behind her, Mrs. Alverez, Mrs. Pearson and Mr. Martin climbed from the windows and children began climbing out.

Her eye to the gun scope, she scanned the trees. A police officer crouched in the woods, not looking at her, but at the roof above her. Sunglasses covered his eyes. A bullet-proof vest with the word police stenciled in white covered his uniform shirt. Hatless and coatless, he crouched beside a tree. She stood, putting her back to the tree line and faced the building, taking five quick steps backward, trusting he had her back. She scanned left and right, then took five more steps. Motion on her peripheral vision warned her.

She dropped to one knee and fired as a black-clad man rounded the corner. She fired again as he yelled in Urdu and darted backward. Behind her, a gun sounded. She jerked her gaze to the rooftop and fired at the man there. He ducked back, and she couldn't tell if he were hit or hiding. Trusting the officer at her back had the children covered from the gunman on the roof, she ran to the corner of the building where the man she'd wounded had disappeared.

In her headset, he called for help between curses.

She took a deep breath and leaned around the corner, trying to take in the entire scene in a glance, aiming and pulling without conscious decision. The man crawling away fell face forward. Two armed men on the stairs opened fire. Her thumb flicked the switch turning the gun semi-automatic as she returned fire. They darted into the doorway, yelling at her to drop her gun. She held her ground.

"This is America," she yelled back "We have the right to bear arms!"

"Go," she yelled to the kids, hoping they would listen and be fast. Eight feet from the edge of the building, she glanced along the left wall. Another shot rang out behind her. She stepped back, letting the corner block her from view of the doorway and peered upward. Too close to get an angle on the roof, she ran backward, holding the gun pointed towards the roof, hoping she'd spotted the gunman before he spotted her.

"I'm out Denali," Sensei yelled.

"Run," she yelled back, not willing to take her eyes from the roof.

Mr. Martin ran after the kids, stopping halfway across the field and firing at the roof.

"I'm Officer Ryan Graham," a man yelled from behind her. "Don't shoot me."

She stepped to the right and leaned, firing blindly then leaned farther to peer around the corner. With frantic haste, she ejected the empty cartridge and withdrew the spare from her pocket and slammed it in.

"Can you cover the roof?"

"Got it," Ryan said.

She ran forward, hugging the wall of the building. In her ear, two men argued in Urdu, either not realizing or not caring their mics were on.

"We should rush the bitch."

"Stay in the doorway, that's an order," Mahir Alfarsi said. "Jabir, go behind the building with Sadiq and see if you can get an angle on the far-right corner. We don't need them anyway. We have our five; the rest were extra. Let them go. Don't blow the mission for revenge."

Denali ran forward as silently as she could and opened fire in the doorway. The echo of the gunshots under the roof of the portico was deafening. A flick of her thumb put the weapon back on single shot, and she pulled the trigger twice ensuring these two men could threaten her family no more.

"What the hell was that?" Mahir Alfarsi hollered. "Jabir— Jabir— check in."

Denali ran forward and peered around the corner, pulling the trigger on the man standing there. He fired back, the bullets catching her on the chest and knocking her to the ground. Stunned, she lay there unable to move.

"Fucking bitch," the man said in English. He kicked the gun from her nerveless grasp.

A choking wheeze was all she managed, not able to draw in a breath to insult him back. "I got her," he said in Urdu, lifting his rifle.

SIX

Let's Go Get the Bastards

A single shot rang out. A small red spot bloomed on the side of the man's head, and he fell in slow motion. Denali gasped, the small movement agony.

"You hit?" Ryan asked.

Denali didn't answer, her entire attention was on forcing her lungs to draw in another breath of air. She expected to feel a bullet any second from the man's partner. He'd waited at the farther corner, but surely, he'd show any second to finish her off. The next inhale came easier.

"Another," she gasped, afraid Ryan would round the corner into the last gunman. She took another deep shuddering breath.

"It's clear. Can you get up?" Ryan held out his hand to her.

"The kids?" she asked as she pushed herself to her hands and knees.

"Behind the small building. The gunman on the roof won't have line of sight." While he spoke, Ryan helped her stand.

She peered into bright-blue eyes framed with black lashes and smiled ruefully. "I'm good. Man, that smarts," she added, ineffectually rubbing the chest piece. "They have at least forty-five kids in the gym already, but they're after just five of them. If I had to guess it'll be Senator McDonald's two boys, Judge Montoya's granddaughter, Jason Pratt, Chester Abrams or Addy Gleason."

While she spoke, she rifled through the dead man's pack, stuffing her pockets with the ammunition and his grenade. Thick flakes of white began to fall, and she realized she was cold.

"How do you know?"

She tapped the headset she wore.

He plucked a headset and radio from the corpse. "Let's go."

Denali headed for the front stairs. "Not without my brother and sister. They plan on killing everyone inside. Mahir is bullshitting the cops to buy time to round up the kids and plant the explosives."

"Yeah, I meant let's go get the bastards." Ryan grinned and followed her, peering back at the tree line and shrugging. "I wasn't supposed to break cover, but too late now. I couldn't just let them shoot you. If what you say is true, we don't have time to wait for rescue or backup. How many and where are they?"

She laughed half hysterically. "Last I saw there were three in the front office. The head guy is there and at least one other henchmen. There'll be three women there and maybe the five kids."

She rummaged in her pack and spread the map out. "The main room here has three smaller offices off it. My sister's office is off this small office," she said, tapping the map. "That will be these windows here and here." Blood smeared the map from her finger.

"There's a bathroom and a closet in that room but no other exit except the windows or main door. Every exterior door and room in the office is alarmed. A tone will sound even if the door is unlocked. I can easily bypass the alarm using the keypad outside the main door."

She stood and handed Ryan the map. Still speaking, she eased towards the main entrance. "At least two men were on the roof, and at least two more are upstairs. The front steps leading to the second floor are mined now, and they're planting explosives to bring down the building but aren't ready for the glorious resolution, whatever that is."

"Our first priority is getting the rest of the kids out. You say the front stairs are mined so that just leaves the back ones, and they're sure to be guarded."

"If we take the interior stairs," Denali said thoughtfully as she eyed the white decorative brick. "You wouldn't happen to have a screwdriver on you, would you?"

Ryan grinned and handed her a Swiss Army pocketknife.

"I love you." Eyes alight she took the small knife and flicked it open. "Let's disable the alarm. I need a minute or two to unscrew the protective case."

He nodded and gestured for her to proceed him.

"Are you in touch with your precinct?" she whispered as she edged along the front of the building.

"Yes, but if I call them, I'm sure to be ordered back—"

"Fuck," she yelled and grabbed his arm, pulling him with her as she ran toward the doorway. "They have reinforcements coming. Head honcho just ordered someone called Nadir to bring a squad up from the parking area and take the perimeter.

"You understand that babble?"

"Yeah, how many are in a squad?"

"Anywhere from three to fifty but usually seven."

"Three, huh?" she said thoughtfully.

"Or fifty," he said quelling.

"I have an idea. Here, take this." A hard grin on her face, she took the pack from her back and removed two grenades, sticking them in her back pockets. "Hold them off at the doorway here. These doors are bulletproof. If you keep one at your back, you'll be safe even if the guys from the office enter the hallway to shoot you. I'll climb in a window and get behind them. If they enter the double doors, we give them a grenade. If they don't, you can use them to hide."

Ryan ripped another headset off the dead man beside the door. "Take this one too; I'll be on channel two."

Denali placed the headset over the one she already wore. "These things have purposefully crap range; I won't be able to pick you up too far away. You okay with this plan?"

"It's good; go." Ryan grabbed an M-16 from the corpse on the steps.

At the corner, she hesitated, peeking quickly to ensure it remained clear. She glanced back; Ryan was stacking the dead men to make a barrier.

"Hope you remembered to take their grenades," she muttered as she sprinted around the corner. Bare feet made the bricks easy to climb. In seconds, she was pulling herself back into the classroom she'd just left. The warmth of the classroom felt like an embrace. She hadn't even realized how cold she was until she felt the heat. Once inside, she took a moment to turn the second radio to channel two. She hated to leave her spare knife, but she needed the nylon to hold the second radio to her shoulder.

"Can you hear me?"

"Loud and clear," Ryan responded instantly, his voice muffled by radio static.

"I'm wearing both; if I ask for quiet, it's to hear the other."

"Roger that."

"Right now, they're checking in. I make it squads are four people, and they have four squads inside, and six left outside." The mirror on the stick laid where she'd left it beside the door. She used it to peek into the hallway. "Two men are escorting a group of children to the gym. If a squad is in the office, and two men are upstairs, where are the other two squads?"

"Roof maybe? Or is there a basement?"

"Yes."

"If it were me, I'd have a squad in the gym with the children," Ryan said.

"Any sign of the four he sent for?"

A sharp blast of gunfire answered her.

"Yep."

She snorted. "Mahir is ordering everyone to maintain positions. Three men just exited the office heading to the doors." She fingered the grenade in her back pocket.

Mahir's voice reverberated over the loudspeaker outside. Walls and distance muffled it, but she heard him clearly.

"The next act of aggression will cost this woman her life." The intercom inside crackled to life, giving his words a slight echo. "Tell them your name." The sound of flesh hitting flesh was loud enough to hear over the intercom. Denali pressed the heels of her hands against her eyes.

"Save the children," Mrs. Ritchie said, sounding confident and unafraid.

Tears trailed down Denali's face.

"Are you sure you want those to be your last words? If you tell her to surrender, she and the children can leave here alive. You can live."

"Denali, do you remember the gift you gave your sister when you were five? I love you and know you feel the same for me. I know you'll listen to me. Save the children."

Another sharp crack of flesh-on-flesh followed. "You have three minutes to surrender or this woman dies," Mahir snapped.

The three longest minutes of Denali's life passed in a haze of tears and self-doubt. A single shot sounded before her. It echoed from the loudspeaker. She jerked and fell back, feeling as if the shot pierced her soul. Another longer blast of gunfire made her shake her head as it echoed through the earpiece.

"See what you've done?" Mahir screamed. "I still have hostages. Shall I kill a child next?"

Denali tuned him out, concentrating on the men in the hallway. Later she could be sorry she'd killed a friend.

"Come on, open the door," she muttered.

Fierce anticipation filled her as the three men entered the double doors. The two sets of doorways formed the perfect trap. "I can get a grenade in the door behind the exiting men. Are you clear?"

"Roger that."

She let the rifle swing from the strap around her neck, took a grenade from her back pocket and pulled

the pin. One man had opened the first door, holding
it open for the other two to pass. She glanced down
the hallway in the other direction. The two black-clad
men still stood there, but they faced the stairs. She ran
toward the front door on her tiptoes and released the
grenade, rolling it like a bowling ball into the open
doorway and darting into the empty classroom; she
ducked behind the door as the grenade went off. The
concussion sounded thunderous and shook the
building.

"How's it looking outside?"

"It's raining men."

Denali snorted.

Ryan laughed at his own joke, then said, "I got
one; the other three retreated. I assume they'll split up
and try to flank me, but I have no visual."

Denali leaned from her doorway and peered at
the end of the hallway. The men at the far end had
disappeared. "I'm turning off the alarm."

She crawled on her hands and knees to the office
door and sat with her back pressed against the wall,
took a deep breath and stood. A bulletproof glass
window faced the hallway. The secretary could
accept packages or speak to visitors in the vestibule
without letting anyone enter the building.

The glass continued passed the door to the edge
of the office wall. Another keypad for the alarm
system sat on the small strip of wall beside the
window, this one without a protective weather cover.
Denali let her breath out in a soft hiss as she reached

around the corner and pressed the first number while keeping her eyes on the office door. She almost hoped a bad guy would open it so she could shoot him.

Each beep sounded like a gunshot to her. As fast as she could, she entered the twenty-five-digit code to override the system. She'd installed this system three years ago. Written in her code, on her machine, she'd left herself access to add to it when the new buildings were constructed.

A sob caught in her throat. Her beautiful sister would never fulfill her dream. Not any of her dreams. Tears clouded her vision, blurring the soft green glow of the keypad. The keypad turned dark as she pressed the last number. It had taken less than a minute.

Denali held a hand to her ear, pressing the headset closer. "Good, they think you threw the grenade from outside, and they're willing to leave you trapped there for the moment. The boss just ordered them to not let you leave. He's ordering a mine placed before this door on the inside. If you're coming in through the front door, now's your chance.

"On three," Ryan said.

"Stay low," she warned in a whisper.

"That's disgusting," he murmured as he crossed the mangled remains in the entrance way. Shrapnel had shredded the men caught between the two sets of bulletproof doors.

Ryan joined her beside the closed office door. She pointed at the stairs to the right of the doorway. After letting him look a second, she took his hand and tugged him toward the nearest classroom.

"They don't realize we're inside. Right now, they're moving another group of kids. There's one more group upstairs. I can get up the steps on the rail and avoid the mines, I've done it a million times at home with my brother Lee; they won't expect an attack from that direction."

"How many are still in the office?"

"Not sure, but I think three."

"Okay, so three bad guys with two good guys and maybe five children. At the other end of the hall?"

"One hundred and thirty-five kids."

"One hundred and thirty-five kids in the gym and?" Ryan rose an eyebrow

"Thirty upstairs. And somewhere there are eight teachers."

"We need to get those kids out. I wish I could report in, but my radio got clipped." He nodded to the mangled remains of the radio on his shoulder.

"Don't forget, the outside is guarded again."

"If I were in charge, I'd put a guy by the cement building."

"It's a pump house." She wanted to smack herself for the inane correction.

"Right, I'd put a guy at the pump house so it can't be used again. I'd replace my sentries and maybe put another guy on the roof. No idea what the ultimate plan is?"

"Details no, but it's always about money. The boss

is yapping about sacrifice and duty, but he's isn't going to sacrifice himself. He must have a plan to escape. We have until sunset to get them out. At sunset, he's going to blow this place. Right before that, he's going to hang the teachers on the crosses and burn them. The time seems real specific. For the life of me, I can't think of any religious or political significance."

"Then something else is planned to happen then. If I were a betting man, I'd say whatever it is he plans to use it to escape."

Denali sat back on her heels. A thoughtful frown crossed her face. "Okay, so the building crashes down, presumably killing all inside, but how does that help him?

"You're sure he doesn't mean to kill himself too?"

"Reasonably sure. He's spoken numerous times of securing the five for transport." Tears filled her eyes." He talks about the two that will be the example. I think he means two children. He calls them small, soulless offspring of the unbelievers." Her voice cracked and she had to clear her throat. "He already killed my sister, my beautiful sister." She sobbed and pressed her hands against her lips.

"Ms. Olympia was your sister? I don't even know your name."

"Delilah Na Abira Leeba Rubinstein-Wong. My friends call me Denali."

Ryan reached out and tucked a strand of hair behind her ear. Sympathetic eyes met hers. "I'm sorry for the loss of your sister, Denali."

"My sister Bee and brother Simon are still inside. God, my parents must be freaking out."

"Don't worry about that right now. We have enough to worry about. I like the idea of surprising them from a direction they don't expect, but then they'll know we're inside. I think we should take the gym first and I have an idea on how to do it.

SEVEN

Movement

Denali stood back and examined Ryan. Now wearing
the black combat pants and black shirt of the second
man she'd killed, from the back he appeared to be one
of them. She poured more soda on the bulletproof
vest and rubbed the blood off with a discarded child's
sweater she'd found in a locker.

She wore Ryan's vest with the word police
emblazoned across it over her stained shirt. Mrs.
Alverez's sweat-shirt covered the vest, and her
sweatpants covered her blood stained ones.

She rummaged in Mr. Fredrick's desk, emerging
with a paper and pen and wrote rapidly while she
spoke. The terrorists had already added fifteen more
children to the group in the gymnasium. Only fifteen

more remained upstairs. They had less than five minutes to get in position before the last group of children was delivered.

She spoke quickly as she stuffed the note into her pants pocket beneath the sweatpants. "Pull down the face mask and put the headset over it. Make your voice as deep as you can and repeat what I say." She grabbed the black grease pencil from the table and put it with the note before handing him the vest and helping to tighten it.

She traced the line of holes where she'd been shot. "Hold the gun up to cover them. The door alarms are off, and the room is almost soundproof. My note tells them to exit through the window of the classroom because of the explosives on the door in case we're both killed. Are you sure police are in the woods?"

"Yes, if they see the children exit, they'll cover them even if you can't get to an upstairs window. They might assume I'm dead." Ryan shrugged and dropped his broken radio into the trash.

He took the damp rag from her and wiped her face. "Let your hair down to cover your face if you talk."

She nodded and pulled the hairpins out, sticking them into her pocket. Ryan continued speaking as she shook her head, letting her long hair fall around her shoulders.

"If I deem the plan won't work, I'll turn and exit the room, and you'll go into the classroom where I leave this." He held up the M-16 she'd been using. "I'll be in the room across from you, and hopefully we can catch anyone who follows in a crossfire."

He tucked strands of hair over the microphone. The headset rested on her neck. The radio was tied to her bra strap on her back.

Denali nodded, knowing as well as he did if the plan didn't work they'd probably both be killed.

"Ready?"

She nodded, reaching to her waistband to make sure the pistol was still secure.

"Don't tuck your hair back," he murmured as they ran down the hallway together.

He paused beside the open door of the classroom before the gym and tucked the rifle behind the door. She held her hands up and marched around the shallow corner to the door of the gymnasium.

A black-clad man lounged against the door jam, eating a protein bar. His rifle dangled behind his back from its strap.

"Too bad we have to waste her," he said in Urdu as he straightened and leered.

Denali pretended to cower away, letting her hair swing forward. Curlier than normal from being put up while still damp, the thick wavy mass nearly reached her waist. She dropped her hands and covered her face as if she were terrified, hoping he'd step forward to prod her inside, letting Ryan get behind him.

The guard laughed and stepped forward, letting the door he leaned against swing closed. Denali dropped to her knees, reached into her sleeve and pulled out the knife duct taped there, hiding the movement by leaning forward.

"I like this one; she knows how to grovel properly," the man said in Urdu.

Denali stared up at him, trying to look terrified and not angry. Ryan had stepped to the side. As the guard leaned to touch Denali's hair, Ryan stepped forward and grabbed the man by the neck.

Denali leaped up and threw her arms around the terrorist's chest, squeezing as tightly as she could. Ryan grunted with effort as the man thrashed and made gagging noises.

"I saw two inside," she said on the radio as she resettled the knife while Ryan dragged the corpse into the classroom. "One at the end near the back door, and one to the right beside the boxing ring.

"Get the guy at the end. I saw a third man sitting on the bleachers, he's my target, then the guy beside the ring." Ryan rejoined her while he spoke. "Wait until I'm in front of the sitting guy."

"*Sit in back,*" Denali repeated a few times in Urdu.

Ryan roughened his voice and mimicked her. "Got it." He hefted his gun.

She glanced at her watch. "One minute."

He grimaced and nodded, motioning her forward.

She went through the door with her arms up and head down, trying not to worry about the other children arriving any minute. Ryan followed, pointing the gun at her back. Thick strands of hair blocked her vision. Before her, children sat cross-legged on the floor.

"Sit in back," Ryan said the rehearsed words in a passable imitation.

"Where's the rest?" the man in the back called in accented English.

"Coming," Ryan grunted.

She walked through the narrow aisle directly toward the gun-wielding man in the back. To either side of her children huddled on the floor crying. This reckless plan could get them all killed. *The odds are good only some get shot,* she reminded herself. *Some hurt or killed are better than all,* she told herself forcefully as her step hesitated as she passed the crying six-year-olds.

'*Be quick, be quick, be quick,*' she chanted to herself and picked up her pace. The best position would be if she could get off to the side of the man. Then, when he fired, only she'd be hit. She didn't need to live, just kill her target.

"Now," Ryan said.

She dropped her hands and reached for her gun. Her target's eyes widened, and he began to lift his rifle. Time slowed, every moment registering in crisp detail. Bee's tear-stained face, her dark braid half undone. Simon, a deep scowl on his face hunched protectively over Bee, glaring at Ryan, Cindy with her head in Ms. Simone's lap. She felt a moment of fierce joy that her siblings were there and unharmed.

"Get down," Denali yelled. "Read the letter in my pocket," she added in French for Simon's benefit.

Simon pushed Bee to the ground and laid over her as the man fired. Denali lifted the pistol and squeezed the trigger right as his bullets impacted, throwing her backward.

Simon scrambled for the gun that fell from her hand.

No, Denali tried to yell, but couldn't draw breath.

A searing pain ripped through her chest as she gasped air in. *She'd cracked a rib that time for sure*, she thought ruefully in one corner of her mind.

Gunshots rang out behind her. Her horrified gaze fixed on her little brother as he rose; she knew he'd go for the gun. Her head smacked into the floor, leaving her dazed.

Three shots rang like a bell. Each echoed, so distinct they were almost musical. She forced herself up and fell forward, landing on her hands.

"He's dead," Simon handed her the gun. "Are you okay?"

"Get Bee." Denali wheezed in a choked voice as she spun to face the two gunmen at her back, but both were dead. She had no idea if her shot had killed the man in the back or if Simon or Ryan had.

Mr. Marshal grabbed a rifle from one of the dead men. Two other teachers grabbed rifles and looted the bodies.

It took Denali a moment to realize Simon still spoke to her.

"I'm okay, just stunned." She hugged her brother, running her hand through his short, black hair.

"Listen up!"

Ryan sounded calm and in charge as if he did this every day, Denali thought.

She removed her sweatshirt, handing it to Bee who only wore a white button-down shirt and shivered at Simon's feet. About half of the children weren't dressed for the cold outside. The girl beside Bee only wore a skirt and short-sleeved blouse. Denali stepped from the too-large sweatpants and handed them to her.

"We're leaving through the window of the classroom next door. Don't use any doors as they've been boobytrapped. I wish we could stay and wait for rescue but that isn't an option. They could blow the building at any moment."

Denali helped Bee put the sweatshirt on and hugged her hard as Ryan spoke.

"Those of us with guns will cover your retreat. Run as fast as you can to the trees. We know there are gunmen on the roof, but SWAT is outside and will be covering us."

"Twenty kids are still inside," Ms. Simone said.

"If anyone knows anything about the missing kids stay behind to tell me, but we need to get out of this room. Exit quietly — but quickly."

While Ryan still spoke, Denali ran to the gym doors, ignoring the stabs of pain from her abused ribs. The gym doors opened out with thick rubber stoppers on the bottom to hold them in place. She opened the right-hand door as far it could go and used the stopper, then open the left twelve inches, leaving an angle she hoped would protect the exiting kids.

The wide stairs leading to the second floor remained clear although she heard crying children approaching. The stairs turned, presenting a wide landing and blocking the view of the top ten steps. She hoped that the armed escort followed in the rear like before.

Ryan laid on the floor beside her and handed her the M-16. She gave him back his pistol. He reloaded it.

Behind them, children ran from the gymnasium and into the classroom next door. Denali kept her gunsight on the end of the hallway.

"This is the last group," she confirmed as Mahir spoke over the radio. They have their two hostages going to the roof." For a minute, she felt relief that it wasn't her brother and sister. A fear that had been nagging her since she'd heard he'd picked two children. The relief turned to furious anger.

"Motherfuckers," Ryan muttered.

She glanced at him. His furious glower matched hers.

"Movement," he warned in a soft voice.

Denali beckoned the children on the stairs forward. The first had halted at sight of them. She pointed to the line of kids still passing behind them.

"Come to me," Mrs. Simone said softly, holding out her arms.

Denali glanced back down the hallway, but there was no movement by the office. She expected that to change when they heard the gunshots.

The children on the stairs ran to Mrs. Simone. She hugged them, then pushed them towards the classroom where another teacher stood, holding an M-16 and hurrying the children along.

"Slow down," the guard on the stairs barked in accented English.

Denali turned back to the stairs as a black-clad knee appeared. She used both hands to grip the gun, took in a deep breath and held it. The crosshairs of the scope traveled the knee as it stepped forward onto the landing. Ryan shot as she did, the sound deafening beside her unprotected ear. The children screamed as the corpse fell. Denali leaped to her feet and raced down the hallway toward the office.

The door to the office opened. Denali fired, making the man who'd open the door jerk back. She let herself sink to the ground, sliding on her knees across the polished wood floor in her silk pants as another man ran from the room firing. Despite the bullets slamming into the floor around her, she took a second to aim and pulled the trigger.

He screamed and clapped a hand to his face. Blood spurted between his fingers. Another man exited the room. Bullets flew overhead. Ryan and the teachers were covering her. She took careful aim and fired. The man she'd shot in the cheek fell backward either Ryan or the teacher killing him. The second man she shot at clutched his neck and sank to his knees. The headset in her ear was filled with Urdu profanity. The boss was still alive and angry.

"One left in the office," she called as she leaped to her feet and ran around the corner.

She glanced in the open office door as she ran passed. A man held a gun to Mrs. Faison's head, his black, hate-filled eyes fixed on her as he rose his pistol and fired. The bullet clipped her shoulder, shattering the radio. Plastic shrapnel cut her face.

A dull burning pain radiated along her arm, but a glance showed she wasn't bleeding too badly. She didn't think the wound was serious. She didn't attempt to return fire, instead, jumping and landing on the thin, left-hand rail and running up it in her bare feet. The glance had also shown Jason and Addy beside a child she couldn't identify in her quick glance, and the edge of Olympia's blood splattered shoe. All three children had been gagged and blindfolded.

She'd run a million rails just like this she told herself firmly as she wobbled. Beneath her feet on the stairs, thin, almost transparent wires, crisscrossed the treads connecting to landmines. A favorite childish pastime had been traveling the house without setting foot on the ground. Running up the curved banister in the main hall of their home had been banned when Lee had fallen two stories and broken his arm, but until then, they'd used the three-inch-wide piece of polished curved mahogany as their highway. This banister had a wall to lean against for balance.

The image of Olympia's bloody shoe haunted her, making her tremble against the wall.

"Please don't really be dead," she whispered, knowing it was futile but needing the comfort of denial to continue.

Access to the roof lay inside a janitorial closet to the right of the stairway. The distant sound of gunfire penetrated the thick walls.

"Be safe," she prayed thinking of her sister and brother exiting under gunfire. Images of their small, terrified faces flashing before her. "Motherfuckers," she hissed and straightened. She'd be damned if any of these psychopaths got away.

EIGHT

One Shot

A man knelt before the door of the supply closet that housed the stairs to the roof. Denali balanced on the rail, turning her body into the wall and fired. The shot pushed her shoulders firmly into the wall, sending sharp jabs of pain along her abused ribs. The dead man fell forward over the expolosives he'd been attaching to the door.

Her gaze traveled the hallway. No one else was in sight. She jumped down as gunfire echoed through the hall below her. She ignored it and ran into the classroom to the left. The windows in this room faced the parking lot. As clearly as she could, she wrote out the position of the remaining hostages in large block print across the window. Tears trailed across her cheeks as she wrote two on the roof.

She checked her watch. In an hour and fifteen minutes, sunset would arrive. Whether the explosives were on timers or would be remote detonated little time remained for negotiations or rescue.

"Denali?" Ryan called from the stairway behind her.

"One more dead man up here, but he boobytrapped the door to the stairs. Two kids are on the roof with an unknown number of gunmen," she called back, not caring if the boss heard. *Let him sweat, the fucker.*

"I killed another on the other stairs, which leaves one more in that squad somewhere; watch your back. Is there any other way to the roof?" Ryan asked.

"Yes," Denali said, thinking of the outside bricks and the cornice that had tempted her to climb months ago.

"SWAT will be coming in— "

"I think you better get out. There's no telling when they'll blow it. Let the boss escape with his hostages. Meet me outside where we met." Without waiting to hear his reply, she ran for the end of the hall.

Windows lined the wall of the last classroom on the right, a foot from the decorative trim she'd used to climb the building before. Bitterly cold wind whipped in the window, chilling her fingers as she slid it open. Thick flakes of snow swirled in the gray sky. Her single hurried glance had shown no sentries.

Already an inch of fresh snow covered the

ground. Two helicopters hovered in the distance. One black, the other bigger and bulkier with camouflage paint. Behind them, a third, smaller, helicopter circled.

"Military, police and news," she muttered as she pulled herself through the window. She balanced on her toes, using the glass frame to steady herself, letting the gun dangle across her back from its strap.

One of the black-clad men appeared below her, just his elbow peeping from the corner of the building.

Clutching the bottom of the window in her right hand, she reached with her left for the brick trim. Once she had a firm hold, she slid her left leg over, released the window and grabbed with her right hand, letting her foot slip from the window. Reaching the cornice was easy. A quick glance showed the man on the corner hadn't moved.

"Just like last time," she murmured, trying to remember the ease with which she'd done this for fun. Toes braced as hard as she could against the bricks, she grabbed the protruding decorative edge of the cornice. The roof overhung about a foot. The decorative, cement cornice stood out six inches from that, ending in a fanciful swirl. To grip the edge of the roof and pull herself up she used the molding, letting her feet dangle as she pulled herself along the shallow grip the molding provided. Her ribs protested viciously with sharp stabs of pain.

Last time she'd done it easily. This time, her arms

shook and her breath came in hard pants. The edge of the roof bit into her hands as she heaved herself over, causing a bolt of agony from her ribs. The skin on her neck tightened, expecting a bullet any second. Nothing happened. No one seemed to notice her arrival.

The snow on the roof numbed her bare toes. Before her, the wooden frame that housed the stairway sat beside a smaller metal box that covered the AC unit. A dead man lay against the wall with his shirt pulled over his face. Another, bigger metal box lay to her right. A row of ceramic exhaust pipes for the furnace and school's ovens stuck from the roof between them. A black-clad man leaned against the corner of the biggest air-conditioning unit. He carried a rocket launcher in one hand and spoke to someone she couldn't see, gesturing to the distant helicopters with the other.

Denali ran across the roof and leaped, catching the edge of the eight-foot roof over the stairs and pulling herself onto it. Slanted sharply to shed rain, the slope offered concealment from the men on the rooftop. She laid flat and slowly pulled herself forward to peer over the edge.

On her headset, men hollered orders and insults to each other.

"Quiet," Mahir bellowed in Urdu. "There are more fucking children to kill, so what if we don't get these. Let's get our five and get out. Make the most of this fucking disaster. Fall back and regroup and stay off the damn radio."

Two wooden chairs had been brought up from one of the classrooms. In one chair, ten-year-old Chester Abrams the Third was zip-tied by his arms and legs. A black cloth covered his eyes. As she watched, one of the men tucked a gray blanket around him.

In the chair beside him, twelve-year-old Mercedes Montoya was tied in a similar manner, except she wore a bright red parka with matching mittens and a hat. A man crouched at her feet attaching explosives to the chair.

"How much longer?" the man with the rocket asked.

"All done," the man at Mercedes' feet said as he stood. Of the three men, only one held a weapon in their hand, and that was a rocket launcher.

He's hardly going to waste a rocket on me, Denali mused and turned her attention to the other two men. One was a clear, easy shot. The wooden chair and Mercedes's body partially hid the other. He would be her first target. Take him, then the other guy while rocket launcher dude dropped the rocket and pulled his sidearm, say five seconds to kill two men before she took return fire. Higher ground gave Denali the advantage.

The children were her kryptonite; she needed to keep the bad guys away from them and the black radio beside the man kneeling before Mercedes.

Every second she delayed was one more second

more men could use to arrive. Two unarmed men she could kill and maybe the third guy, but more… She took a deep breath and sighted.

"Call Mahir and let's get out of here. He can detonate them anytime with this controller. Let the helicopters come and get good pictures. We will show the world— "

The man dropped mid-sentence as she sighted on the second guy. The children screamed. Her target stared at the roof she lay on in shock. She shot him as he went for the pistol on his hip. Once again time slowed, each detail crystal clear. Cold snow seeped through her pants and the thin sleeves of her shirt, numbing her fingers and toes.

Gunsmoke overlay the scent of fresh coppery blood. The children screamed, their shrill voices galvanizing her. She rolled and shot without aiming. The man holding the rocket launcher had dropped it and drawn his sidearm.

"Fucking whore," he shouted.

"Mercedes, Chester, stay still!"

She shot again. His return fire impacted the wall of the stairs right below her head, splintering the wood. A quick glance showed he was running toward the kids or maybe the remote controller. She flicked the switch to make the rifle semi-automatic and opened up on him, praying to hit something vital but willing to settle for chasing him away from them. It worked, he retreated to the safety of the air-conditioner unit. She slithered backward off the slanted roof, dropping to the rooftop and ran as fast as she could toward the back of the unit. Her rib throbbed with each breath and pain made her shudder.

Her back to the air-conditioner, she slapped a fresh clip into the gun. Her last clip. Cold seared her feet as she ran behind the unit, hoping to come upon him from a direction he didn't expect.

With any luck, he'd think she remained on the roof, waiting for him to show himself. She ran into him on the corner to close to lift her gun. He lifted his. She dropped hers and threw herself forward, grabbing his arm and twisting in a move her brother Lee had taught her.

He swore and dropped the gun, reaching for the knife on his hip with his other hand. Denali kicked out, connecting with the back of his knee, throwing him forward into the snow. On his hands and knees, he kicked backward unaimed. Her gaze flicked to his gun as she dodged the kick, and she leaped for it. As her hands touched it, fingers tangled in her hair, yanking her back.

"Fucking whore!"

"You fucking said that already. Repeating insults is a sign of a lack of intelligence," she gasped out as she reached for the knife taped to her arm. The tape released with a loud rip, pulling out the fine blond hair on her arm, leaving the cold metal in her hand.

She rose a hand to block his knife while stabbing at his face with the other as she turned into him, sliding her right leg behind his. When he jerked back, she'd already dropped her knife to use both hands to grab him and throw him over her shoulder, using her leg as a fulcrum.

He hit hard, letting out a loud 'oof' that changed to a piercing scream as she fell on him, and kneed him in the balls. Instinctively, he curled and grabbed his crotch. With both hands, she grabbed the hand that held the knife and twisted, stabbing at his descending face while grinding her knee into his groin.

He shrieked again, trying to buck her off, releasing her hair and gouging at her eyes. Blood streamed down his cheek.

In her earpiece, Mahir screamed threats and obscenities. Somehow, she had the knife in her hand, but he was rolling them over, grabbing at her neck. Black spots and golden sparkles danced before her eyes. With all her strength, she stabbed.

The hands on her neck relaxed. Cold air pierced her lungs, every breath a fresh pain. He was a dead weight on top of her. She didn't know if she'd killed him, or he'd passed out or played possum. For a moment, she didn't care. His body heat warmed her. Fire traversed her abused ribs in increasingly painful waves. Eyes closed, she took shallow panting breaths until the fire settled to a sharp throb. Harsh grunts escaped her as she slithered out from under him. Just to be sure, she slit his throat, then wiped her knife on his pants before sticking it in her waistband.

She wished he wore a jacket, but she settled for his too large boots and socks. The numbness in her toes quickly became painful tingles as she clomped back to the kids through the bloody snow.

"We're okay," she gasped.

The children continued to sob.

"Mother fucker!" she snarled when she saw the mercury switch.

She winced apologetically, not taking her eyes from the wiring connecting the children to the bomb. "Observe, plan, act," she mumbled as she traced one finger along the path of the wire without touching. "Okay, guys, give me a second, and I'll get you out of here."

"Ms. Denali?" Mercedes asked in a voice thick with tears.

"Yep, hold on and don't try to move."

"They're going to kill us."

"No, they're not. We'll remain calm and choose right action. I'll untie you in just a minute."

"We're strapped to bombs," Chester said.

"I know, sweetie. But I got this, just sit still and give me a minute." While she spoke, she fumbled in her pockets, removing the bobby pins and Swiss Army knife. "I need to make the loop of wire bigger, but you need to be very still while I do." She pulled the knife from her waistband and cut off the blindfolds and zip ties.

"Don't move until I say, okay?"

A wire attached to a level crossed the children's

laps. She wasn't too worried about that one. As long as they didn't move, that one wouldn't blow; it was the one attached to that, going to the explosives beneath the chair that worried her.

"Watch the level there." She pointed at the liquid-filled glass vial. "Tell me if it moves."

The dead man still carried a spool of wire and the tools to cut it. She cut off a three-foot piece and made small loops on each end. Wind whipped her long hair into her face. She muttered an obscenity as she gathered it in both hands, twisted, and tucked it into her shirt.

These wires were much thicker than the ones she normally worked with on her computers, the plastic coating easier to strip. In seconds, she had the ends of the wire ready. The cold numbed her fingers, making her clumsy; she had to tuck her hands into her armpits to warm them before attempting to strip the wire leading to the bomb.

The children watched her with wide, terrified eyes.

Gunfire in the distance made her shoulders tighten.

With slow, careful movements, she removed the plastic coating on the wire leading to the explosives. She returned to the dead man, tugged off his vest and placed it beneath the bomb to keep the wire from the snow, and went back for the shoelaces. She debated a second about getting the vests from the other men for the children and decided the vests wouldn't make much difference but the time getting them might.

"Okay, Mercedes, give me a hand here. Just hold this without moving, okay?" Denali said as she gingerly handed the girl the wire loop.

The girl swallowed convulsively and nodded.

As Mercedes held the wire taut, Denali placed the loops she'd made around the cleared piece of wire, then used the plastic-coated bobby pins to hold them in place. She took the wire from Mercedes and stretched it out along the bulletproof vest she'd placed on top of the snow.

"Chester, don't touch the bare wire. After I cut the bottom one, I'm going to pick up the wire across your lap. I want you to stand slowly on the chair, trying your best not to bump the wire. Stand there until Mercedes stands too. Then I'll count to three, and you both step off the chair to the side. Try really hard not to rock the chairs. We need to keep this glass vial steady. Are you ready?"

"Yes," he said in soft, scared voice. His wide brown eyes shone with unshed tears.

"You guys are doing awesome. This is just like no touch we play in gym, but easier because I'm not calling out math problems.

Chester's laugh caught on a sob, tightening Denali's throat.

"Okay, stand nice and easy." Denali grasped the level and slowly lifted it away, making sure the mercury inside touched both ends to keep a steady flow of electricity.

One foot at a time Chester stood on his chair, clutching the blanket.

"Throw the blanket, sweetie, so it doesn't trip you."

Chester wadded it up and threw it into the snow. A loud explosion made the kids jerk and cry out.

Denali placed a hand on her heart and laughed shakily. She wiped her sweaty palm and brow, then grasped the level again in two hands. "Wasn't us. Okay, your turn, Mercedes. Nice and easy. On three, step off. Once you're off, get behind the stairs. I'll be right there. Don't try to use the stairs; they boobytrapped them. Ready?"

Wide, terrified eyes met hers as they nodded. Gunshots sounded in the distance. Denali winced, hoping Ryan was okay.

"One-two-three."

Both children stepped down and ran. Denali heaved a heavy sigh of relief and gently lowered the glass vial to Mercedes's seat. She grabbed the man's shoelaces and tied the wire to the chair legs.

"Stay there," she called as she backed away from the chair.

She'd hoped the police in the helicopters would see what she was doing and that the children were free, and come get them, but neither approached.

"Let's see what's holding you back," she muttered and dropped to her stomach to crawl to the edge of the roof.

The smoking wreckage of a police car in the

parking lot drew her eye. Emergency vehicles lined the road leading to the school, their lights competing in a dizzying array. Directly before the main entrance, eight upside down wooden crosses gathered a coating of snow. Two black vans, each with a man on the roof, parked on the small strip of lawn separating the school from the parking lot. Anti-aircraft missiles rose from the van's roofs.

Her gaze darted to the rocket launcher in the snow on the rooftop.

She only had one shot.

NINE

I Love that About You

"*How many more of* you bastards are there," she muttered as she peered through the snow, trying to see into the woods that separated the parking lot from the front of the school.

A clock ticked in her head, counting the seconds until sunset. She didn't know if the boss meant true sunset or just dark. She didn't know much at all except that the entire building was rigged to blow.

She had to get the kids off the roof. On her stomach, she wriggled backward until she was sure no one on the ground could target her before she stood and ran to the kids. A continuous shiver shook her. Cold winter air pierced the front of her clothing, wet now from the snow. She eyed the dead men thoughtfully.

"How were you planning to get off, or were you sacrifices too?"

Her fingers trembled from cold as she snatched the radio and turned it to channel two.

"Ryan?"

"Denali, thank God! Did you find a way to the roof?"

His voice steadied her. "I have the kids, but we can't get off. Can you get to the window in the last classroom on the right on the second floor?" While speaking, she tugged off the men's belts and holsters.

"Yes, but it will leave the boss uncovered."

"Okay, do it. Let's get these two safe, then worry about the others."

Denali threw the holsters over her arm, grabbed the blanket, and ran to the kids. She found them hugging behind the wall. Mercedes had removed her jacket and given it to Chester. Long strands of straight, black hair caught in the tears on her cheeks, but her expression was determined.

"Braid these strips together as tightly as you can," Denali said as she cut thin strips from the blankets. "Don't let the ends where we knot them together match up. Chester, hold the ends for her and let her braid them," she added as Chester tried to make a braid.

He gave her a wan smile. "Yeah, Mercedes does awesome braids."

Denali grinned at him and squeezed his shoulder. "That she does." She turned to Mercedes. "You wouldn't happen to have a hair elastic, would you?"

The wind wiping her hair into her face was seriously annoying her. Mercedes nodded and handed her an elastic from her wrist.

"I let my hair down 'cause I thought it'd be warmer."

"Smart, girl." Denali took the proffered elastic and pulled her hair back into a ponytail. "I'm going to make a harness and lower you to the window. A police officer inside will pull you in. Once you're inside, watch the door and warn him if you see or hear movement, but don't stick your head in the hallway."

"I'm here," Ryan said in her earpiece, sounding out of breath.

"We need another few minutes. I really love how dependable you are. I'll lower Chester to you. Chester, take Ryan's hands and let him pull you in. I promise I won't drop you."

She placed a holster around Chester's waist and buckled it then looped a belt through it. With her knife, she bored a bigger hole through the leather and forced the end of her blanket rope through it, tying a knot on the end so it couldn't slip back through. She took the last belt and attached it the holster she wore the same way, giving herself about six and half feet of rope between them.

"Grab the rope, Chester. I'm going to lower you over, then release you. You'll feel a sharp jolt when I do. Don't worry, if you let go of the rope, the belt will hold." *I hope*, she added to herself.

She knelt a foot from the edge and gave Chester a quick hug before clasping him under the arms and leaning forward. A groan of pain she couldn't contain burst from her as she fell forward, letting herself fall onto her chest as she lowered him over the side. She let her hands slid up his arms and grabbed the rope between them. Chester screamed when she released him.

"I got you," Ryan said. "More slack."

Denali lowered him.

"He's inside," Ryan said unnecessarily.

She'd felt the weight release from the rope.

"Okay, Mercedes, you're up," Denali said as she pulled the belt back up and buckled it around the girl's waist. "Can you grip the edge of the roof in front of me? I'll have the rope; you're taller than Chester, Ryan can probably reach your feet. You can grab the rope when you let go of the roof if you want to. We won't let you fall.

"I can do it, Ms. Denali."

"Ready, Ryan?"

"Yep, piece of cake." He sounded cheerful and confident, just listening to him settled Denali's nerves.

"Well, Da, I meet a guy I like, too bad we're both going to die," she muttered as she lowered Mercedes over the side of the building.

"I got you," Ryan said.

The muscles in Denali's arms strained and the cracked rib protest viciously with sharp stabs of pain.

Mercedes was a good thirty pounds heavier than Chester.

"Hurry up," she muttered, not sure how long her makeshift rope and strength would hold. She sagged in relief as the weight left the rope. "Get them to the bottom floor window. I'll meet you there."

"How will you get—" Ryan stopped speaking as Denali kicked off the too big boots, swung herself over the edge, and grabbed the cornice, feeling for the decorative brick with her sock covered toes.

"I'm good, go." She glanced at Ryan wedged in the windowsill, one leg inside the classroom the other tucked between his chest and the wall keeping him in place and leaving his hands free.

With her toes curled into the brick, she shimmied along the decorative cornice with her hands and had reached the wall as she spoke.

He nodded and disappeared inside.

"I love that about you," she said into the mic.

"What?" He sounded amused.

"That you believe me when I say I can do something with no macho bullshit."

"So… wanna go for drinks later?"

She laughed. "I really do, but I can't."

"Damn. Married?"

"No, too young to go to bars. I'm only twenty."

"Phew, I was worried I'd missed my chance."

She laughed again as she dropped the remaining five feet to the ground. "I'm outside the window."

He grinned at her and lowered Chester into her

arms. "So, dinner then?"

"Yes."

His eyes lit. "I'm glad I met you, Delilah Na Abira Leeba Rubinstein-Wong."

"I'm glad I met you too, Officer Ryan Graham."

He lowered Mercedes down to her and leaned out the window. "They should be able to make it to the trees. We could escort them, but if we do, we won't be allowed to return to the school. I'm conflicted and frankly confused on why SWAT isn't in the building with us already. I really want to get in touch with my chief to find out what's going on."

Denali handed Mercedes her radio. "Give this to the first officer you see and tell them it has a range of about one thousand feet." She kissed the girl's cheek. "Run straight to the woods. Police officers are hidden in there and maybe military. Stay together. Tell them to call us."

She kissed Chester on the forehead and gently pushed them. They grabbed hands and began running. Both glanced back. Denali waved them on, praying the good guys waited in the trees and not the bad.

Ryan leaned down and offered her a hand to the window. He pulled her up and into his arms. His legs inside the window, hers out, they sat pressed together in the tight opening. His blue eyes met hers as his breath misted her cheek.

With all her soul, she wanted him to kiss her. As if he read her mind, he lowered his lips to hers. The kiss was light and gentle, and she felt it to the soles of her throbbing feet.

One finger moved a strand of hair from her face and tucked it behind her ear.

"I think we left radios on the dead guys in the entrance way," he said.

She laughed. "You're so romantic. I really love that about you."

"I love everything about you." He tightened his hold on her. "Is it too early to propose?"

Her heart jumped. "You're exactly the man I've been waiting for."

"Is that a yes?"

"Are you serious?"

"As a heart attack."

Denali drew back and examined his face. A smile lit her eyes as she pulled him down for another kiss. This one she deepened and didn't pull away until he moaned. "If you ask me again, I'll say yes, but I'll mean it, so don't ask unless you do."

Delilah Na Abira Leeba Rubinstein-Wong will you—" An explosion interrupted him. Glass shattered, tinkling shards fell past them as the building shook. He pulled her into the building, falling backward, landing on the floor hard with her on top.

She screamed and grasped at her ribs as she scrambled off him. "Missile launcher or maybe anti-aircraft. Jeez, I hope they didn't get one of the copters. "I could climb back up and try to take one out. Should

I?"

"No, we stay together from now on." He rose and brushed himself off, stifling a groan.

"Are you hurt?"

"Just my pride. How about you?" He jutted his chin at her shoulder, which, now that he brought it to her attention, began to throb.

"Just a graze. I guess we should go see what the boss is up to, he hasn't said a thing except for swears in ten minutes."

"Think he realizes you understand him?"

"Maybe. Mrs. Ritchie knew I speak Urdu. While I'm sure she wouldn't volunteer the information…"

Denali straightened her shoulders. Mrs. Ritchie had been a friend of the family for years. When Olympia had first decided to build this school, she'd asked her to work for her before the first brick was laid. The two women were longtime friends. She forced her thoughts from her sister. She couldn't dwell on who would miss her or the pain her absence would cause.

Ryan kissed her forehead. "They'll pay."

She nodded and wiped her eyes. "Let's get the bastard." Together they ran down the dim hallway.

TEN

Together Forever

A trail of blood led from the wide-open office door. Footsteps tracked through the blood, all heading outside.

"The kids are with them," Denali whispered pointing to the small sneaker prints.

"Let's make sure no one is left inside, then get the hell out."

Ryan entered the doorway crouched with his gun extended before him. He waved her forward as he straightened and darted past an open door, placing his back to a wall. Denali stopped inside the doorway, her horrified gaze lingering on a large puddle of blood. Her sister's blood. A sob escaped her. She slapped a hand over her mouth and swallowed convulsively, forcing her gaze away from the floor to Ryan. He gestured with his chin to the open door, then ducked low and entered.

"Clear," he said as he exited the room and entered the adjoining one. One-by-one he cleared the rooms. Denali stood with her back against the wall beside the door, covering him.

"All clear." Ryan put an arm around her and kissed her temple. "One dead, a woman."

"Which room? Denali asked in a breathless voice. Ryan pointed with his chin.

Denali ran to the room. "Not Olympia." She fell to her knees beside Mrs. Ritchie and closed the staring gray eyes in the bruised face. Blood had matted her graying blond hair. Her expression was deceptively peaceful. Bloody gunshot wounds crossed her body on an angle.

Ryan ripped the flag from the stand in the corner and laid it over the woman's face. "We need to go, sweetheart."

"Where's my sister?" Denali stumbled to her feet, wiping her face with her dirty sleeve. "I can't go. Maybe she's in another room."

"No. I'm sorry, but… they dragged her outside while you were upstairs."

"She's really dead?" Tears streamed down her face.

She let the gun swing from the strap, using both hands to wipe her eyes as sobs racked her.

"Denali, we need to go."

Denali nodded and grabbed the purse hanging

from the back of the chair. Ryan took her hand and pulled her from the room, the purse bumping her side as they ran. Her mother had given it to Olympia two years ago for her birthday. Inside would be a beaded change purse made by Denali when she was five. Another sob escaped her, and she began crying again.

Ryan pulled her into her classroom, he eyed the corpses but stepped over them and headed to the window.

Denali began taking off the vest she wore, which said police in bright white letters. "Switch vests with me so you don't get shot."

She removed the vest, getting tangled in the gun and purse. He had his off before her, pain in her ribs made her slow, and settled it over her head. His warm lips briefly touched her cold ones. They each slid open a window and climbed out, dropping to the ground.

Distant machine gun fire ripped the air. Hunched over, Denali and Ryan ran for the trees. Something stung her arm and Ryan grunted, falling to his knees less than forty feet away from the tree line that promised safety, but she was too weak to carry him.

"Get up," she begged as bullets kicked up dirt beside them. A sharp weight hit her back as she bent over him. Not able to raise him, she gave up and pushed him flat, laying alongside his body, using hers to block the bullets. Two more shots hit her back, feeling more like sharp taps then bullets.

"Don't you dare die!" Her voice caught on a sob. Blood oozed from his neck. She slapped her hand over the wound.

"Run," he wheezed.

"Together forever."

Before he could answer, a hot wave of air rolled her over. The noise was so deafening and encompassing it didn't register as noise. She felt it; she didn't hear it. It shook her bones and made her head spin. A cloud of choking dust covered her as sharp pieces of shrapnel rained down, too many to pinpoint individual pains. Arms outflung, she swept the ground feeling for Ryan. The dust was too thick to see through. She kept her eyes tightly closed and clapped a hand over her nose and mouth to breath.

"Ryan!" her scream sounded muffled and weak.

She cried out wordlessly when she felt his hand. Her right leg wouldn't support her. She felt no pain, it just wouldn't respond to her mental commands, so she dragged herself to him. Blood spurted from his neck, warm on her cold fingers. Dust sifted across them thicker than the snow.

It took her two tries to release the Velcro that held the vest on. She didn't bother trying to unbutton her shirt, she just ripped it off. Stiff with cold, her fingers fumbled on the clips that held the strap to the gun. Wadded up shirt in one hand, she felt for the wound on his neck and pressed the fabric against it.

"Denali," he gasped.

"I'm here; don't talk.

"My leg is bleeding. I love you."

"Don't you dare die! And stop talking!"

She'd intended to use the strap to hold the bandage in place on his neck. Instead, she ran her hands down both his legs until she felt wetness. The dust was clearing but night had fallen, and snow continued to fall. She couldn't see much. Her sister carried a tiny flashlight on her keychain. Before searching for it, she placed the strap around his leg as high up by his groin as she could and tightened it, making him groan.

"Sorry," she sobbed as she rummaged one-handed in the purse.

Her searching fingers encounter a thin rectangular box. Olympia's cell phone. The screen lit as soon as she touched it. The flashlight app on the first page bathed Ryan's neck in a bluish glow. Blood trickled from the wound when Denali pulled the soaked cloth away. She didn't know if that was good or bad. She replaced the cloth and examined his leg. A bullet had traveled through his leg, leaving a hole on the inner and outer thigh. Both spurted blood when she released the tourniquet, so she tightened it again. Not knowing what else to do, she called her father.

"Olympia?" her father's hopeful heartbroken tone made her cry again.

"No, Da, it's me. I have her phone."

"Oh, thank God. Are you okay?"

"No. I need help."

"Where are you?"

About forty feet from the trees on the right-hand side of the school."

Gui spoke to someone with him, repeating what she'd said.

"Don't hang up."

"I won't; I love you, Da."

"Don't give up either."

"I won't. Are the kids okay?"

"Sensei is with us. Bee and Simon are in police custody. All are fine."

"Olympia is dead."

Saying the words tore a sob from her. It felt like the words tore her soul too.

"I know." Her father sobbed once, then cleared his throat. "Mom is with Neil. Tianzi and Clare are coming home. How badly are you hurt?"

"I don't know. I can't move. I'm getting married, Da. You'll like him. His name is Ryan Graham."

Ryan snorted a bare breath of laughter.

"Stay alive," she said to him and kissed his cheek.

She released the tourniquet for a moment then tightened it again.

"This is sudden."

"He's perfect, Da."

"Nobody's perfect; settle for faults you can live with."

Denali almost laughed, her father sounded so normal, the kind, wise tone comforting.

A helicopter passed overhead, playing a

searchlight over the ground. It passed them, then returned.

"I'm so tired, Da. I could sleep for a week."

"Don't sleep yet, my beautiful mountain."

The use of his nickname for her brought tears to her eyes again. She closed her eyes and relaxed against Ryan's side no longer feeling cold but comfortable. She didn't remember falling asleep.

ELEVEN

Glory Hog

When Denali woke, her sister Anya hovered above her frowning. Everything hurt from her hair to her toenails. She groaned and lifted a hand to her head. "Stay still," Anya said, sounding annoyed.

"Ryan?"

"In surgery, but the prognosis is good."

"Olympia's dead." She started crying.

Tears sprang to Anya's dark eyes. "We know."

Meteora leaned over Anya's shoulder. "Rest. Try not to worry about anything. You scared us."

"Am I okay?"

"You will be… If you listen to medical advice. You're probably dumber now from the hypothermia, but that's no great loss."

Denali snorted then winced, grabbing at her ribs.

"What did you do to me? They didn't hurt this bad before."

"You have four cracked ribs and one badly broken one. The graze on your shoulder is nothing. The one on your waist is a little more serious, but it only needed stitches like the one on your arm." Meteora smoothed Denali's hair back. "The bruising worries us a bit. Your vest stopped the bullets, but the impacts damaged you. The swelling on your back is compressing your spinal cord. We think you'll regain feeling and full range of motion when the swelling diminishes. Plan on being sore for a while. You have a million small scrapes and bruises, but all should heal with minimal scarring."

Meteora's words washed over her with no real effect. She felt dazed and disconnected, unable to even worry about possible paralysis. The door to her room swung open, admitting her mother and brother Danxia.

"Mom." To Denali's embarrassment her voice came out a thin wail and she started bawling.

Her mother appeared to have aged ten years since she'd last seen her. Dark circles ringed the eyes sunk into gaunt cheeks. Her salt-and-pepper hair was caught up in a loose, messy knot on the back of her neck. Her brother Danxia held her elbow as if afraid she'd collapse.

Anya and Meteora stepped back to let their mother reach her side.

"Hush," her mother said and stroked her hair. She

switched to Hebrew. " Thank you for the gift of my children. May the Lord bless you and keep you; the Lord make his face shine upon you and be gracious to you; the Lord lift up his countenance upon you and give you peace."

"Amen," her siblings replied.

Denali cried quietly while her mother held her. When she finally pulled herself together, she and her mother were alone in the room. "Sensei, Bee, Simon?"

"All well. Sad over the loss of a beloved sister and angry, but physically well. Your father tells me you're to marry?"

"I hope so, Ma."

"Then I have lost a daughter and gained a son?"

"Is Neil…"

"Brokenhearted. The family is with him."

"His family?"

"Arriving soon. Shiloh is here. Talk to him before speaking with the police."

"Am I in trouble?"

To her surprise, her mother smiled. The smile made her appear years younger. "You're always in trouble. We should've called you trouble. Your entire life you encouraged your siblings to reckless behavior, always running and jumping. Your father and I worried so for you. But if you hadn't been trouble those children would've died. I'm so proud of the daughter we raised."

Hester kissed her cheek and rose. "Your Father and I will visit later, after you've spoken to your brother Shiloh and rested." She paused at the door and turned back. "From what I saw of your young man, I liked him very much."

The door swung closed behind her before Denali could ask what she meant. It occurred to her she had no idea how long it had been. She was almost too tired to care. Her brother Shiloh entered, appearing as tired as she felt. Tall and broad-shouldered, his blue suit fit him to perfection. Deep creases in the elbows and knees told her he'd been wearing it quite a while. Long, black hair tied back with a leather thong and an eagle feather left his high Navajo cheekbones clearly visible. His sad black eyes met hers.

He kissed her cheek and sat on the bed beside her. "Meteora says you'll be up and about as soon as tomorrow. How you feeling?"

"Tired." They were both silent a moment. "And angry."

"Yeah, me too. Those goddamned bastards." He picked up her hand and examined the bandaged tips.

"What happened? I mean after the building fell," Denali asked.

He snorted and kissed her hand before replacing it on the bed. "Mahir Alfarsi exited the building with four henchmen each holding a child." He shrugged. "You can watch the news footage. Tristin McDonald was shot, friendly fire, but not fatally. He's here undergoing surgery. The other four are fine. Frightened and probably scarred for life, but physically fine."

"And the secretaries?"

"Marion Cole has minor injuries. Mrs. Faison is dead. Everyone is accounted for except Mrs. Ritchie who we assume died in the explosion.

"No, she was already dead." Denali closed her eyes. Mrs. Ritchie's face was clear in her memory—the purpling bruise around her eye, the small bullet hole in her temple, the large exit hole on the back of her head, the line of bullets holes crossing her torso, fired after she died. "They shot her in the head. Did any get away?"

"They aren't sure. It's possible. The FBI arrested sixteen men. Twenty-nine more are in the city morgue, and they're still pulling bodies from the rubble." He held up a hand as she started to speak. "I'm acting as your lawyer, anything you tell me is completely confidential. Tianzi will be here soon," he hesitated a moment then said, "I think he'd do anything for you, but don't put him in a position where he must break his word. Client confidentiality won't work for him. He'll want to help you, Denali, don't let him."

"Do I need help?"

"I'm not sure. What I *am* sure of is Tianzi's work as a DA in Boston could be seen as a conflict of interest. Let me represent you.

"Okay."

"The police and FBI are waiting to question you. I'll be blunt, the media is vilifying you, calling you everything from reckless to a glory hog. Tell me what happened and leave nothing out."

"I didn't realize anything was wrong until Mahir came on the intercom. While he was talking three of his men spoke in the background. The spoke Urdu, but I understood them. I knew the boss had no intention of letting us go, they said so. They said we'd all die."

"So, you knew about the bombs in the building?"

"I knew they were planting bombs. I knew they planned to kill the children, but not how." Denali shrugged. "What was I supposed to do? Let them? I killed the guy who came for my kids and took his gun. I killed the next guy. By then I knew they planned on taking five kids with them and burning the teachers alive. I got the kids on my floor together and out the window after killing the guy outside. A police officer helped me. He covered them while I went after the guy I knew was patrolling outside. I killed him and his buddies. The officer killed another right as he shot at me."

She tapped her chest. "These bruises here. The two of us went back for the other kids. Most of them were already in the gymnasium. The bad guys didn't realize we were back inside. I disabled the door sensors that would've told them. We took out three more in the doorway, four in the gym, and one on the stairs. I killed one guy upstairs while he was boobytrapping the stairs to the roof. Then climbed up the building to get to the roof, killed the three guys there, got the kids to the ground and went back in for the last five kids, but they were gone already. The building blew up as we were getting away."

Shiloh leaned forward, searching her face. "But you knew they planned on killing you?"

"Yes, I knew they'd wired the building and planned something horrid for the two kids on the roof. They bragged about leaving no survivors more than once."

"Do you have any proof of that?"

"No. Ryan heard them but wouldn't have understood what they said. Well, Sensei might have heard and understood. And maybe Simon. I hope they didn't... Do I need proof?"

"When you speak to the police and give your statement, make it clear you knew. Be as specific as you can about what was said by whom, when, and where. Write it out for me, and we'll go over it."

"They think I went crazy and attacked?"

Shiloh nodded. "Yes, the media is saying you attacked in revenge for your sister's death, not caring who you put in danger. The fact none of the children was hurt they're counting as luck. I'm afraid some are calling you a murderer for killing the men outside."

"Idiots," she said and closed her eyes.

"Yes, but idiots with loud voices. "I can handle this though. You have nothing to worry about."

"Except Olympia."

Shiloh leaned down and hugged her. The two cried over their dead sister. Denali cried herself to sleep in her brother's arms. When she woke again, her mother and father were there with Iggy, Tianzi, and Clare.

Gui hugged her gently, careful of her sore ribs. "You're not to worry about anything. Your mother and I will take care of you."

"That bad huh?" she asked, smiling ruefully at Tianzi.

Clare laughed sadly, took her hand and kissed her cheek. "It's a mess, but I'm sure it'll get straightened out. Meanwhile, lay low."

"Did you have to give Sensei a gun?" Tianzi asked, sounding affronted.

"Sensei is very proud of himself." Gui gave Tianzi a pointed stare.

"Should I have sent him out defenseless because I was afraid of upsetting a cowardly man?" Denali said, glaring at her oldest brother.

"No." Tianzi sighed deeply. "You did the right thing. The only thing you could do. I'm sorry, it's just such a media nightmare. Mom and dad are being inv—"

"Tingzhe Zihao Israel," Hester snapped, using his full name, a sure sign she was very angry.

"Sorry," he repeated.

Denali rubbed her brow. The IV in her arm caught on Clare's jacket.

Clare readjusted the pole and handed her a black bag she took from her shoulder. "Toiletries and clothes. I brought the softest dress I could find in your closet. No shoes; I'm afraid the bandages won't fit in anything you own."

"Thanks, Clare."

"Your welcome, my sister." Clare's eyes filled with tears and she turned away. Tianzi hugged his wife, staring at Denali unhappily over her head. Olympia and Clare had been best friends since preschool. Clare's heartbreak hurt. Neil's would hurt more. She dreaded seeing him.

She pasted a false smile on her face for Iggy. "Hey, sweetie, can I get a kiss?"

Iggy started crying and reached for her.

Denali held up her arms. "I got her."

Her mother let her take her.

"We're okay, and it's all over."

"I'm glad I'm not six. Bee is so scared," Iggy mumbled into her neck.

"I know, sweetie, I'm glad you aren't too. We'll be extra nice to Bee to help her feel better."

"Mommy's sad too," Iggy whispered.

"We're all sad, sweetie. We'll all be extra nice to each other."

Denali held her youngest sister as she cried. The hole Olympia left in their lives was impossible to fill or traverse. It gaped, a dark emptiness, a bottomless well of sorrow, so deep you could fall in and drown. And it held currents, pulling her family in, threatening to destroy them all. Her father threw a lifeline.

"Tonight, we will light a candle for Olympia. While we live and remember her shining brightness, she lives on."

"I'd rather have her here," Iggy said.

Clare's laugh caught on a sob. "Me too, sweetie."

"How's Ryan?" Denali asked.

"Surgery was successful, and he's resting comfortably now. Meteora assures me she'll look after him," Hester said as she picked Iggy up with a grunt of effort.

Tianzi took Iggy from her. "Let's go, gang. Denali needs rest." He turned to Denali, his expression serious. "Shiloh can't hold back the authorities forever. You'll need to make an official statement soon. No matter what he said, I'm your brother first. If you need me…"

"Thanks, I'll be fine. I didn't kill them out of anger."

Tianzi nodded and headed to the door. Clare kissed her forehead and followed.

Alone with her parents, Denali relaxed against the pillows and closed her eyes.

"When you're well, you can tell us what happened," her father said as he leaned down to kiss her brow. "Shiloh assures me he can help you." He smoothed the hair from her face, his smile sad. "I pray to God you don't need help. Whatever happens, the Rubinstein-Wong's will stick together."

"Come," her mother said, taking her father's arm. "We love you, Daughter." She kissed Denali's cheek and drew her husband from the room.

To Denali's surprise, she immediately dozed off.

A dark room met her eyes when she woke again. She felt more alert, more herself, and hadn't realized she'd felt muzzy before until now. Trying to sit made her moan in pain. Her entire body throbbed or itched or both. Moving like an arthritic old lady, she sat and swung her legs to the side of the bed.

Each small movement brought a fresh lance of pain with it. She wanted to go to the window but wasn't sure her feet could take it. The thick bandages around them intimidated her. For the first time, she wondered if she'd lost toes to frostbite.

Meteora hadn't mentioned anything like that though, and they really didn't hurt too badly; more a tingling itch as if she suffered from pins and needles in the feet. While she debated trying to stand, a nurse entered. She wore light-blue scrubs and a shy smile.

"Ah, you're awake. Shall I help you to the bathroom?"

"Yes, please. What time is it?"

"Five-thirty. February sixteenth. You've been here a day now."

The nurse flipped the light on, making Denali raise a hand and squint.

"I'm Jean, and I don't care what anyone says, you were amazing. Thank you. My cousin's daughter was in there." She offered Denali a shoulder to lean on. "The feet might be sore. I'll check the bandages after our bathroom break."

Denali tentatively stepped down, cringing in anticipation of pain, but felt fine. The ribs hurt more when she straightened. Her feet felt bulky and awkward but standing didn't hurt. The moist oozing sensation was a bit disconcerting.

"Are my feet bleeding?"

"No, they shouldn't be." Jean sounded alarmed and leaned over to peer at them.

"They feel oozy and weird."

Jean straightened and laughed, brushing her short, brown hair behind her ears. "That's the antibiotic gel. Do they hurt?"

"Tingles and itching."

"All good signs." Jean walked her slowly to the nearby bathroom and flipped on the light. "Want help, or can you manage?"

"I can manage, thank you." She glanced in the mirror and gasped. "Holy crap. I'm a mess."

"Nothing time won't fix," Jean said sympathetically.

"Can I shower?"

Jean pursed her lips a moment, then nodded. "I don't see why not. I was going to rebandage you anyway. Pull the cord if you need me. I'll change the bed while you're in there."

"Thanks; can you hand me my black bag?"

Jean retrieved the bag and laid soap, shampoo and a washcloth on the tray in the shower. "Take your time. I'll bring towels. Any problems at all, don't hesitate to call."

Denali nodded her thanks and closed the door, then stared in the mirror. Small nicks and scratches covered the left side of her face. Her hair made her shudder. Bits of grass and dirt stuck to other unidentifiable pieces in her blood-matted hair. She almost had to call for help to remove the hospital gown. Some sadist had tied it closed on the right side of her lower back. The knot remained stubbornly out of reach of her left hand and trying to use her right sent a bolt of agony through her ribs. After numerous attempts, she finally released the knot and dropped the robe.

Deep purple and green bruises covered her chest and stomach. Another dark purple bruise adorned her shoulder. From what she could see in the mirror, her back was the same. She tentatively fingered a bruise under her left breast. The skin was sore but touchable. Only touching the deep purple center made her wince.

"I can live with this," she murmured.

Small nicks and scratches covered her randomly, none very deep or painful. A longer cut held closed with butterfly tape on her left thigh made her pause. She didn't remember getting it.

She sat on the toilet and unwrapped her feet, expecting to see gangrenous toes and sighed in relief. All toes present and accounted for. Both small toes were a deep, angry looking red, but the rest were just mildly pink.

"I can live without little toes." Relieved, she turned the water on and took the longest shower of her life.

Guilt finally prodded her from the shower. Quick showers had been drummed into her since she'd begun taking them. Hot water was rationed in a family as big as hers. Even when she'd shared an apartment water and shower time had been strictly enforced to ensure everyone got equal time in the apartments only shower.

Her houseboat had limited water tanks, leading to the continuation of fast showers. Today, she wallowed in the water and used all the soap and shampoo before finally getting out with pruned fingers and toes.

She was happy to note some of the bloody scrapes and nicks appeared much smaller with the crusting blood gone. Some had disappeared entirely, not cuts just dried blood. Even her face looked better, *a little cover-up and she wouldn't scare small children.* Her flippant thought saddened her. She had scared small children. She'd scared them badly, maybe scarred them for life.

Subdued, she dried herself and her hair before taking out the dress Clare had provided. Deep blue, shading to dark indigo, the cotton sundress fell to the floor in graceful folds. One of her favorites, the color reminded her of Ryan's eyes. A built-in bra provided modesty, which the plunging neckline did it's best to negate. Clare had put in a soft, thick sweater in a matching blue. A sweater Denali didn't own. She must've bought it or brought it from home. The sweater hid most of the bruising. Clare had also provided makeup. Normally not one to bother, Denali gratefully applied it.

Ryan's bright blue eyes and handsome face were motivation to look her best. An excited twinge fluttered her heart at the thought of seeing him again.

"Maybe he didn't mean it. Maybe he thought we were both going to die," she said to herself in the mirror. "You're smart, get him to mean it."

She stuck out her tongue at herself and turned away. Her soul thought he'd meant it, that Ryan's word was his bond. Truth and integrity were so deep a part of him he shone with it.

Jean greeted her with a smile and waved her to the chair. Denali sat gingerly, keeping her spine straight.

"Bending will be out for a week or two," Jean said sympathetically. "Get help with your shoes." Jean reapplied the bandage to her arm over the graze and asked her to lift the dress to apply one to the wound on her side.

"I'll get it myself." A red flush covered her cheek. She hadn't bothered putting on any underwear.

"Okay, let me check the cut on your thigh."

Denali lifted the dress, and Jean reapplied fresh butterfly tape. She touched each small cut with the tip of her gloved finger dipped in antibiotic cream. "Now for the feet. You'll be tempted to try shoes and forgo the gel and bandages. Don't. Two days minimum, but better for three. If the tingling persists after tomorrow, call your doctor. You came very close to losing your feet. The paramedic on the scene had advanced training and saved them."

"My feet?" her voice sounded breathless.

Jean nodded grimly. "You didn't but take precautions. Stay off them as much as you can to let them heal." She applied gel and wrapped them as she spoke, then put bulky white slippers with gripper bottoms on over them.

"Is Ryan okay?"

"Recovering. He lost a lot of blood."

"His leg?" Dread filled her. The leg had been badly wounded. She still wanted him though, one leg or two, he was exactly who she'd been looking for, kind, smart, brave, and strong both mentally and physically.

"The doctor thinks he'll be okay." Jean grinned suddenly. "The doctor's a bit annoyed to have three doctors examining all his notes and double checking everything. I assure you, everything that can be done is. Everyone from the police commissioner to Senator McDonald has been here checking on him."

"Can I see him?"

"Yes, but… once you leave this room a swarm of police will descend."

"Give me two hours, then bring me to him."

Jean nodded and left.

Denali spent the time writing her report, including every detail she could think of except she didn't mention Simon had picked up her gun. Let the world think she'd killed that man. It was a blur anyway. All that was clear were the three musical shots. She made no mention of them. It took her longer to write out what had happened then to experience it. She was just finishing when Jean returned with a wheelchair.

Jean wheeled her past busy nurses and orderlies serving breakfast and helping patients ready for the day. Doctors in white coats stared at clipboards in their hands, not glancing up as they walked.

"That was easy," Jean muttered.

"You expected it to be hard?" Denali half laughed.

"Well, I wasn't sure if we'd be stopped. You're not under arrest or anything, but the police come by and lurk until we shoo them away. And some of the staff are…" Jean shrugged and glanced away, two red spots appearing on her cheeks.

"I see," Denali said. Butterflies bloomed in her stomach.

A police officer sat in a metal folding chair before the ICU cubicle. He stood as Jean approached. He appeared to be in his thirties and prematurely balding. Unshaven pale cheeks and dark circles ringing his eyes attested to his worry. Ryan was clearly someone he cared about. His hand dropped to the gun holstered at his hip when they approached.

"Ms. Rubinstein-Wong is here to visit," Jean said.

"No visitors except family." The officer glared at her. He crossed his arms and leaned back against the wall with a smug smile at Jean.

Denali pursed her lips and examined the man.

Clearly, he didn't want her to visit. While she wasn't sure if his hostility was personal or generated over worry over his friend, she still wanted to see Ryan. Her gaze lit on his name tag and she smiled, giving him her brightest smile. "Ryan's my fiancé, Officer Ortega. I think that counts as family."

"No fucking way." He straightened from his relaxed pose and glared, clenching his fists at his sides.

So, the hostility was for her personally, Denali thought and pondered the best approach. The Rubinstein-Wong endowment funded a sizable portion of this hospital, and her mother's position on the board would grant access; she was sure of that. While she could raise a fuss and invoke her family name, Ryan would be working with these men a long time, and she didn't want to antagonize them.

"Is he well?"

"No thanks to you. What the hell did you think you were doing? You could've gotten him killed!" Officer Ortega took a deep breath and spoke in a calmer tone. "Officer Graham is not receiving visitors, any visitors. He and I are personal friends, so I know he wasn't engaged to you or anyone else, and I've met his girlfriend."

Denali's heart thudded painfully. "I'm sorry to disturb you. I'm sorry about the entire mess. I did the best I could." She peered over her shoulder at Jean. "We can go. I'll wait for him to wake."

Jean nodded and rolled her away. "I'll tell him

you came," she offered. "Are you really engaged?"

"I hope so," Denali mumbled and lifted her hands to rub her stinging eyes.

TWELVE

She Really Wanted Him to Mean It

Shiloh waited in her room with her brother Dai and two men in black suits and one in blue.

"I'm here unofficially," Dai said as he leaned down to kiss her cheek. "Agent's Raul Bowen and Matt Santos from the FBI would like to speak to you." He nodded to the two men in black suits.

Raul smiled, a polite empty expression. Short, neatly combed black hair tinged with gray framed a weathered face. Matt nodded. Younger by about five years than Raul, his eyes seemed kind in his round, boyish face. A light mustache matched his thin, sandy blond hair. He offered his hand.

"Ms. Rubinstein-Wong?"

"You can call me Denali."

She shook his hand and peered up at the last man. He reminded her of her brother Tianzi, tall and muscular with short-cropped black hair. Even the face was similar with high cheekbones and big eyes. This man had a broken nose sometime in the past and a thin scar on the side of his face.

"Commissioner Alden Westfall," he said and offered his hand for her to shake. "Are you well enough to answer some questions?"

"Yes—"

"We'll come down to the station," Shiloh interrupted. "I've spoken with her doctor, and she can be discharged." He glanced at his watch. "We'll be there by noon today."

"Very good." The commissioner hesitated at the door. "I'm asking that you make no public comment until we speak. The city is panicked, and I'd like to speak to you before you address the press."

"She'll make no comments at all," Shiloh assured him.

The commissioner rapped the door with his knuckles and left.

Shiloh rose an eyebrow at the two men who remained.

"Commissioner Westfall is rightly concerned. The populace is afraid, and not just of the terrorists. Threats have been made against you, Ms.— Denali; for your own protection, we'll be accompanying you."

Shiloh nodded. "Please wait outside the door

while she speaks to her doctor. I'd intended to stop somewhere to eat, but maybe it would be better to bring her something?"

"We'll see to it," Raul said.

He and Matt left the room.

Denali hugged her brother, then handed him the report she'd written. "This is the best I could do. I can add some sketches later."

Shiloh sat on the bed and read the report. Dai peered over his shoulder, reading along.

"Jesus, Denali." Dai squatted before her and took her hands. "Are you okay? I mean… so mean deaths."

"Only one mattered."

"Olympia," Dai said softly.

"No, Mrs. Ritchie. I couldn't do a thing to stop what happened to Olympia. Mrs. Ritchie…" Denali lowered her head and stared at their clasped hands. "He was going to kill her anyway, no matter what I did. And she wanted me to save the children. How would handing myself over to him help her?"

"It wouldn't. The sick bastard was really going to burn them?"

"So they said. That's what the crosses were for. They planned to nail the male teachers upside down on them and tie the women there and burn them. Somehow the sunset mattered. It had to be done thirty minutes before sunset. The boss said —"

"Mahir Alfarsi," Shiloh interrupted. "The boss's name is Mahir Alfarsi."

"Right, Mahir said they'd blow the building and

126

take their five as the world watched and cowered in fear. I don't think he's finished. He said that would start the war. There must be more crazy people with plans."

"We'll find them and stop them. Hell, you made a big dent in them already. Al-Jadr must be embarrassed as hell with the pictures of their operatives being taken out by a girl."

"Pictures?"

Dai drew back in surprise. "You didn't know?"

"Know what?"

There's footage from a news helicopter. They got some great long-range shots. All that practice paid off. I especially liked the footage of you climbing the building like Spiderman."

Denali covered her face with her hands. "Olympia told me not to fall off the roof. She knew I was climbing it, and I didn't stop even though I knew it aggravated her."

She'd be glad you can now," Dai said and put an arm around her.

"She won't be anything ever again," Denali said angrily, dropping her hands.

"The entire nation is mourning her." Shiloh placed the notebook on the bed and rose. "Our family will never be the same. Olympia was a second mother to all of us." His voice broke and he turned away. "God, Neil is a mess. His wife and baby…"

Dai left Denali and hugged his brother. "We'll make them pay. We'll make them all pay."

* * *

Denali straightened the blank sheaf of papers before her, aligning the pencil precisely along the top edge. Her brother Shiloh sat beside her in an immaculate, blue pinstripe suit. His shiny, black hair was braided and tucked beneath his suit collar leaving his chiseled profile visible. A black leather briefcase laid open before him on the table.

Twelve men sat around a table covered with recording equipment. Half empty coffee cups littered the surface.

Denali's stomach roiled, the coffee she'd drunk turning to acid.

To the left of her, a grizzled balding man stood and stretched. Harry Aldridge, the district attorney, gathered his notes and stuffed them into his briefcase. "As of this moment, you're not under arrest. I'm asking that you return at eight a.m. for further debriefing."

Around the table, other men stood and began gathering their belongings.

Shiloh sat back in his seat and arched a brow. "Arrested? For what? Defending herself against armed men bent on killing her?"

Harry paused. One hand rose to straighten his tie as he set the briefcase on the table. He leaned forward, his expression serious.

"Ms. Rubenstein-Wong attacked, escalating a

situation already fraught with tension. The end result was three deaths of innocent bystanders, and as of the last count, thirty-two gunmen."

"That's ridiculous. Denali didn't kill the secretaries or nearly that number of terrorists."

"Her actions caused those deaths."

"Again, that's ridiculous. The actions of Al-Jadr caused those deaths. Denali didn't ask for them to come and threaten her life!"

"We only have her word that her life was threatened." Harry held up his hand when Shiloh started to speak. "I believe her, which is why she isn't under arrest right now, but Mahir Alfarsi is in custody claiming he had no intention of doing any of the things she claims he planned."

Denali snorted. "So how does he explain the bombs or crosses? How does he justify tying two innocent children to chairs rigged with explosives?"

"I said I believe you. The problem is proof. Al-Jadr has a long history of protesting women in the workforce, but they've never taken hostages before. The CIA reports they've been calling for jihad against women not in their rightful place. Reports of heightened recruitment in Pakistan and Afghanistan had Al-Jadr on the watch list, but they weren't a priority before this. They believed Al-Jadr had faded as a threat when their leader, Komar Alfarsi, was arrested. Instead, Komar's children hatched this plan to retrieve him.

The Pakistani government is investigating

training camps believed to be supplying men. We know Al-Jadr has connections with both ISIS, Al-Qaeda and a number of Mexican cartels. My point is that the world sees them as misguided fanatics, not dangerous criminals.

"Mahir Alfarsi is claiming the violence is a result of Denali's actions. He's claiming that while trying to kill him, she killed the women in the office."

"He said I killed Olympia?" Denali half stood and leaned on the table before her, so furious she shook. "And you think that's true?"

"No." Harry held up his hand in a placating gesture. "He admits to her murder. A murder he claimed he did to prevent more violence."

"So, I shot the other two then? That's ridiculous. Ryan heard him kill Mrs. Ritchie. Speaking of that, what was in the change purse?"

"What change purse?" Harry furrowed his brow.

"Mrs. Ritchie told me to get the change purse I gave Olympia." Denali glanced at the seated men, her gaze narrowing on the two FBI agents who exchanged quick glances. "I reported that" –she glanced at her watch— "Ten hours ago. Mrs. Ritchie specifically told me to get it. It was inside Olympia's purse."

"As far as I know nothing of substance was found in her purse." Harry turned to Raul. "Mr. Bowen, has the FBI discovered differently?"

"The purse and its contents are still being investigated. You'll be informed when our superiors deem it's appropriate."

Harry narrowed his eyes and straightened, tapping his fingers lightly against the handle of his briefcase. "I see." He cleared his throat and picked up the briefcase. "Everyone could use a good night sleep. I personally think what Ms. Rubinstein-Wong accomplished was heroic, but the law is the law. It's illegal to kill people unless they present an active threat. And yes, being held at gunpoint constitutes an active threat despite what the captors claim is their intention. The problem is, she risked the welfare of minors in her care. My office must proceed cautiously."

Shiloh nodded and rose, offering his hand. "We're happy to help in any way we can."

Harry snorted lightly. "Speak to no one about this case outside of this building, excluding your lawyer of course. This investigation is ongoing. That was an official command. We're releasing you on your own recognizance. If you make a statement or speak with any victims, charges will be brought." He strode from the room.

Denali wanted to lay her head on the table and go to sleep, but more than that she wanted to see Ryan. She'd been at the police station since noon the day before. Most of that time she'd spent being questioned by a dizzying array of people. For four glorious hours, she'd napped on a couch in the commissioner's office, awakening stiffer than when she'd fallen asleep.

The two FBI agents said nothing, sitting in the back, listening to each interview with recorders running. The hostility with which she'd been greeted had lessened, which relieved her. She thought the police believed her story, at least most of them did. The entire station was still in an uproar. The policy decisions that had held SWAT back were being examined, and Denali was aware the blame was being pushed onto her for that bad call. *The police wanted the escalation to be her fault,* she thought bitterly as she returned the glares she received as they exited.

Shiloh pushed her wheelchair to the waiting town car. She dozed as the driver took them back to the hospital.

"Tianzi is meeting us. Say nothing about the case," Shiloh warned when they arrived.

She nodded tiredly and happily left the wheelchair behind. Her toes squished in her gel-lined socks with each step but no longer tingled or itched.

"Ryan's been moved to a private room on the third floor." Shiloh stopped to speak to the nurses at the desk. Denali greeted Tianzi with a hard hug, resting in his arms a moment before kissing his cheek and hugging Iggy whom he carried.

"Hey, sweetheart," Denali said.

"Da, says I shouldn't bother you by crying."

Tianzi laughed, tossed her in the air, and kissed her cheek. "No, he said seeing you cry will bother her. There's a difference."

A woman walking past, carrying a small bouquet

of flowers, gave a disapproving sniff, narrowing her eyes at Denali.

Denali smiled at the woman, she reminded her of a poor copy of her mother. Where her mother wore expensive pantsuits and real pearls, this woman's polyester suit had seen better days. Large fake pearls encircled an age-spotted neck, but the no-nonsense stride was exactly the same. The haircut was also the same shoulder-length bob. The color was different. Her mother's naturally graying dark hair shone with health. This woman's dyed blond hair looked brittle. A wide smile lit Denali's eyes. There was nothing fake about her mother. She was a rock.

"When will you be home?" Iggy asked petulantly.

"Soon, I hope." Denali turned her attention back to her sister. Lots of people had glared and stared as she entered. The attention unnerved her, but the flowers reminded her.

"I need flowers for Ryan."

Tianzi rose an eyebrow.

Denali blushed and he laughed.

"Like that, is it?" He smirked and took her arm. "The gift shop will have some, and maybe buy a comb." He snickered when she glared.

Twenty minutes later, she paused before the door of Ryan's room. Officer Ortega glared at her from half-lidded eyes.

"Hello," she said tentatively. The large bouquet of roses she carried rustled as she nervously shifted her grip.

"He'll see you." He lifted his newspaper, snapping it open and burying his face in the folds in clear dismissal.

A heavy sigh escaped her. *Later,* she told herself. *I'll fix this later.*

"Oh, excuse me, I didn't realize you had company," Denali said when she stepped inside the room. She hesitated right inside the doorway. The dyed blond woman who'd glared at her stood by the window arranging the flowers she'd brought in a hospital water jug. A tall man built like Ryan with wide shoulders and narrow hips stood beside her, staring from the window. He peered over his shoulder, smiled, and turned, offering his hand. From the front, the resemblance was unmistakable. Same kind blue eyes and high cheekbones. His hair was a lighter brown then Ryan's and speckled with gray.

"You must be Ryan's father." She balanced the flowers against her chest and shook the proffered hand. Nervous butterflies made her hands shake. She really wanted him to mean it.

"And you're Denali. Ryan's told us—"

"Ryan's told us nothing," the woman snapped. "He's delirious. Now isn't a good time for visitors."

The smile fled Denali's face.

"Mom, be nice. Denali isn't a visitor, she's my fiancé."

Her heart began to beat hard. He still wanted her. She turned to face him. Love shone from his eyes. Tension she hadn't realized she carried slid from her shoulders. For a moment, she thought she might faint so great was her relief.

He held a hand out to her. A smile bloomed on her face, and she laughed as she took his hand. The flowers forgotten, she leaned down to kiss him, drawing back with a sharp groan of pain.

"Sorry, bad ribs. These are for you."

His free hand traced her face, his thumb brushing her lips. "I love you."

"I love you too." Again, grinning like a fool, she stared at him, wanting to kiss him badly, but her ribs constrained her.

"Rubbish," his mother snapped. "Don't be ridiculous, you don't even know her."

"I know everything I need too," Ryan said.

The simple, confident tone soothed the hurt from his mother's harsh words.

"Son," his father said and paused to clear his throat.

"Dad, I do know, and I want her strength and passion. A man with a wife like Denali can rest easy knowing nothing will break her. What she sets out to do, she accomplishes with her whole heart. It isn't her physical beauty, it's her soul I want." His voice lowered, and he turned to Denali. "I want all of you."

Tears filled her eyes. She rubbed them from her cheek with the back of her hand, smearing her careful makeup. "Your mom is worried because she doesn't know me."

"No, I'm worried because I do. I know the kind of

girl you are. Hot tempered and rash. A handsome man like my son sees it as passion and you pounce, knowing what a good catch he is."

Denali shrugged and grinned. "I can't deny that he's handsome and a good catch."

"See?" his mother said in triumph. "I told you she was a gold digger."

Denali burst into laughter and grabbed her side. "Oh God." She moaned between snorts of laughter. "Believe me, we didn't talk about finances."

"I saw you kiss that man in the hallway and your little girl."

"We have a daughter?" Ryan sounded thrilled.

Again, her eyes filled with tears. His trust in her was so perfect it left her breathless.

"Not yet, someday I hope."

His eyes darkened, and his gaze traveled her body. Unconsciously, she leaned toward him.

"The man was my brother Tianzi, and the little girl is my sister Iggy.

"Those two were not related to you; they were black."

"Mother, stop it." Ryan turned and glared at his mother.

"Everyone, calm down," his father said. "Ellen, your son is going to marry her; open your eyes and look. They're in love. It isn't our choice; it's his. Let's start over." He smiled and held out his hand again. "I'm Nelson Graham, and this is my wife, Ellen. We're delighted to meet you, Denali. Ryan told us you had siblings and that he assumed you were adopted. How many do you have?"

She shook Nelson's hand and returned to Ryan, sitting stiffly on the edge of the bed. "Eight brothers and six sisters now. The reminder of her loss hurt, a sharp pain to the heart that brought tears to her eyes.

"Fifteen!" Ellen exclaimed, looking horrified.

"All adopted. My parents have no natural children."

"And your parents are okay with you marrying a stranger? Of course, they are," she answered her own question, pursing her lips and glaring at Denali. "They're probably delighted with one less mouth to feed."

Denali giggled, then groaned and grabbed at her ribs. "My parents trust my judgment. I support myself, I won't need your son's money. Everything I have will be his."

"Everything I am is yours," Ryan murmured and brought her hand to his lips.

The small contact sent a tingle through her entire body.

"How old are you?" Ellen asked.

"She's twenty. And before you say it, yes, I'm six years older. The math isn't hard. I figured it out as soon as she told me. I'll wait as long as she likes."

Ellen quirked an eyebrow. "Twenty? How are you a teacher? Or are you an aid?"

"I'm not really a teacher. I still go to school." She turned to Ryan. "I go to school in Boston, but I'm willing to commute. My house is mobile, so we can park it halfway. I'm willing to do whatever we have to, to stay together.

Ellen drew in a deep offended breath. "No! Absolutely not! No son of my mine is living in a trailer park. What will my friends think? That's just ridiculous."

"Mother," Ryan said, sounding aggravated.

Denali glanced between them and patted his hand. She really didn't want to cause a rift. "I'm sorry, I wasn't clear. I live on a houseboat. It's really nice. If you give it a chance, you'll like it, but if Ryan hates it, I can move."

"How many more years of school do you have?" Nelson asked. "Washington to Boston is a long, expensive commute."

"Well." A blush climbed Denali's cheeks. "My da says I'll likely go forever, and he might be right."

Ellen's glare deepened. "Hmmph, and you expect my son to support you?"

"Not at all," Denali said hurriedly. "I work at the school, and they let me take classes free. There are lots of schools though. Ryan and I can figure out what one works best for his career, or he could quit. I could easily support him."

Nelson laughed and put an arm around his wife." She's got you there. A teacher as a daughter-in-law will be nice."

Denali nervously cleared her throat. "Well, as I said, I'm not really a teacher. I work in a lab there. My sister was the teacher, and I worked for her as a favor when Mr. Rand died unexpectedly."

"You're a scientist?" Ryan asked in interest.

A wave of relief flooded her. Only his opinion really mattered, and he didn't seem to care that she wasn't a teacher from Washington. "I work with computers writing codes and programming mostly. Some of what I do is classified."

"What school?"

"MIT."

He grinned, his grin widening when he glanced at his mother.

She snorted, then laughed. "You can't blame me for being worried."

"I don't at all," Denali assured her, lightly squeezing Ryan's hand. "I'd be worried too if I were his mother, but I assure you, I'll take very good care of him and try my hardest to make him happy."

Ellen nodded slowly.

"She probably makes more than I do," Ryan said.

"My finances are a bit complicated, but I'll walk you through them when we get a chance. I really could support both of us though. My boat is paid for and almost finished. I've been upgrading it slowly as time permitted."

"Yourself?" Ryan asked, sounding interested.

Denali grinned at him, hoping he liked tinkering as much as she did. "My family helps, but most of the work I can do myself. I like gadgets and electronics, so my house is full of them. Right now, I live at our family home, and the boat is docked in Boston. Tianzi looks after it for me. He lives there. Do you have any siblings?"

"Nope, just me. Your family sounds fun." Ryan kissed her hand again, making her heart flutter.

"Your mother must be crazy," Ellen muttered.

Denali laughed. "People have said as much."

"Let's leave the kids to visit. I'm sure they have things to talk about." Nelson took his wife's arm and drew her from the room.

THIRTEEN

Alone at Last

"Alone at last," Ryan said, heaving an exagerated sigh as the door closed behind his parents. "I'm so glad you didn't change your mind."

She ran a finger over his stubbled cheek. "I never will."

His eyes glittered with unshed tears. He closed them, lifted her fingertips to his lips, and kissed them. "I know. I feel like I've always known you." His eyes opened, showing his sincerity. The look in them fluttered her stomach. "I've never met anyone in my life I trusted as much. You can trust me the same way."

"I already do." She sighed unhappily and grabbed her ribs. "I really want to kiss you.

"I can't lift the bed to a more upright position yet, doctor's orders. One more day of lying flat to ensure the neck wound stays closed."

"How's the leg?"

"Sore and itchy."

"You have a lot of bruises?"

"You show me yours, and I'll show you mine."

She laughed and groaned. "God, I really want to but…" The thought of seeing him naked and touching him made her breath catch. Heat flushed her body.

"Yeah, me too." He ran his hand over her hair. "We have the rest of our lives. There's no rush. When we make love for the first time, it's going to be perfect."

Denali groaned and lowered her body slowly, supporting her weight with a hand on either side of him. His hands laid softly on her hips. She never wanted the kiss to end.

"Get off my boyfriend, bitch!"

The words jerked Denali from the daze his kiss induced.

"You aren't my girlfriend, Gail," Ryan snapped.

"Well, she can't be either. She's crazy; everyone knows that. She's a crazy, vicious murderer."

Denali pushed herself upright with slow, careful movements. The girl at the door wore a tight white miniskirt and four-inch heels. The pink tank top left nothing to the imagination. Long, dyed-blond hair teased to within an inch of its life curled around her heavily made-up face. Denali wondered how she hadn't frozen to death crossing the parking lot.

Pretty as a snake, Denali thought, pondering what Ryan saw in her.

As if reading her mind Ryan mumbled, "What did I ever see in you." He squeezed her hand and cleared his throat before saying loudly.

"Denali and I are getting married."

"Did you tell her you fucked me just three weeks ago?"

"No, surprisingly your name never came up."

Denali giggled and clapped a hand over her mouth.

Gail glared. "He'll forget to call you too. Don't believe his bullshit lines. You think you're special. You're not."

"Gail, cut it out. What the hell do you hope to accomplish? You and I had no relationship. None."

"Liar."

"Look, it's clear you guys need to talk. I'll give you privacy." She gave Ryan a rueful smile as he winced. "She changes nothing," Denali murmured as she ran a finger lightly along his bottom lip, wishing she could kiss him, and turned to the door.

"You can't have him. I'm so much better than you for him." Gail's hand dropped into the enormous gold purse hanging from her shoulder as her eyes narrowed. "You'll see, I'm just as tough as she is." Her hand emerged from the bag clutching a twenty-two.

"Are you crazy?" Ryan yelled.

Denali stepped forward and grabbed the hand

pointing the gun, pushed it into the air, and punched Gail hard in the kidney.

Gail dropped the gun. "You bitch," she sobbed as she scanned the floor for the fallen weapon.

Denali punched her again and yanked the bag from her shoulder. A harsh groan escaped her as she bent to retrieve the gun.

"Gail, cut it out. Do you want to go to prison? Jesus!" Ryan sounded aggravated and worried.

"She's a murderer; everyone knows that. You don't go to prison for killing murderers." Gail clutched her stomach and backed away from Denali.

"You will be too if you shoot her. Don't be a stupid ass."

"Wow," Denali said as she handed Ryan the gun and bag.

Ryan flushed bright red.

"Did you know she was this stupid," Denali whispered as she leaned on the edge of Ryan's bed and cradled her ribs with both hands.

The flush on his face deepened.

She turned to Gail and spoke louder. "I won't press charges but smarten up. What you just did could earn you serious jail time. And what's the point? Even if I didn't exist, he wouldn't want you. I'm sorry your hurt, but it has nothing to do with me." She pushed herself upright.

"Damn, I'm so sorry, Denali. Give us a minute. As you can see she's a bit overwrought. I love you, and only you — forever. Please..."

"Together forever." Denali gave him a sad smile and turned away, his relieved answering smile lightening her heart. Gail was his problem. Ryan's prior relationships were something they could deal with later, privately.

Gail slapped at her as she passed, her long nails scratching her neck and tangling in her hair.

Denali tried to push her away. "Get therapy. You're out of control."

"I hate you," Gail sobbed and threw herself at Denali, yanking her hair and slapping at her.

"Get off," Ryan yelled.

"You're going to hurt him," Denali shouted as she punched Gail again. "Ryan, stay down, don't break your stitches. Are you trying to kill him?"

"No, you, you stupid bitch. I hate you."

A sharp bark of laughter escaped her that changed to a hissing moan as she considered telling her only stupid people repeated insults. Gail pressed her hard against the wall, trying to scratch her face.

"Gail, stop it right now, or I'll never speak to you again," Ryan snapped.

Gail released Denali's hair, taking strands with her caught in her jewelry and fist. Tears had smeared the mascara on her eyes. Black streaks trailed across her cheeks. Teeth clenched in a furious scowl she shook her fist.

Denali wanted to hit her again but couldn't release her ribs or the wall that held her up.

"Please, Gail? Ryan asked softly.

Denali's heart caught; she'd do anything he asked if he asked her in that tone.

It worked on Gail too; her shoulders lowered and she stepped away.

"Sorry." Both hands rose to rub her eyes, smearing the makeup there across her nose and cheeks. "I'm sorry. I'm acting crazy. Can you just talk to me?" she pleaded to Ryan.

Denali lifted a hand in a small wave and limped from the room, each step a piercing agony of stabbing pain. The fight, small though it was, had injured her already hurt ribs more than any of the proceeding fights.

Officer Ortega glanced at her and laughed. "Told you he had a girlfriend. Looks like she doesn't like poachers. Sent you packing, did she?"

With both arms clutching her ribs, Denali leaned against the wall opposite the door. "What did I ever do to you?"

Officer Ortega folded the paper and placed it on the floor. "Nothing. Ryan's my partner; it's my job to look out for him. I haven't decided yet if you're a hot-headed psycho, a glory hog, or what, but I know you're bad news. He had a good life before he met you. Now he's clinging to life in a hospital bed."

Denali snorted and slid down the wall. Black spots became swirling blooms that covered her vision. Blood thrummed hard in her ears. She missed what he said next.

"— fault but maybe he wouldn't have been if you

hadn't attacked."

She nodded numbly as tears of pain filled her eyes. White-hot agony stabbed her chest.

"Don't try that bullshit. Tears? Really? You're a crocodile. I saw you kill three men without batting an eye; don't pretend my words hurt."

"Why let her in while I was there?" Her breath came hard, making her words tremble when she'd meant to sound angry.

"Hell, if an old flame makes you buckle and run, good riddance. Ryan does a tough job and doesn't need a delicate wilting flower who's going to leave if he stays out all or night, or a crazy woman who makes threats."

Denali lifted an eyebrow and snorted.

"Yeah, I heard her. I don't like her either. It happens to police officers a lot. The crazy can follow us home. If you can't hack it, go now before you break his heart. But if you cared about him at all, you'd leave him the hell alone, not drag him down with you."

Denali closed her eyes and leaned her head back against the wall. *Was she going down?* At the minute, it felt like it. She wanted to leave but lacked the strength to stand. Sweat sprang up on her brow, and she thought she might vomit.

"Nobody's ever hated me before," she said in a small voice.

"Lots of people hate you now."

"Ryan doesn't," she said the words in a bare

whisper more to herself than him. "I did the best I could," she mumbled, wanting to defend her actions so Ryan's friends wouldn't hate her, but lacked both breath to speak and permission.

"No, he doesn't," the officer said thoughtfully.

The elevator at the end of the hall dinged. Officer Ortega rose, a frown on his face as a dull moaning cry echoed down the hallway.

"Maria, I told you to leave her home." He hurried to the woman carrying a young girl. Fisted hands laid atop two skinny, brown braids tied in pink ribbons that matched the frilly pink dress. The girl cried in a rhythmic moan, banging her forehead on her mother's shoulder.

Denali stared after Officer Ortega, then closed her eyes, letting the monotone sound soothe her. No stranger to autism from Anya's work, she recognized the signs and her heart went out to the family.

Pain skittered over her ribs in waves. To distract herself, she concentrated on the girl. Her head jerked up, and her eyes opened. The noise was a clear pattern, a desperate try to communicate. Eyes on the girl's hands, she fumbled for her cell phone.

"You aren't autistic at all are you," she mumbled as she typed on the tiny keyboard. She lifted two fingers to her lips and blew shrilly. The loud whistle stopped everyone in the vicinity and made her groan and pant for breath.

"Carry on," she gasped to the nurse and orderly who paused and stared and then she clapped sharply three times.

Cally turned her tear-streaked face to her.

Denali clapped again, varying the pattern. Cally stared. Denali clapped. Cally clapped.

"Stop it," Officer Ortega ordered, his face bright red. "We don't encourage her. She's autistic and can't help it.

"She isn't autistic,"

"The hell you know."

Denali shrugged." I'm betting she was diagnosed an autistic, but she's repeating meaningful patterns. Hell, maybe she is autistic, but it isn't a type I've seen before. My sister Anya would love to meet her. I bet she could teach her to communicate."

"What the hell are you talking about. And stop clapping."

Denali altered her pattern of claps, then tucked her hands beneath her legs. Cally laid her head on her mother's shoulder and put her thumb in her mouth. Her eyes never left Denali.

Denali leaned back and closed her eyes. "My sister Anya is a specialist in autism. A doctor and a good one. Call her, what could it hurt?"

"Jeff?" Officer Ortega's wife asked uncertainly, her voice laced with hope.

"You're a real asshole, aren't you? You don't know anything about my family and look how you're upsetting my wife.

"I'm sorry. My sister's number is in my phone. You're right; I know nothing about you, but I've done work with Anya, and we've published two books on this. What Cally has is different. She's obviously smart. Look what we just did here. Think what I could do if my chest weren't killing me. I'm an expert at languages. I have a doctorate from Boston College for it and another from MIT in computer science with a minor in mathematics. My specialty is codes — patterns. I can't make you get Cally help." Denali gave up, lacking the air to speak and let the phone tumble to her lap.

The black spots had taken over completely, leaving her blinded by pain. The pain was a fire each movement fanned higher.

"I need help. Can you call my sister?" *How ironic,* Denali thought as the room seemed to rotate. *I'm going to die unattended on the floor of my family's hospital.*

"What?" Officer Ortega asked, glaring over his shoulder at her.

Denali screamed, the sound emerging as a hiss as she slid to the side unable to hold herself upright. Cally began to cry. Blackness engulfed her.

FOURTEEN

How'd She Get by You

When Denali opened her eyes, Ryan leaned over her, his unshaven cheeks drawn, his eyes circled with dark rings.

"You scared me to death." He kissed her lips. "Are you awake?"

"Yes." The harsh croak of her voice surprised her. She lifted a trembling hand, meaning to touch his face, and let it drop, the effort exhausting her.

"Don't move. You've been unconscious for twelve hours. Twelve hours!" Ryan repeated angrily. "I thought you were going to die. I've never been more terrified. Are you okay?" he smoothed her hair and took a deep breath. "Sorry, I'm babbling. Don't you dare die while I call the doctor."

She wanted to laugh and reassure him but lacked the energy.

Her brother Danxia entered the room a minute later. He examined the machines hooked to her, then poked and prodded her.

"Cut it out," she mumbled as he shone the light in her eyes for the second time.

"That's better." He grinned at Ryan. "When she's all passive, you need to worry. This is the real her."

"What time is it?" Denali asked.

"Seven thirty, but who cares? You aren't going anywhere."

"I have to be back at the police station by eight."

"Denali, you even try to sit, and I'll restrain you. I'm not kidding. I've lost one sister this week and I'm not losing another. Lay there and get better!"

"Danxia… I'm so tired I want nothing more than to lay here, but I'll be arrested…" She closed her eyes and moaned more from annoyance than pain. She felt kind of floaty and good.

"Sweetheart, you won't be arrested, I promise. Go to sleep," Ryan said.

"Stay with me?"

"Forever." Ryan ran his thumb over her lower lip. She smiled and closed her eyes again.

"How'd you do that?" Danxia asked in amazement as she drifted into the dark.

The next thing she knew bright midday sun streamed across her face. Ryan slept beside her, his breath on her temple filling her with joy. The heat from his body where it lay against hers comforted her. She brought his hand to her lips and kissed it, settling it against her cheek, her gaze lighting on the gaudy gold purse on the nightstand. For a moment, she wondered what happened to Gail, but she didn't really care. He was hers now; she felt it in every fiber of her being.

Not for a second did she doubt his love for her or the truth of his words. She pitied Gail, it would kill her to lose him too. But she believed him when he said Gail had never been a girlfriend, and she believed him when he said it would just be her forever.

She drifted to sleep again feeling safe and loved.

She woke again when he stirred. "This is nice, waking up with you."

"Mmm," he made a small aroused sound and kissed her neck.

For the first time, she realized he was shirtless, his chest broad and smooth under her palm. Until this moment, she'd never experienced desire, not true desire. She wanted nothing more than to run her hands over him and explore his body. The curve of his shoulder under her hand made her gasp.

"Kiss me," she breathed.

He leaned across her and really kissed her.

"Huh-hum!" Someone cleared their throat loudly. Flushed and breathing hard, Denali stared into Ryan's eyes as he reluctantly pulled away.

"I'm striking out in the romance department," he whispered, making her laugh.

"You're doing just fine," she whispered back and moaned as heat leaped into his eyes.

"Standing right here," Meteora said and snapped her fingers.

Denali blushed and pulled the light blanket up.

"I need a bathroom. Be right back," Ryan said.

"Wow," Meteora said softly as the bathroom door closed behind Ryan.

Denali giggled.

Meteora grinned at her. "I'm happy for you. He seems like a really decent guy."

He's perfect."

"Remember that when he leaves his dirty clothes on the floor and the toilet seat up. How you feeling?"

"Still tired and woozy. Did you give me something?"

"We gave you a lot of something. Doctor Reynolds operated under Danxia's watchful eyes and half the staff of the hospital. Your seventh vertebrosternal rib on the right-hand side is now held together by a small flexible metal plate and four screws. A minor tear in the pulmonary artery has been stitched closed. Another small puncture of the chest wall led to a Tension-Pneumothorax, which required a chest tube."

Meteora took her hand when she reached to feel her chest and laid it at her side. "Don't worry about it. We'll do x-rays again to make sure it remains clear, but you're doing much, much better. In a day or so we'll remove the tube."

Meteora kissed her cheek. "You almost died. No more stupid chances. Listen to your doctors! We mean it when we say take it easy."

"I meant to," Denali said sulkily. "His girlfriend pulled a gun on me. What was I supposed to do? Let her shoot me?"

"Oh jeez, this could only happen to you. She almost killed you. Call me right away if you're hurt again. We wrapped the ribs. Keep them wrapped for twenty-four hours to give the surgery a chance to heal, then we'll unwrap them so you don't develop pneumonia. No sex! No strenuous activity at all."

"Maybe you should say that louder so the people next door hear."

Meteora snickered. "Will you be good, or do I need to speak with him?"

"No need; I heard you," Ryan said as he exited the bathroom. "We'll be good; scouts honor." He held up two fingers and winked at Meteora. "How hurt is she?"

Denali couldn't help grinning at him; he looked so good standing there in the sleep pants with his hair messy and five o'clock shadow on his cheeks. And he was hers. She couldn't wait to be alone with him.

Meteora frowned, her narrowed gaze traveling

between them. "Seriously, so listen to me. The ribs shouldn't hurt that bad now that the badly broken rib is being held together, but they remained injured. Let them heal. If one nicks an artery, you're all done. No bending, lifting or straining of any kind. No more gunfights!"

Denali rolled her eyes.

"Drink the broth the nurse brings you. Ryan, I'll have a meal sent here for you. We're going to discharge you with the same instructions. No lifting or straining. See your doctor in three days for the throat and five for the leg. The stitches are barely healed and breaking them could kill you, so when I say take it easy — take it easy."

"For how long?" Ryan asked.

"Until you're completely healed." Meteora said in exasperation. "The neck injury should heal quickly. The leg might require some therapy." She sighed and laughed. "What you really want to know, but don't want to ask her sister, is how long until you can have sex."

Denali blushed and giggled as Ryan turned red.

Meteora snickered. "Her ribs won't be fully healed for six to eight weeks." She laughed when Denali groaned. "But, in a week, you should be breathing much better. And as long as the pain is tolerable, and you're careful, light contact would be okay. No vigorous exercise of any kind. Keep your torso as still and straight as you can. You'll need help dressing and caring for yourself for a few weeks at least."

Ryan saluted. "Got it, Doc. I'll take good care of her."

Meteora hesitated, a troubled expression on her face. "Denali, I know you want to stay with him, but Mom and Dad need you home. If you wouldn't mind, Ryan, could you stay there while she recovers? My parents really need her. You know they'll never ask, Denali, but they do need you."

"Yes," Ryan said before Denali answered. "We can stay there. I don't even mind if we can't share a room. Thanks for inviting me. You sure they won't mind? Space at your home must be tight or are most of your siblings older?"

"They won't mind, and we have room. I'll leave you two to get better acquainted. Don't stay up too long talking. Danxia ordered more blood work, and the nurse will be in with more pain medicine in an hour or so. It will make you sleepy. Don't fight it, sleep until morning. Sleep is the best thing for you both right now.

Meteora paused at the door. "Ryan, your doctor will be by to discharge you, and I'll have your belongings brought here. Should I send for clothes for you?"

"When will Denali be discharged?"

"Maybe tomorrow, it depends on the blood work."

"My mom will bring me clothes if I can stay here until tomorrow."

"You can stay as long as you like. Don't worry

about visiting hours." Meteora grinned at her sister. "You two have a lot to talk about. Welcome to the family, Ryan." She returned and kissed his cheek, then her sister's.

"No more fighting," she said over her shoulder as she closed the door behind her.

Denali reached for him. "Can we talk later? I just want to hold you and feel you breathe."

"Sounds perfect," he murmured as he carefully lay beside her and smoothed her hair back.

The weight of his hand on her skull sent a tingle through her entire body. He pressed his lips to hers, the brief contact making her hum with pleasure.

"I feel really good."

He laughed, his warm breath fanning her face. "Good pain meds." His voice deepened as he ran a hand lightly over the curve of her side. "You feel really good to me too." He snuggled closer, resting his face on her pillow and placing his injured leg over hers. "Too close?"

"Perfect," she sighed and ran her hand through his hair, pulling his lips to hers again. They lay with their foreheads touching, fingers wound in each other's hair, just being together. Denali dozed off and woke again when Ryan's doctor entered and examined him. She drank her broth and gave more blood to the nurse as Ryan signed his discharge papers. The nurse injected the IV in her arm with pain medication.

"No more until seven. So, try to sleep until then,"

she warned as she left the room.

Denali drifted to sleep as Ryan spoke with his mother on his cell phone.

When next she woke, a bright slice of light from the hallway illuminated her dark hospital room.

"What time is it," she asked muzzily.

Ryan sat, swinging his legs to the floor as a nurse entered.

"Routine check, Ms. Wong." The girl said cheerfully "The doctor ordered more pain meds."

Without turning on the light, she approached the IV pole, setting down the clipboard she carried and reaching into her pocket.

Denali exchanged a confused glance with Ryan.

"What doctor order it?" Ryan asked and flipped on the light over the bed.

The nurse frowned. "You shouldn't be here; visiting hours are over. The patient needs rest." While she spoke, she removed a vial and injected a clear liquid into the IV bag.

Denali ripped the IV from her arm.

The nurse dropped the bottle as Ryan reached slow and clumsy over the bed to her. The nurse's hand darted to the waistband of her pants.

Denali pressed the call bottom while trying to force her sluggish body upright. "We need help in here; send security."

Ryan swore as he snatched Gail's gold purse from the small table beside the bed and grabbed the gun it held.

The nurse darted for the door, removing a small pistol from her waistband. She paused as the door to the room swung open, glancing at it unwittingly, giving Ryan time to grab the gun and fired right as Ryan did. Raul caught her crumpling body.

FIFTEEN

Tell Me About Your Family

Denali felt slow and disconnected. "What's happening?"

"Are you okay? Ryan leaned over her, his anxious gaze scanning her body.

"What the hell was that? Was she another x-girlfriend?"

Ryan laughed and kissed her. "You're okay." He sounded relieved.

"Are you?"

"Fine," he said as he sat shakily on the edge of her bed. "What gave her away?"

"No one in this hospital would call me Ms. Wong or try to kick my guests out." Denali laid back and closed her eyes. Now that she relaxed, she noticed the throbbing of her chest.

"You sure you're okay? You're all pale and sweaty."

"I've felt better," Denali said without opening her eyes.

In the hallway, men spoke in loud, angry voices.

"Danxia," Ryan called. "She needs a doctor."

"Damn it, let me through to my patient! Has she been shot again?'

Her brother sounded really angry, Denali thought. She wished she had the strength to holler back she was okay, but she didn't. She lay there and panted.

Four men entered the room. Her brother, Raul the FBI agent, and a man she didn't know but assumed was another agent by his dress, and Stan, a security guard. Stan was long familiar to Denali, escorting family members anywhere her mother deemed unsafe.

"Shall I throw these men out, Ms. Denali?" Stan asked, laying a hand on his holstered gun.

She had to take a deep breath and force the words out. "No thanks, Stan. Call my mom though, please."

"Yes, Ma'am." Stan nodded his head and left the room, closing the door behind him.

Danxia leaned over her, listening to her breath through his stethoscope.

"How'd you get here so fast?"

"Shut up and let me listen." Her brother glared at her.

Denali rolled her eyes and did as he bid. He examined her completely before placing the stethoscope over his neck and speaking.

"Meteora and I are taking turns sleeping right next door in case you need us, and good thing we are. You're okay; she shot the bed. I want another X-ray to be on the safe side, but you're taking years from my life." He turned and glared at the two FBI agents. "How the hell did she get passed you?"

Raul shrugged. "She checked out as legit. Right name, right badge, doctor's orders, all appeared genuine. She even stopped and spoke with the other nurses at the desk. Nothing seemed off at all."

The tightness in Denali's throat eased, allowing easier breaths.

Ryan handed Raul the IV bag. "She put something in here."

"We'll find out what." Raul handed the bag to his partner.

"How did you know she wasn't legitimate?" Raul asked.

Denali shrugged, then winced and grabbed at her chest. "No one here would call me Ms. Wong. Well, maybe a new person, but I doubt I'd get assigned a new person, and my sister told me no more meds until seven."

Ryan nodded. "That's what tipped me off. Did I kill her?"

"No, hospital security has her, and they're taking her to the ER," Danxia said. "Who the hell was she, and why did she want to kill my sister?"

"Both good questions," Raul said. "The FBI will be

finding out the answers. Did she say anything? Make threats or demands?"

"No," Ryan said.

Denali shook her head.

Danxia snapped, "Out! My sister needs rest, not more interrogations. I'll call her lawyer if I have too, but I want you out of here."

Raul held up his hands and stepped backward toward the door. "We don't mean her any harm, just doing our jobs."

Danxia snorted derisively. "Do them later. She needs rest. Get out!"

"When will she well to enough to speak with us?"

Arms out held to the sides, Danxia shooed the men from the room. The door closed cutting off his, "When I say," in mid-sentence.

Denali snickered and clutched her ribs.

"Did you hurt yourself?"

"No, they hurt much less than they did. I'm okay. Thank God you were here."

Ryan snorted. "Who'd of thought Gail would come in handy.

"Don't make me laugh," Denali gasped as she tried to stop laughing.

Ryan smiled and ran a hand through her hair. "I can't believe you're not angry about her or jealous or ..." he trailed off, an unhappy expression on his face.

"Why would I be?" The laughter faded, his unhappiness making her sad. "We didn't even know each other three weeks ago. I hate the thought you had sex with anyone except me, but I can't change it. I do question your judgment though."

Denali frowned thoughtfully at him. "She seems really stupid, not like someone I picture you with."

Ryan ducked his head and rubbed his cheeks, avoiding Denali's eyes. "This makes me sound bad, but I wasn't looking for a girlfriend when I picked her up, just sex. The second time we had sex I knew it was a mistake, but I'd had a few too many and thought I was real clear that it wouldn't happen again."

Ryan slumped back on the bed, resting his elbow on the pillow to prop his forehead on his fingertips, turning to facing her. "Three months ago, I went to a party. She was there, and we hit it off. She took me to her place afterward. I realized she wasn't for me. In the morning, I thanked her, told her I wasn't interested in a girlfriend and left. She called me a few times and stopped at the precinct once. Three weeks ago, she showed up with friends at the bar we hang out at. I'm not stupid, I realized she wanted to date me, but I told her I wasn't interested."

A flush climbed his cheeks and he covered his eyes with his hand." She offered a no strings attached night. I should've known better from the phone calls and whatnot, but… anyway, I felt like a shit the next day and made plans to meet her for coffee after work. I didn't want to just walk out. I mean she was nice to me, the least I could do was break it off nicely."

Ryan turned on his side to face her. "I hurt her; I

know that. She pretended she was fine with it and offered to meet me again 'no strings attached' I turned her down as nice as I knew how."

"Have you had a lot of girlfriends or…one-night stands?"

Ryan winced. "Two serious girlfriends. Six women who I had no intention of having a relationship with. Most of those affairs were very brief although one lasted for six months."

"What happened to the serious girlfriends?"

"Julie met someone else. At the time I was heartbroken, now I realize I made a narrow escape. She's on husband number two already. I dated her from sixteen to twenty. From twenty-two to twenty-four I dated Janice Helms. I liked her a lot and wanted to love her, but never did. She was kind and fun, but something was always missing. When she gave me a marriage ultimatum, we broke up. I'm so glad we did."

"Me too." Denali kissed him.

His smile made his blue eyes sparkle. "I love that you believe me so easily."

"You've more than earned my trust. I'm sure we'll have problems—"

Ryan laughed; he rolled onto his back and grabbed his stomach, laughing so hard his eyes teared.

"I meant relationship problems." She giggled and laughed with him.

"I know what you meant, but if we can handle

crazy killers we can handle toothpaste caps or missed dinners."

"I love you," Denali whispered.

"I feel it." Ryan laid his hand along her face. "When you smile at me, hell, when you glance at me, I feel your love. I hope you feel mine the same way."

"I do."

"Let's get married really soon. I know I said I wouldn't rush you, but I really want you to be completely mine. Is there an x-boyfriend I should worry about?"

"No. I've never had a serious relationship with anyone. I've barely dated." She laughed lightly and gave him a rueful grimace. "That's why I was here working with Olympia. My parents were concerned I was too withdrawn with no friends or lovers and wanted to make sure I was okay."

"Were you okay? Did someone hurt you?"

"I'm fine. Just picky. I was waiting for you."

"You're a virgin?" he sounded dismayed.

A dark blush scalded her cheeks.

"I'm so sorry I'm not." He kissed her lips then trailed kisses to her neck, making her heart beat fast. "I really want to hug you tight," he murmured against her hair.

"Me too."

His voice deepened, "I really want to make you mine."

"I am yours."

He groaned and kissed her again. She didn't

know it was possible to be that aroused from a kiss. He made her feel trembly and weak. Her entire body felt feverishly hot. The palm of his hand skimmed her side, cupping her breast for a moment before coming to rest on her hip, fanned the heat. He groaned when he pulled away.

"You need rest."

"I need a shower," she disagreed. "Want to help me?"

"Stop; you're killing me. I really do want to help, but I don't trust my self-control. Tell me about your family."

He settled her against his side and played idly with her hair as she spoke.

"Well, you've met Danxia already, he doesn't actually work at this hospital although he has rights here. He's a thoracic surgeon and sees patients at MedStar; his full name is Doctor Darsh Xianliang Li Doran Rubinstein-Wong. Danxia is a nickname. Like me, he's nicknamed for a mountain. Mountains in my father's culture are revered as places of power. I got my nickname for being tempestuous as a child, 'not easily crossed' as my mother would say. He got his for his strength and colorful genes.

"His childhood was rough. My parents adopted him at eight-years-old. He spent the first eight years of his life trying to deal with the cruel taunts of other children over his mixed heritage and scrounging food from dumpsters."

"What is his heritage? I've never seen a skin tone

that unique color of red-brown before."

"Mostly Indian. Not American Indian like Shiloh although Danxia has some Cherokee blood. He also has Spanish ancestors, but his exact parenting is unknown, also like me. The red tone of his skin remains a mystery. If he spends time in the sun his skin tans to a beautiful shade of mahogany, but he never makes time to spend outside anymore. Danxia and I both had genetic testing done.

"Let me guess; you're Irish."

She laughed. "Scottish, English, and French mostly."

"Olympia looked Indian to me, are a lot of your siblings Indian?"

"Olympia…" Denali took a deep breath.

"We don't have to talk about her if it hurts," Ryan said apologetically

"Olympia was a second mother to me. The best big sister anyone could ever have. Named Pia Ling Shu Rubinstein-Wong, my mother called her Olympia by the age of three because she did everything so well. At fifteen she won a silver medal in the Olympics for archery, and her nickname was adopted by everyone, not just family. When she finished graduate school, my parents bought the property Olympus sits on. When she received her doctorate, they gave it to her and helped her build her dream." Tears filled Denali's eyes. "She was thirty-nine and expecting her first child."

"Oh, Denali." Ryan's voice caught on a sob.

Denali wiped her face. "I haven't seen Neil yet. He's sure to be angry with me."

"Her husband?"

"Yeah."

"Nothing that happened was your fault."

"It sort of is. I designed the security for the school."

"What would you do differently now?"

"Each door should be able to be locked from the inside with bars or something."

"That wouldn't have saved her."

"Maybe it would have. There were cameras in the parking lot and doorways. If she knew in time, she could've locked them out even if they had keys."

"They had keys?"

"Let's not talk about this. I'm not supposed to discuss what happened with anyone."

Ryan nodded. "Who lives with your parents still?"

"Sensei, Bee, and Simon, who've you sort of met. My sixteen-year-old sister Iaia and five-year-old sister Iggy. My brother Zane is home from school. He's eighteen. We were really close growing up. My next closest sibling is Jeremy Liam Li Jie, but everyone calls him Lee. He's twenty-two and in the Navy but likely will come home for the funeral. The three of us were inseparable until I went away to college.

She grinned at him." I was twelve. I lived with my brother Tianzi in Boston while I got my first doctorate. My parents gave me the houseboat when I got the second one."

"So, your parents are wealthy, and you're a super genius?"

"I have a thing for numbers and patterns and an eidetic memory which makes me really good at languages. My sister Anya, who you've met, is also a doctor. She and I work together sometimes. Her specialty is autism, and we're trying to figure out how to communicate with autistic children. I also work for the government, examining codes. Both of those things I do mostly from my lab at school."

"You take classes and work at the school too?"

"Yeah, mostly programming. Computers speak their own language, and I'm working on a new one. Occasionally, I do translations for different departments, mostly giving opinions on already translated texts. My brother calls me in sometimes to help in his office if he needs to speak to a client in a hurry. The local police and hospital also call occasionally if they need a translator. I do that for free but only for really obscure languages."

"Which brother and how many languages do you speak and how do you have time for all that?"

"Tianzi is the DA in Boston. He doesn't need help a lot, he speaks six languages. I'm fluent in six middle eastern languages, all the romance languages and Swahili, Hindi, and Bengali. I'm working on the Indo-European languages, and while I'm nowhere near fluent yet, I'll get there eventually. I'm fluent in Mandarin, everyone in my family speaks that because of Da. I can get my point across and understand

Japanese, but I'm still learning it. The Sino-Tibetan languages are complex but stable, not incredibly hard to master. Russian, on the other hand, is an evolving language and incredibly hard to master as each region has its own idiom. While I can speak and understand, I'm by no means an expert.

"Believe it or not English is also a difficult language. For a non-native speaker, it's very hard to master our slang. If I say I have a bad ride, you know if I mean I have a fast car or a junker depending on the inflection of my voice. Because our slang changes so rapidly and leaves general usage quickly, it can be very confusing. Before I worked for Olympia, I began studying sign languages. Body language and hand gestures can be universal clues to meanings of sound. It will be years before I'm even close to mastering that. It's a complex subject."

"So basically, you study language."

"I study communication. How people communicate, what they say versus what they mean. Communication is what sets us apart from the animals. True communication is the only thing that makes us different. By communicating, we can better our situations and the situations of others. I'm not talking about the noise we make. Animals make noise; they bark, and growl, and whine and while that is communication, they can't convey complex thought to develop that thought to action. Hence, they're animals."

Denali grinned and laughed. "My mother argues

that not all humans aren't animals. Those unable or unwilling to use true communication do no more than grunt and growl their way through life never truly speaking."

"Your family is sort of intimidating. All these doctors and lawyers and you…"

"We're just people. People trying hard not to be animals the same as you." Denali sighed hard. "Olympia taught those kids how to think, not what to think. That was the difference in that school. In the long run, teaching a child the dates of battles by rote is meaningless. If we tell them about a war and say memorize who was in it and when and where it happened, what have they really learned? She didn't do any of that. No long boring classes on history or science or anything. She taught them to think and seek knowledge. Her loss is a great blow. Given time, it would've been obvious to the dimmest-witted person her methods were far superior."

"Can't the other teachers continue?"

"Sure, but who'll lead them? You have no idea how hard it is to keep a group on track and not get caught up in test scores and politically correct nonsense. I was there less than a year and saw how she had to constantly remind them they weren't competing with other schools, they were teaching the children to think. By high school age if a child can't think they're basically doomed to be animals for life. Sure, they can get along in our society, which caters to the weak, but they'll jump off the cliff if their peers do without a thought in their heads on the way down."

Ryan snickered. "Man, your sister must have been so unpopular with other teachers."

"Yeah, but she mostly ignored it. The students proved her point. Hers all excelled, and while the high schools and colleges tried to take credit, a clear trend was developing. In our society, grammar school isn't taken nearly as seriously as 'higher' education, and that's a major flaw in our system. We have a lot of flaws in our system, but it's still the best one on Earth."

"How many kids do you want?" Ryan asked.

Denali grinned at him. "I love how calm you are about that. Aren't you at all worried I'll want twenty or more?"

"Nope, if you do, you'll tell me why you think it's a good idea and probably be able to convince me."

"If we had a boy and girl I'd be happy with that. But not soon, I'm too busy now."

"What if we had two boys or two girls?" Smiling into her eyes, he ran his thumb over her bottom lip.

"We could try again? I'm really not set on any number."

"Okay, me either. One for sure, maybe more but not soon. I'm good with that."

"We still have politics and religion."

"Yikes, politics can start fights even in people who agree on the party. What about religion? Is your family very religious?" Ryan asked.

"Sort of, not in a traditional sense; we're more spiritual. My mom says prayers and means them but isn't a practicing Jew. My dad practices Buddhism but isn't a Buddhist. We attend no church, but we pray and believe there is a God. Whenever five or more of us gather for dinner, we light a candle to honor our ancestors. We celebrate Christmas, but not really as the birth of Christ more Santa Clause."

"Hmm, sounds pretty normal. I was raised Catholic but haven't been to church since I was thirteen. My mom goes weekly. Dad goes on holidays or when forced by my mother, but I think she goes for the social aspects, not to worship. I've never seen her pray at home although I've seen her cross herself."

Denali snickered.

"I pray occasionally," Ryan continued. "Usually using traditional Catholic prayers, but honestly, I don't know too much about my religion. We can raise our children in whatever religion you like. I like the idea of stealing the best parts from all of them like your family does. It is comforting to have symbols and traditional prayers."

"I'm good with that, we let them learn by example and find their own way. My brother Shiloh practices Navajo ceremonies. Some are very beautiful. We both learned to speak the language, and I used to go with him sometimes."

"What will be done for Olympia?"

A lump formed in Denali's throat. "I have no idea.

We've never held a funeral. Let's not talk about that either."

"Sorry, you should be resting anyway."

"Tell me about your family, its traditions, how you grew up. Tell me about your friends." Denali dozed off as he described a typical Christmas at his house.

SIXTEEN

I'm Bait

Danxia hadn't released her from the hospital for three days. She'd gone straight from there to the police station where she'd answered the same questions continually to faceless strangers in suits. It was the second day of interrogation now, and she was exhausted.

At times hostile, others kind, the men bit out questions and accusations in an unending storm. She felt dull and lifeless. The repetition and constant criticism were wearing. She didn't know if she cared anymore if they believed her or not if they would just let her go sleep after she saw Ryan. The thought made her smile.

"Are we amusing you, Ms. Rubinstein-Wong?"

Harry Aldridge, the district attorney, asked.

"No, sorry, I was thinking of something else? What did you ask?"

A woman dressed in police blues knocked on the door and opened it. "A package for Mr. Rubinstein-Wong. The messenger said it was urgent and you were expecting it."

"Thank you," Shiloh said and grinned, taking the box.

The policewoman smiled back.

Denali bit back a snort of laughter. Shiloh could charm feathers from a snake. A prosecutor like their brother Tianzi, Denali thought it was Shiloh's ability to manipulate jurors more than his legal skill that won him cases.

"Gentlemen. If I might provide corroborating evidence to my sister's testimony?"

He withdrew a USB stick from the box and inserted it into his computer.

"What evidence?

"Tracy Aims recorded everything she heard on Denali's phone. Including what was said over the intercom. I've had experts going over those tapes to eliminate everything except what the men are saying in the background."

"By all means…" The commissioner made an expansive gesture and leaned forward, placing his elbows on the table.

The two FBI agents exchange dismayed glances.

"You knew," Denali said.

Agent Santos winced.

Shiloh sighed and drummed his fingers on the table. His eyes narrowed on the agents as he hit play. A spate of Urdu in three different voices interspersed with laughs and expletives in English followed. Pauses filled the recording where the background remained unclear enough for a certain translation.

"What good is that? We need a translator."

"One moment please." Shiloh held up a hand." I hadn't heard the recordings until now. My assistant has had them translated, and you're welcome to have them translated yourself, of course, but Denali can interpret as she did that day. Let her translate so we have a clear record of what she thought was said before she hears the official version."

The commissioner waved his hand, and Shiloh restarted the recording.

A chill shivered her skin with remembered horror. In an expressionless voice, Denali translated. "None will remain alive to taint the Earth with their presence. Deaths of the capitalist's spawn will bring many to our cause. Children of infidel dogs. We do the world a favor. Send Rahiq for more explosives. The map of the gymnasium is off, we'll need more to ensure its total destruction. When they see the fate in store for succoring the spawn of capitalist pigs. Quiet, let Mahir speak." Denali waited out the muffled the laughter on the tape, then said, "I will light the torch, and God will reward me. We should burn the children too. No matter, let them search for the bodies in the wreckage. No survivors. Our five. We'll make an example no one will ever forget. A glorious triumph over our oppressors that will weaken them forever. I brought the marshmallows. Kill both the bitches, we can still burn them later. I still think we should place cameras in the gymnasium so the world can watch them die. You're not paid—' that's it," Denali said.

The men at the table sat back stunned.

"Later they spoke of hanging the male teachers upside down and how they'd make two examples on the roof, but I already knew they planned to kill everyone there. Some of them expected to die there as martyrs to their cause, but not all of them. They spoke of leading the fight in the coming war."

"Gentleman, I'll play our transcription now," Shiloh said.

Shiloh played another clip of a man speaking. He said almost exactly what Denali had. "As you can see, Denali knew the gymnasium was a death trap and acted courageously, at great risk to herself, to keep the children in her care safe."

The commissioner leaned back in his seat.

Raul spread his hands on the table. "I'll admit we knew. Our experts have gone over those recording in great detail. We retrieved similar recordings from a voice recorder placed in the purse Denali carried from the building. Whether we knew or not had no bearing on this questioning though."

"It had great bearing on the validity of her word,"

Shiloh argued. "Not to mention the media vilifying her."

"They did it on purpose," Denali said tiredly. "They want to see who causes the biggest stink. This isn't about me but finding out what groups are radical enough to take action. I'm bait.

A red flush climbed Shiloh's cheek. Denali winced, her brother was furious.

"It's fine," she added hurriedly, placing her hand on his. "I wish they'd supported me privately, but I understand. I too want the radicals watched closely. I've been thinking, and I hate to say this, but someone inside must have helped them. I can't think of any scenario where all the guards are taken out and no alarm trips. They had the keys to the rooms. How would they even know they needed them?"

"We think so too," Raul said. "In fact, we have a suspect. Our experts, who went over the recordings, note that Marion Cole never once cries out. Mrs. Ritchie and Mrs. Faison both can be heard in the background pleading for the children, but not a peep from Ms. Cole.

Denali drummed her fingertips on the table as she thought. "She was hired a year ago. Olympia vetted her employees thoroughly because of the security issues some of the children presented. A good portion of the children came from either well-to-do homes, political families, or both. Besides the two guards on the door, three more patrolled the grounds and another manned the gate on the drive. I'd assumed the door guards were killed before they had a chance to hit the emergency button to lock the outer doors, but now… Ms. Cole had that code and the code to the office doors." Denali slapped her hand on the table.

"Damn it! If I'd thought to look, I could've checked to see whose code was used."

"The records are destroyed then?"

"I assume from the explosion. Was any hardware recovered?"

"Some, mostly useless fragments."

"Have everything sent to my mother's house, and I'll do what I can to retrieve the information."

"Thank you," Raul hesitated.

"Yes, I'll cooperate any way you need."

"No!" Shiloh said, glaring at Raul. "We do *not* use my sister as bait. We especially don't use my sister as bait in the home with my young siblings and parents. Enough has been done to them. Release the tapes or I will. Let the world see she didn't risk those children on a whim or in anger."

The commissioner cleared his throat and tapped the tabletop with the military class ring he wore on his right hand. "The populace is afraid, both of another attack, and frankly" –he nodded apologetically at Denali— "of the teachers running amok. If we can show them concrete proof she acted with reason, it should calm them."

"These recordings are public and already being played by the media. To protect my family, I'll release the transcripts whether you like or not." Shiloh said as Raul opened his mouth to speak.

"I was going to say, we can't keep it quiet indefinitely, but we held back, not just to use Denali as 'bait' but, also, the plans they had were so gruesome we didn't want to cause a panic. But I agree. The truth needs to be told because it is the 'truth.'

Raul turned to Denali, a puzzled expression on his face. "What I don't understand is how you did it? I realize how you understood, your doctorate in languages, but you've had no training, yet you managed to kill fourteen hardened men."

Shiloh smirked and tweaked Denali's ponytail. "That's easy to explain. Our parents taught all their children everything they could about self-defense. Not just because they were wealthy and concerned, but because they believe all people should be able to protect themselves and those in their care. All of us can fight and shoot. Not all of us can climb or run like she can, that was the younger kids. They drove Mom nuts climbing everything in the house. My brother Lee started that; I think to get away from his pestering little sister."

Shiloh tweaked Denali's hair again. She batted his hand away, making him laugh. "It didn't work, nothing stops her when her mind is made up."

"Back to business." Harry turned to the commissioner. "Prepare a statement for the press. We'd better warn them first, privately, so they can be ready. God knows what they'll do if we make them look bad. Sometimes I think they don't care if they whip the nation into hysteria as long as they get good ratings."

"I'll see to it," the governor said. Until then, he'd said nothing, sitting quietly, observing the proceedings. "I'll admit I was angry; my granddaughter was in that school. Now I'm sorry for my thoughts. Thank you. You saved her life. This isn't the time or place, but Olympus was a great school, and I hope it can continue to be one. I'm unsure who to contact to offer my support for the rebuilding."

"Neil, I suppose," Denali said doubtfully. She hadn't considered the children's need for continuing education at all until then.

"Someone will be in touch," Shiloh said. "We haven't discussed it yet. Arraignments will be made to finish out the school year. Counselors are being provided for the children. The family plans on contacting the parents of all the children, but, as you can imagine, things are hectic in our home right now."

"Ah, yes, the funeral."

Denali winced.

"The funerals," she corrected. "Mrs. Ritchie was a dear friend of the family."

"Please have whoever is in charge of the funeral contact me about that too," the governor said. "The public will wish to pay its respects."

Shiloh nodded and made a note.

Denali cleared her throat. "I've given my testimony to the best of my ability, may I be excused?"

Shiloh laid a hand on her arm. "Are charges pending?"

"No," Harry said. "We won't be filing any charges against you." He rose and gathered his briefcase and turned to glare at Raul. "You on the other hand— I'm considering charging. Withholding evidence is a serious crime. You wasted all our time with this…" he gestured around the table. "Not to mention the stress on her and her entire family. I better see some compelling mitigating evidence on my desk by morning." He nodded to the seated men and left the room.

Denali rose stiffly, her too large sneakers making her awkward. The gel between her toes squished unpleasantly.

"Excuse me for a moment, gentlemen." Shiloh rose and escorted her to the door." You okay?"

"Yes. I just really want to speak with Ryan."

Shiloh took her elbow and glanced back to the table as he ushered her from the room. "I'll be right back." He closed the door behind them. "About that. An intense experience can make you do things you wouldn't ordinarily do. Emotions are high, leading to poor decisions."

Denali grinned at him.

He sighed and hugged her. "I don't want to see you hurt. Death can make us seek life. He might not be who you think he is."

"I know him. He's exactly who I think he is, and everything I ever wanted in a mate."

"You think you know him." Shiloh drew back and framed her face with his hand and heaved a deep, unhappy sigh. "Like the rest of us, you'll have to learn the hard way and make your own mistakes. The heart can make you see things that aren't there. It can blind you to faults. Be smart, little sister, and use your beautiful mind."

She searched his face. "What? this is more than general anxiety."

Shiloh dropped his hands and squared his shoulders. "I met his parents, and I have to say, I didn't like his mother one bit. I'm just worried you're rushing without looking. This is so unlike you, we're all concerned. Just promise me, you'll really look before you leap."

"I will. I love you too."

SEVENTEEN

Way Out of My League

Ryan picked her up outside the police station in a black, dusty jeep.

"Damn, I should've borrowed my mom's car," he said as he helped her in.

"This is fine." Denali bit back the groan pulling herself into the seat caused. "I have no idea what happened to my car. Last I saw, it was in the school lot. I like your jeep. Do you like camping and hiking?"

"Yep; I know you like climbing, and I'd love to learn. I swim, fish, and hunt. In my free time I go to the gym and catch a game of whatever's being played, basketball, tennis, even boxing. I jog occasionally but not daily. I don't watch much television, preferring movies or video games.

Hmmm, what else?"

He flashed her a grin that made her pulse pound.

"What's your favorite food?" she asked.

"Pasta, pizza, lasagna, basically anything with sauce. I love steak and chicken and tolerate fish. Pork I almost never eat because it's usually so dry. I'm a good cook but don't do it too often. What about you?"

"French fries, I love French fries and eat them almost every day. I can cook but usually eat takeout. My favorite meal is anything my Da cooks. No matter how hard I try, I can't make fried rice as good as him."

"Does your mom cook?"

"Not that I've ever seen. Most of my siblings are passable cooks but never ever eat anything Lee prepares."

"That bad, huh?"

"He adds hot sauce to everything." Denali grinned at him. "I want to kiss you. Not being able to sucks."

"I want to kiss you too." Ryan glanced at her, a wry smile on his face. "Will your parents let us share a room?"

"Yes."

"What? You sound nervous."

Denali rubbed her sweaty palms on her knees. "Money can be a big problem in relationships. I don't want it to be a problem for us."

This disclosure had been worrying her. Her family's wealth could overawe and turn people away. She wasn't worried he'd become fake and try to ingratiate himself in the hopes of some of their wealth coming to him as others had in the past; she worried he'd think he didn't fit into her world and leave her for own good.

Ryan pulled into a gas station parking lot and switched off the jeep. "Me either. Your family is well to do. Mine is middle class. I'm guessing you make more than me. I could get a better paying job, but I love my work. I spent four years in the Navy and have health benefits and education credits which expire in a few years. Are you okay with being a cop's wife?"

"Yes, I love that about you. That you want to help people. I really love living on my boat though. Will you try it? I can move it here."

"I already notified my landlord I'll be subleasing. We can live wherever you want. I'll apply for a job in Boston. It doesn't matter to me what city I work in, but I do want to be a police officer in a big city. I'll keep applying until one closer accepts me. We can pool our money and decide major purchases together."

She sighed heavily. "I really want to kiss you."

He chuckled, leaned closer, and kissed her for a long time before sitting back and taking a small box from his jeans pocket. "I wanted to wait and give you this after a romantic dinner or moonlit stroll, but I can't wait."

He opened the box and removed the small diamond ring. "Delilah Na Abira Leeba Rubinstein-

Wong, I love you with all my heart. I promise to love, honor, and cherish you as long as we both shall live. Will you do me the great honor of becoming my wife?"

"Yes." Tears clouded her eyes as he slipped the ring on her finger. "I can't wait—"

A rock impacted the window by her head. They both jerked as if it had been a gunshot. Denali laughed nervously and scanned the parking lot. An overweight woman, clutching a small dog under her arm, bent and picked up a crushed soda can, which she threw at the car. It only made it halfway.

"You could've killed them, you crazy, selfish bitch," she screamed as she reached for another rock. "I'm sorry your sister was killed, but you had no right. You should be in jail! I can't believe they let you walk the streets!" Another rock dinged off the side of the jeep as the woman ranted. A man ran up yelling, at first at the woman, then at Denali. Two men on motorcycles yelled at the two throwing rocks at Ryan's cars.

"Time to go," Ryan muttered. "If I try to stop her, it's just going to escalate, and I don't want to spend the rest of day explaining this at the precinct." Not able to back out because of the people surrounding the jeep, he pulled over the curb.

Denali couldn't hold in the groan from the sharp jolt of crossing the curb.

"Sorry," Ryan glanced in the rear-view mirror. "This is crazy. My mom is being such a pain in the ass over this too."

"She thinks I got mad and attacked?"

"Yes, I told her that isn't how it was, but… I hate to say this about my own mother, but she believes the news doesn't lie."

"Well, she'll have something to think about then because my brother is releasing a recording of the first conversation I heard. Tracy got the entire thing on my cell phone. I've got to say I'm relieved. I hate how everyone is so angry at me. But really, it's so dumb to be angry at the victim for fighting back. I mean— so what if I was mad…"

"Well, I see your point, but the public is worried about the children and rightfully so. Anger or fear isn't a good enough justification to risk their lives."

Denali rubbed her face hard. "I know, and I would've let the authorities handle it but there wasn't time, and I knew those men were lying assholes." She directed him absently to her parent's house as he spoke.

"We never talked about that either. The deaths I mean. I keep expecting to suddenly feel bad, but I feel nothing for them," Ryan said

Denali giggled and slapped her hands over her mouth. "Me too, I almost feel bad that I don't feel bad. Maybe someday it'll hit me, I mean, they must've had people who loved them, but they were evil men intent on evil deeds. I feel no remorse at all for killing them."

"Good. If that changes though, tell me. I don't

want you to worry about upsetting me or making me feel bad."

"Okay, I promise. You promise too. Turn here. "

"Hmm." Ryan's gaze flitted over the large homes set back from the road peeking through the trees. "Your family might be richer than I thought."

"Seems likely. Hardly anyone thinks we're as rich as we are."

She giggled at his expression. "I personally am not that rich. I couldn't afford this house. Turn into the next driveway on the left." She pointed to the cobbled driveway. "The gate code is three-four-seven-nine-two. I'll get you a remote so you don't need to stop at the gate." She waved out the window at the security guard sitting inside the small stone building beside the gate.

He lifted his hand and waved back, resting a hand lightly on the gun on his hip. Denali gave him a thumbs up, and he settled back in his chair and opened his newspaper.

"Always give the gate guard two acknowledgments, if you only give one, he'll call the police and hit the silent alarm."

"Got it," Ryan said and slowed the car even more. "Holy shit, this isn't a house it's a mansion."

Denali peered at her home through considering eyes. Three stories of peaked roofs interspersed with chimneys and round turrets of varying heights gave her home a fairytale air. She'd always loved this house. More for the people inside it, but the outside charmed with its fanciful gables and turrets.

A large marble portico held up by round marble columns fronted the main section of the house. The two wings sported balconies, overhangs, and decorative trellises. Greenish copper roofs of outbuildings peeked through the trees in the distance. On the edge of the manicured lawn, white fencing separated the horse pasture where Bee's pony, Feathers, meandered beneath spreading oak trees. A corner of the red barn was visible at the edge of the field.

"Yeah, I guess it is. It's just home to me though."

"I'm way out of my league with you." Ryan turned and frowned at her.

"Don't, you'll break my heart," Denali said softly. "It's only money and not even my money. My boat wouldn't even take up a fraction of this space."

"You're right, but I feel like a pauper next to you." He snickered suddenly. "My mom is going to freak. Let's have her here for dinner."

Denali chuckled then sobered and said, "Your mom and dad will likely feel the same as you. This house and my parents can be intimidating, and I want your parents to like me. I want them to like all of us, to join us for family events and feel welcome—not inferior. I've lost friends in the past who couldn't get over my parent's wealth. Fake friends, people that just want to use us have always been a problem. Others who have money but not as much sometimes treat us badly because we're adopted.

"My mom comes from a 'good' family, and some of that crowd look down on us because we aren't purebred enough. My father's family was well off, but he's the last. He can trace his ancestry to Emperor Puyi, the last Chinese emperor, so he's accepted in social circles. Not that they're overtly rude..." Denali sighed. "You'll see. It can be uncomfortable, but we learn to ignore it. My point is, let's not embarrass your mom. As fun it would be to see her be shocked, warn her."

Denali bit her lip. "I'm going to be blunt here. Our family doesn't give a hoot in a half about materialistic things, but that being said my mother is a reverse snob. She wouldn't give a lick if you show up in jeans and T-shirt, but she'll snicker behind her hand if you wear fakes in the hopes of impressing. Tell your parents to dress normally, not formally, unless invited to a formal event."

"You have those a lot here?"

"Fairly often. My mother's work requires she observe large groups of people. She hosts parties here all the time with a very eclectic guest list. Sometimes its politicians, sometimes businessmen, sometimes homeless. Last week she threw a party for the local VA. The week before she sent a bus to the local homeless shelter. The week before that it was the Chinese embassy, that party got rowdy. We needed security to clear them out."

"Where should I park?"

"Right here in front is fine. You can call for the car

to be brought around or ask where they park it. I have no idea what the parking situation is at the moment with all my siblings home. Actually, I have no idea what room to use. I share a room with Meteora when she's home. It has twin beds, and I don't want to do that with you. I'll need to pick a new one."

"Well, there appears to be plenty to choose from," Ryan said cheerfully.

Denali's brother Lee ran down the front steps as Ryan opened his doors. Dressed in faded jeans and a red T-shirt that had been washed so many times it was almost pink, Lee's straight bearing and short brown hair marked him as active military.

"Lee." Denali held out her arms. Her brother hugged her gently, then stepped back to examine her. "You look tired."

"I am. I need a nap. Lee, this is Ryan. Ryan, my brother Lee."

Ryan extended his hand, and the two men shook.

"How long are you home?" Denali asked as she stepped gingerly from the car, being careful to keep her back straight.

"One week. You almost gave me a heart attack. I watched live. It was terrifying.

"I haven't seen it yet. It actually wasn't that scary; I didn't have time to be scared."

"Speak for yourself. I was plenty scared," Ryan said.

"You didn't appear scared. It looked like you had

training," Lee said admiringly.

"Some, I've been taking ERT training." Ryan grabbed a faded blue duffle bag from the back of the jeep and swung it over his shoulder.

"Mom had your things moved to the second-floor guest room with the round study. She told me to tell you to take the elevator, that if she sees you on the stairs, she'll be very angry. She also told me to tell you, you can pick any room you like if that one displeases." Lee sniffed. "Everyone knows you love that room. I think she's trying to bribe you to stay."

"I'll stay as long as they need me."

Reminded, Lee saddened. He placed an arm around his sister's shoulder and offered her a hand for the stairs. "Weird how wounds hurt more later." His glance flicked to Ryan. "I thought she was dead when that man shot her and knocked her down. Thanks for not letting him finish her off. Is that where you cracked the rib?"

"I don't think so. It hurt, but not as bad as the guy in the gym. I hate to admit this, but it was his girlfriend who took me out."

Ryan snorted with laughter. "Not my girlfriend, never let her even think it." He paused inside the front door and whistled softly, his gaze traveling the inlaid tile floor and wide marble stairs. He tilted his head and examined the curved rail of the staircase. "You ran up that? No wonder your mom almost had a heart attack. You're lucky you didn't break your neck," he added to Lee.

"Ah, she told you, did she. Did she tell you about the month we spent climbing the elevator cable until mom caught us and put a stop to it?" Lee escorted them across the polished floor to an elevator made to appear as part of the decorative paneling along the wall. It opened onto a wide hallway on the second floor.

"The balcony back there overlooks the ballroom. It's the favorite hangout of everyone." Lee gestured to a small grouping of shabby couches set before an elaborately scrolled iron rail. Two children jumped up and rushed over.

"Denali!" A young girl with white-blond hair grabbed Denali.

Lee pulled her off. "Easy, Iaia, she has hurt ribs."

"Hi, Bee, remember me?" Ryan squatted before the other girl who stood back wringing her hands.

"Yes, thank you."

"You're welcome. We're going to be family now."

The girl's eyes filled with tears.

Denali made a soft sound of distress. "I really want to hug you, Bee, but I can't because of my ribs. Can Ryan hug you for me?"

Ryan hugged Bee, then picked her up so she could hug Denali.

"Let's go tell Mom she's home. Denali needs a nap. Bee will come get you for dinner," Lee said as he took the two girls by the hands. He led them away, talking softly.

EIGHTEEN

Security

"Poor Bee," Denali murmured. "You don't know, but this is a big change for her. We call her Bee because she buzzes around always chattering and into everything. To see her quiet and sad breaks my heart."

She led Ryan down the hallway and a short corridor that ended in double doors of dark, rich wood. "This room is fancier than most of the bedrooms and usually reserved for favored guests." She opened the door and ushered him inside.

Fresh flowers sat in a cut-glass vase atop an antique table set into a round alcove beside the door. Two blue and gold striped padded armchairs sat beside the table with a bank of windows behind them. Built-in shelves of paneled dark-wood framed the windows from floor-to-ceiling. Leather bound books with gold writing and small glass and crystal sculptures lined the shelves. Heavy, gold velvet drapes puddled on the dark, hardwood floor. A crystal chandelier glittered above the table.

On the opposite side of the room, a large marble fireplace framed with dark, heavy wood, sat across from a king-size four-poster bed. A woodland scene bordered by a chunky gold frame hung above the fireplace. Matching drapes tied back with blue cords draped around the bed. The light blue walls shimmered in the sunlight streaming through another large window to the right of the bed. Barely visible gold lattice patterned the blue walls, catching the light. A couch sat in front of the window upholstered in a darker shade of blue covered with plush gold pillows. The bed linens matched the couch. Thick, potted ferns squeezed up against a tree in the corner of the room, the twelve-foot ceilings giving ample space for the leafy branches. An empty birdcage composed of fancy scrolled metal dangled from a tarnished, gold chain beside the potted plants.

"Wow," Ryan said.

"Wait until you see the bath." She gestured with her chin to an ornately carved door beside the couch. Ryan went to the door as she laid carefully on the bed and sighed in relief.

"We have got to let my mother stay here."

Denali laughed and grabbed her ribs. "She can stay in the fancy guest room."

"There's a room fancier than this?"

"Yes, this room is meant to be comfortable, that one is meant to impress. It's a great room with a private balcony, and it has a private seating area to overlook the ballroom. Mom hired a designer for that room, this one she did herself."

"This house must've been amazing to play hide-and-seek in."

"It really was. We still sometimes do, but, don't tell my mom, we play it on the outside. This house is great for climbing."

"I'm not sure I want to know that. Are you going to kill yourself climbing buildings?"

"I hope not." She patted the bed beside her. "Come lay down with me. If I fall asleep, feel free to explore."

She had to wake him when Bee knocked on the door.

"Da cooked dinner," Bee said as she escorted them to the elevator.

"Can you show Ryan around after dinner?

"Sure."

"No stairs though, even if he wants to. Take good care of him for me."

"I will. Iaia can drive him around outside if he wants." Bee sounded so jealous Denali had to hide a laugh.

"A few more years and you can drive around unsupervised too. How's Feathers?" she asked, referring to Bee's pony.

"Great, all better now. The vet says to keep up the

compresses, but he's good as new. I'm going to be a vet when I grow up."

"That'll be awesome; we don't have one of those yet."

"What other pets do you have?" Ryan asked.

Bee chattered happily all the way to the dining room. Denali's parents greeted Ryan warmly. Denali grinned at her father who sat beside her holding her hand as the younger kids bore Ryan off after dinner, Bee's happy chatter leading the way.

Ryan glanced back and smiled before turning his attention to Iaia.

"Do you like him, Da?"

"Very much. I wish to meet his parents."

"I'll ask Ryan to invite them."

"I was thinking, you should ask them to stay here if they wish." Hester set her wineglass on the white tablecloth and rose, taking Ryan's discarded chair. "Security here is tight. Dai is concerned over the number of threats."

"Once Shiloh releases the recordings— "

Gui said, "I don't wish to alarm you, but you need to be cautious; Al-Jadr has made threats against you."

Denali tightened her grip on her father's hand.

"Just me or my family?"

"You— and Ryan."

"Have you set security on her boat?" Lee asked. His worried gaze traveled his gathered siblings.

"Yes. The FBI is also watching it and this house," Gui said. "Neil and his family will be arriving tomorrow for the funeral and will stay with us one night before returning to Texas. Neil has taken leave from his job and will be going with them. I've hired security for them. I wish he'd stay here with us, but I understand it's too painful right now."

Bottom lip pinched between two fingers, Denali stared down at her dirty dinner plate. "Is he angry with me?"

"God, no. None of us are angry with you," Dai said. "Denali, none of this is your fault. No matter what happens, I want you to remember that."

"It was my security system, Dai."

"Yes, and its only flaw was the humans who knew about it. Marion has confessed she altered the security feeds to allow them on campus. She gave them the keys and the codes."

"If I'd thought to incorporate bolts on the doors…"

"You would've been blown to smithereens. I'm not saying that isn't a good design improvement, but it wouldn't have helped in that situation. That wasn't a hostage attempt, it was a murder attempt. Those men had no intention of letting any children go. What you heard was only a fraction of the evil they had planned. Mrs. Ritchie slipped a recorder in Olympia's bag. What it captured was chilling."

"When did you hear the recording?" Gui asked angrily.

"This afternoon, Da. Family comes first. I would've told Shiloh if I had proof sooner."

"The amount of sheep disguised as people worries

me," Hester said. "All these people so angry with Denali for standing up to those bad men."

"Watch the news tonight, Mom, the tide will turn," Shiloh said soothingly. "Nobody can argue she did the wrong thing once they know she understood what was planned."

"Still, doesn't it worry you, son, how many people would rather rely on others to care for them?"

"Yes, but it's a fine line from self-reliance to anarchy. I don't want to live in a vigilante state either."

Denali smiled to herself as her siblings began arguing politics and human nature. The familiar conversation comforted her. She dozed off in her chair. Bee's laughter woke her. Hester glanced at the gold Rolex on her wrist and rose. "Zane, see the youngsters settled please before coming to the media room."

"Yes, ma'am." Zane grabbed Bee and threw her over his shoulder and swiped at Iggy who shrieked and ran to Simon.

Hester beckoned her family to follow and headed to the elevator.

Ryan took Denali's hand. "I didn't see much of the inside, but Iaia gave me a quick tour of the grounds. I feel like I'm at a resort. Tennis courts, stables, pools, ponds, a basketball court.

"Did you see the gazebo?"

"No, I must've missed it somehow."

Denali grinned. "Iaia saved it for me to show you.

She thinks it's romantic. Of course, she thinks everything's romantic. I'm willing to bet she asked about what we planned for the wedding. I bet she even offered to help."

"Hmm, we need to talk about that, betting I mean. I'm partial to back rubs. What do you get if I lose?"

"I like back rubs too; not right now, but you can owe me. I'll settle for IOU's

Ryan pulled her into a doorway and slid his hands under the back of her T-shirt. "This is good too," he murmured as he ran his thumb along the underside of her breast. I wouldn't mind rubbing your front instead of your back."

She moaned into his mouth when he kissed her, sliding his thumb over the lace of her bra.

"Denali, you coming?" Lee hollered.

"Be right there," Ryan hollered back. "I need a minute," he whispered and tugged her back.

She kissed his neck and ran her hands under his shirt, caressing the muscles of his back.

"That isn't helping," he half moaned as he grabbed her hands and kissed them before putting them on her waist. "You go, I'll follow and don't make that noise."

"What noise?" She said and sighed softly again.

"That one. How long did Meteora say we needed to wait?"

"A week, but I'm a fast healer."

"Go, your killing me."

She took his hand and led him to the media room.

Part of the original basement for the house, the low-ceilinged media room had no windows. Four rows of stadium seating, consisting of mismatched armchairs and two couches sprinkled with small tables made up the back of the room. In the front, a wall of monitors lay before a conference table surrounded by leather office chairs. Two vending machines sat beside the door. The room smelled of popcorn.

"There's a big screen that can be lowered for movies, but generally we don't bother, the seventy-inch television in the center is big enough. The vending machines work but cost money. Mom isn't against snacks, she's against waste, and kids who have to buy their own sodas tend to not waste them or drink it too often.

"Holy crap, I want to come here for Super Bowl." Ryan sat with an exaggerated happy sigh in a worn leather armchair and kicked his feet up.

"You can come whenever you like. Your family now," Gui said and clasped Ryan on the shoulder, sitting beside him in the matching recliner. Denali sat on his other side in a smaller blue velour recliner.

"Who wants a soda? My treat," Tianzi asked. His wife Clare began handing out soda without waiting, already familiar with drink preferences.

Dai squatted before Denali. "This might be upsetting, it's okay if you want to leave. We've all seen the news footage before, but we didn't live it. This is the first time we're hearing Tracy's nine-one-one call."

Clare handed her a soda and a blanket from the back of the couch. Shiloh entered and drew his mother aside. Her face whitened, and she nodded. He handed her a box of tissues.

"This special report will be played unedited exactly as Denali heard it. They're going to be using the transcription she gave during the relevant portions. That includes Olympia's murder." Tears filled Shiloh's eyes. "Every time I hear it, I cry. I don't think Mom and Dad should hear this, but it's their choice." He turned to his mother. "Please reconsider."

She shook her head, sat beside her husband, and clutched his hand.

The news logo appeared on the screen with special report in large letters across it. The room quieted, all eyes on the television.

NINETEEN

The News

The man on the screen said, "This is Ronald Hill, coming to you live from Washington DC. New and disturbing information regarding the attack at the private grammar school Olympus has been brought to light. And while we don't wish to panic the American people, they have a right to the truth."

A picture of the school as it was a week ago appeared behind Ronald. "This photo was taken two days before the attack and was supplied to us by Shewster Security, the firm who lost six employees that day." The photo changed to portrait shots of the six men killed.

"First, let me be very clear. These six men were murdered most foully. I'm aware of the rumors that the company was corrupt or incompetent and nothing could be further from the truth. What they were, was betrayed. Marion Cole, a new employee of the school, purposefully manipulated the security system to allow the security team to be murdered. Without inside help, this wouldn't have been possible. She supplied keys, codes, and false data. It was her job to monitor the live footage. She let the armed men walk in."

Ronald glared at the picture of a smiling Marion that appeared on the screen. "Her motive was greed. The cost of six men and three women's lives and the betrayal of two hundred and twenty-six children…" He paused dramatically. "Five hundred thousand dollars. For that measly sum, she agreed to let terrorists into the building, and while she didn't realize their true intentions, she saw the guards be murdered.

A stock photo of one of the classrooms appeared behind him. "What you're about to hear is a translation of the Urdu spoken in the background of the recording supplied by Tracy Aims, one of Ms. Denali's students. Tracy is just ten-years-old, and this is her nine-one-one call. What you may not be aware of is Delilah Rubinstein-Wong, called Ms. Denali by her students, has a doctorate in communications. She works as a translator in Boston and at MIT where she uses her expertise in languages and her doctorate in mathematics to devise new ways to communicate with autistic children.

"She has co-published two books on this subject with her sister Doctor Ananya Rubinstein-Wong. Ms. Denali is widely regarded as an expert in African tribal language. She speaks a wide range of languages fluently, including Arabic, Urdu, Pashto, and Dari as well as a smattering of the lesser known 'tribal' languages of the area."

Ronald pointed to the screen. "At the bottom is a running time clock, which we'll pause as we break for explanations. This line shows the actual time of events. It took her less than a minute from the moment Mahir Alfarsi first spoke until she handed Tracy Aims the phone. What follows took place in under three minutes. In that time, Ms. Denali checked all possibility of exit and determined none were viable without violence. Her students report she appeared calm and moved quickly, getting them behind a barricade. She asked them to hide their heads and climbed on her desk, which she'd had placed by the door of the classroom. Armed only with a pen, she killed the man who appeared.

"She's been widely condemned as being a hothead or acting rashly in anger over her sister's death, but she'd already decided on this course of action and here's why."

Denali closed her eyes as the recording played. Ryan squeezed her hand.

Ronald stopped the tape. "Her sister has not yet been murdered, but she heard them, from their own lips, say there would be no survivors. She sent a message saying so on the tablets the school used, trying to warn the others. She gets her classroom into their winter clothes, knowing they'll have to run for it despite the armed men waiting outside.

"Fifteen minutes has passed. A police vehicle has blown up, and Ms. Denali learns they have the keys to the rooms. Here is what the men say in the background right before they kill her sister. Words that horrified her because she understood them."

Ronald gestured, and the screen behind him darken. White text formed on the screen while the sound played. '*A glorious triumph over our oppressors will weaken them forever.*'

Ronald said, "Another man says this next bit," and he played the audio while the writing on the screen changed. '*I brought the marshmallows.*' "And yet a third says," Ronald gestured to the translation as a man said in Urdu, "*Kill both the bitches, we can still burn them with the others.*"

Ronald stopped the recording. "What follows is horrifying. She knew what they had planned for the children was death. What she learned over the next thirty minutes was the truly gruesome nature of that death. The FBI has confirmed they possess other recordings that corroborate what she heard. Mrs. Ritchie, the school secretary, heroically planted a recording device at the cost of her life and told Ms. Denali where to find it.

"We ask that small children not be present for this. We'll play the recording in its entirety, including what she heard after the shot which took her sister's life before she attacked with her bare hands, the only weapon she possessed against men armed and armored and bent on killing.

Denali closed her eyes and moaned when they shot Olympia. She cringed at the desperate sound of the struggle, her heavy breathing, and how cold she sounded ordering the children. Most of the conversation she had with Mr. Fredrick was inaudible, just Tracy and the rest of her students crying, then Tracy telling them to be quiet Ms. Denali would get them out.

You've all seen the footage from the news copter. We'll show it again and you can watch it with fresh eyes. This wasn't a woman bent on revenge. This was a woman desperate to save the children in her care.

Without sound, the footage played like a bad comedy act, Denali thought as she watched herself fly backward and land in the snow. The camera crew had gotten a great shot of Ryan's expression as he shot the man about to kill her. *He looked hard and dangerous,* she thought approvingly, so happy a man like him loved her. On screen, SWAT appeared on the edge of the woods and fired at black-clad men as the children ran from the building.

She was embarrassed by how hard she made it look to climb the building when it really wasn't that hard. She'd done it with ease numerous times. Of course, those times she'd worn shoes and wasn't scared to death.

The fight on the roof scared her. That man had been closer than she liked to remember to killing her. The next pictures shocked her.

The main doors opened, and two men appeared and threw Olympia's lifeless body down the stairs. One shot at her corpse while the other waved his gun in the air, grinning at the helicopter. Ryan appeared on the corner of the building and shot the man shooting Olympia's corpse. The terrorist grabbed his leg and stumbled forward, landing face first and remaining motionless. The other man turned and fired. Bullets kicked up puffs of dirt and splintered the brick wall beside Ryan's face.

Ryan took careful aim and put a shot through the man's eye. He slung his stolen gun over his shoulder, ran to the steps, and picked Olympia up. The anguish on his face was clear as he glanced up at the helicopter. He swung back to the building, then hesitated, peering over his shoulder. Olympia's dark hair trailed over his arm as he ran to the flagpole to the left of the main entrance and laid her in the snow-covered garden, straightening her clothes and folding her hands on her breast. Wind whipped the flag as he lowered it and covered her, tucking the edges under her body. The flag covered her from head to toe.

On one knee, he knelt and crossed himself before jumping up and grabbing his gun. He glanced back toward the school and ran backward, staring at something in the distance. The helicopter swung around, and four armed men could be seen running toward him.

They shot at the helicopter, which peeled away, then they turn to the flag-draped body. Ryan stepped out from behind the pillar on the portico and opened fire. One dropped his gun and fell backward, the other three turned and fired back.

Even knowing he was well beside her, it was terrifying to watch. On the screen, Ryan ducked back. Marble chips exploded from the pillar, leaving deep holes. Smaller holes appeared in the brick of the building. He didn't return fire.

The helicopter was too far to show their faces now. But they seemed confident with swaggers in their step as they approached the pillar. Suddenly, Ryan ran for the main entrance and darted through the door. Denali grabbed his arm as if she could stop the Ryan on screen from passing through the interior double doors and triggering the explosives on them. He stopped at the first set and held them closed, casting a terrified glance behind him.

The three men charged the door. An explosion knocked them back. Before they could stand, Ryan opened the door and opened fire, three shots at close range. He twirled the grenade pin on his finger, then saluted the helicopter before running around the corner of the building.

"A ruse to draw them in," Denali breathed relieved.

She clutched his hand, angry he'd risked himself, and angry with herself that it upset her so much.

Tears trickled down Denali's cheeks. Not for her sister, but herself, that she should have such a brave, strong, man.

"If I didn't already love you, I would after seeing that. Thank you for treating my sister with such respect."

Ryan wiped the tears from her cheek with his thumbs. "I'm sorry I never got to know her. She seems like an amazing woman."

"She really was," Hester said in a tear-choked voice.

Her father began to cry when she laid down in the snow beside Ryan. A dusting of snow had coated her naked back before the EMT's showed up. "I thought you'd died. I'll never forget that horrible feeling or my joy when your sister called to say you lived. Danxia, Anya, and Meteora had immediately gone to the hospital to prepare for causalities when they heard. They were there when you were brought in." Her father sobbed and covered his face with his hands. "I thought you were dead," he repeated.

"I'm okay, Da." She glanced at Shiloh. "When I die, I want a Navajo burial for a life well lived."

"If I survive you, I'll make sure of it," Shiloh said.

Hester rose and faced them. Tears had tracked across her pale cheeks. "No more talk of funerals. We'll bury the dead, not the living. Olympia would be proud of you and so grateful you saved the children. When Neil is more recovered, we'll speak to him about the school and do what we can to keep her dream alive. Tomorrow is sure to be a hard for everyone. Try to rest. We leave at ten." Hester kissed Denali's cheek and hugged Ryan. Tianzi and Clare escorted her parents out.

"Shiloh—"

"I left you ash and feathers in your room. I'm sorry, Denali, but it couldn't wait."

"It's okay. Olympia would've liked that you did it properly for her even though she didn't believe."

"It isn't about belief, but tradition. We honor the dead to rest our souls, not theirs."

Lee sat beside Shiloh and put an arm around his shoulders. "I'm sorry I missed it."

"I saved you ash and feathers too. Mother came and gave us the blanket from her bed, the most prized possession Olympia left behind here. She believes in comforting rituals too."

Shiloh leaned his head back on the chair and closed his eyes.

Zane kissed his forehead before kissing Denali's cheek. "Neil brought the baby's bassinet," he whispered.

Denali had to swallow twice to force the lump in her throat away. She kissed her siblings and pulled Ryan from the room. "We'll leave the ash and feathers with Olympia tomorrow to take to the underworld."

Ryan gave her a dubious glance.

"No, we don't really believe she can take the ghosts of her favorite possessions with her, but it is a comfort. I wish I was with them when they burned them."

"I really like your family. I'm sad to meet them all this way."

"I like your dad; I'm not so sure about your mom."

Ryan laughed and ruffled her hair. "She'll grow on you, I hope. She's a good, kind woman just a bit too worried what others will think."

"My mother is the opposite; she couldn't care less what others think. Well, most others, she cares about what we think. Will your parents come stay tomorrow?"

"Yes, more to support me and meet your family than because of security issues. My dad say's no one is mentioning me much. His officers are keeping their ears to the ground, listening for rumors, but so far haven't heard anything they consider credible.

"His officers?"

"He's a police officer, Captain Nelson Graham."

"I had no idea. What does your mom do?"

"Real-estate, part time. She does some charity work for the Red Cross too. I think she'd like to do more but isn't sure how to go about it."

"My mom is the queen of charity work. She could get your mom on any committee she liked. I'm not above using my connections to buy my future mother-in-law's affection. Our family has seats all over town from the opera to the Smithsonian. Any event she wishes to attend, we could get her in."

"And she was worried you were after my money. People are going to think I'm after yours."

"I don't care what strangers think. They're usually wrong. You're going to get people hounding you who think we brainwashed you into our cult, and others will be sure we're using you in our secret labs for breeding experiments, and there are others who are certain my parents live off their children."

He quirked an eyebrow, and she laughed.

"The family has a pact, and I'm in it. I joined when I was twelve, which is young, but I knew what I was doing. I'll show you the paperwork, but basically, I give my family ten percent of whatever I make, and they pay for education and any medical bills."

"For how long?"

"Forever. It's how we send all our siblings to school and ensure they're cared for if something happens to Mom and Dad. We get a lot of cult rumors because of it."

"What happens to all the money once everyone is done with school?"

"We'll send our children to school. We can spend it on whatever we want with a majority vote. The pact funded Olympus. Technically, the school is in the black, but Olympia hasn't paid back that loan; she was saving for the expansion with our complete support. So really the family owns the school. Or I should say the rubble."

"Didn't you have insurance?"

"Yes…" Denali opened the door to their room and waved him inside. "Let's not talk about any of that in here."

"Let's make our first rule. No business talk in the bedroom."

Denali laughed. "Okay, but let's pick one of the other rooms for our bedroom; this one, as much as I like it, feels like a guest bedroom to me."

"Can we do that tomorrow?"

"Yes, we can do it whenever we want."

Ryan strode to the window and stared out over the moonlit grounds for a moment before closing the heavy, gold drapes. "I'll be honest. I'm finding this a bit awkward."

"Sharing a room?" Denali asked in surprise.

"Yeah. I want to be with you, I'm just not sure my willpower is up to resisting you unless we go to bed fully dressed. On opposite sides of the bed," he added when Denali grinned.

"Do whatever you normally do. No one is here except us; we can do whatever we want."

"That's just it, you're not medically ready. I want your first time to be perfect, not wincing in pain."

"Our first time. I'll stop you if it hurts. My ribs I mean." A hot blush scalded her cheeks. "I'm going to take a quick shower. I should warn you water is rationed to ten-minute showers between the hours of five a.m. to one p.m. and six p.m. to eleven p.m. Don't try to cheat, or you'll be taking an ice-cold shower. There's a hot tub and a sauna in the gym if you want to soak. And if you want, you can take a longer bath or whatever between those times, but Mom made that rule back when the water heaters couldn't keep up, and she stuck to it when we got the new water heater."

Denali emerged from the bathroom with a towel wrapped around her body, using another to dry her hair.

"Have I told you yet how beautiful you are? Even with these bruises." His finger traced the swell of her breast above the towel, then skimmed along the green bruise on her shoulder before trailing to the edge of the darker purple one on her shoulder blade. "How many times did you get shot?"

"I lost count. Only three drew blood. What about you?" Denali asked as she ran her hands under his T-shirt and removed it, letting it fall to the floor.

"Four that drew blood." His breath caught in a hiss as she leaned forward and kissed his chest. "Denali…"

She dropped the towel in her hand and ran her hands lightly over him, tracing his bruises with her fingertips. The small bandage on his neck she brushed with her thumb. "I would kiss it if I could reach." The two stitched wounds on his arm she kissed. She lowered her hands to the waistband of his jeans. "I know you'd never hurt me."

He moaned when she undid the top button of his pants. The towel wrapped around her body fell unheeded to the floor as she slid her hands under the waistband of his boxer shorts.

"Don't let me hurt you," he whispered as he kicked his pants off. "A moan of pain won't be enough; you'll have to tell me. Good and bad moans can sound alike."

She made a small aroused sound as he pressed her against him and kissed the top of her breast. "That was a good moan, do it again."

He chuckled and complied.

TWENTY

A Hard Lesson

"Denali, sweetheart, time to get up."

Ryan sounded both happy and anxious, and she didn't know how he managed it. Her body hurt. As if he read her mind, he handed her a glass of water and two pain pills.

"Last night was too much, wasn't it?"

"Last night was perfect. I love you."

"I love you too, but you're in pain now, and I caused it."

"Well, to be fair, I helped." She laughed when he frowned. "Please, let me have this without guilt. I'm sore, but not too bad. It's true, I lose my common sense when you touch me, but we were careful. We can be careful again later, maybe tonight in the pool?"

Ryan's warm hands on her bare back with his body pressed against hers made her sigh hard and closed her eyes, pressing as tightly as she could against him. "You make me feel so safe and loved. I want to lay naked next to you for hours— days— weeks."

"Every night for the rest of our lives and some days too," he added as she giggled.

"We belong together. Last night was the most amazing night of my life. We connected on a level I didn't even know existed." He paused to kiss her shoulder. "After today, let's spend a few days somewhere alone just us. I want to take you somewhere warm and make love in the sun."

"That sounds amazing. It might have to wait though. My parents might need me home a few days."

"I could wait forever for you." He chuckled quietly, ruffling her hair. "This room isn't a hardship."

"I wish we could sleep late and make love all day." Denali kissed his chest where her head lay. " I sort of feel guilty I'm so happy with you. How can I be happy to have met you when we met so horribly?"

Ryan heaved a deep, unhappy sigh, and sat on the side of the bed, absently rubbing the wound on his thigh. "Never regret us, Denali." On his hands and knees, he crawled on the bed, leaning over her. "What happened was terrible, but we're amazing. Your sister wouldn't begrudge your happiness. From what I've heard of her, she'd be happy you had comfort."

"She would." Denali smiled a sad, soft, smile as she ran her hands over the planes of his back.

"I want to stay here and all day and comfort you, to feel you breathe and know your safe, but duty calls." Ryan kissed her lips lightly, then carefully moved away before getting off the bed and stretching.

"Ryan?"

"Hmm." He glanced back from the bathroom doorway and smiled.

"Thank you for everything. I never thanked you for saving my life and my brothers and sister. From the moment I saw you, you've been exactly what I needed."

"You take my breath away," he murmured as he entered the bathroom.

Denali closed her eyes and pulled the blankets that smelled like them up to her face. "I'm so sorry, Olympia. If I could've saved you… You'd like him though. Somehow it feels like a trade, and it wasn't; I'd never have traded you."

Zane knocked lightly on the bedroom door as Denali slipped her foot into the low-heeled, knee-high, black leather boot.

"Come in," she called.

Ryan peered over his shoulder from his spot

before the mirror in the bathroom as he adjusted his tie.

In his dress uniform he looked even more handsome, Denali thought as his eyes met hers. She pulled up the zipper of the boot and stood, letting the long, black skirt settle around her ankles.

"Da wants you to carry this." Zane handed her a twenty-two. "Ma, wanted you to wear a vest but we talked her out of it. But be careful, please. Stay with us."

"I will. Thanks." She nodded her thanks for the gun and slipped it into the top of her boot. "Has Anne called?"

"You know she won't." Zane hugged her quickly. "It's better if she doesn't. Mom and Dad don't need her drama."

"I keep hoping she'll change her mind someday."

Zane snorted. "What mind?" He winced and hugged her again. "Sorry, she just gets me so mad. She called me last year when I went to school. I have no idea how she got my number. She didn't ask how anyone was, just if I could spare a few bucks."

"Your sister?" Ryan asked.

"Yep, our black sheep," Zane said cheerfully. "She barely completed grammar school. By the time she was fifteen, she'd run away three times. She dropped out of school at sixteen and not to work. She drove our parents nuts laying around the house. It got so bad they had her arrested for stealing. She'd take anything not nailed down. She spent the next two years in and out of juvenile detention centers."

Ryan glanced at Denali and frowned. "Maybe she just couldn't keep up with the rest of you guys?"

"She never tried." Zane shrugged. "At eighteen they kicked her out and cut her off." His eyes flicked to Denali then away. Pink covered his cheeks.

Denali shrugged and hugged him quickly. "I know she was selling herself. She came to our apartment in Boston and tried to guilt Meteora into giving her money. Meteora offered to pay for school for her. Anne stormed out. She never even said a word to me as if I didn't exist. I don't understand how people can treat others so badly. Mom and Dad were so good to her. They really tried.

"I guess some people just don't share well. Honestly, I was glad when she was gone. I was afraid for the younger kids."

"She was violent?' Ryan asked.

"Not to us; we could kick her ass, and she knew it." Denali exchanged fleeting smiles with Zane. "We learned to ignore her insults. It wasn't hard, she avoided everyone, staying in her room. By the time she was sixteen, Mom and Dad had given up and just let her stay there. Her behavior was really disruptive. She couldn't even be civil at dinner. She really hated us. Every child Mom and Dad adopted made it worse. She'd scream about her inheritance like we were going to take everything from her when it should've been clear our parents weren't planning to leave her a thing. But still, I thought she'd come home for Olympia."

"Maybe she'll come," Zane said, but his eyes were sad.

*　　*　　*

Neil sat beside her in the limousine on the way to Saint Patrick's Cathedral. He'd hugged her and kissed her cheek while assuring her he wasn't angry, but he'd been cold and distant. Ryan took her hand in his gloved one. Seated beside her, he offered her a reassuring smile.

Ryan's parents sat across from them, beside Neil's parents. No one said a word. A large crowd had gathered, comprised of mourners, gawkers, and reporters. The limousine slowed. Police, dressed in their best uniforms, lined the street on both sides, directing traffic.

Overhead, police and news helicopters passed, adding their noise to the din.

"This is a nightmare," she murmured as she took Ryan's hand to exit the vehicle.

Reporters yelled her name as flashes nearly blinded her. Calls of, 'Officer Graham, Mr. Bachman, could we get a statement,' competed with shouts of, 'murderer, hero, reckless, Ms. Denali.' Police whistles blew as the officers pushed the surging crowd back. She was grateful when the cathedral door closed behind her, shutting them out.

Three white coffins and six black ones lay at the front of the church, their tops covered with flowers. The cloying perfume of lilies filled the air. Beside her, Neil stumbled.

She offered him an arm, which he accepted. Those already seated peered over their shoulders as they walked down the aisle to the seating reserved for family. Denali stared at the floor at her feet. The hard, wooden bench pressed against her sore ribs. She sat ramrod straight and folded her hands in her lap.

Ryan placed his hand on her knee and squeezed. "This is nothing," he murmured. "A few hours and we can go home; no one is even shooting at us."

She snorted and took his hand, holding it in both of hers. Neil's mother grasped Neil's hand. Her tear-filled eyes met Denali's for a moment before she closed them and turned away.

Denali heard nothing of the service. Mrs. Ritchie's crying family distracted her attention. A dull throb built in her temple until it became a sharp, stabbing pain.

"Hello, my name is Tracy Aims, and I'm speaking on behalf of the students of Olympus."

Denali opened her eyes. Tracy stood in her school uniform at the podium. She met Denali's gaze and smiled sadly before returning to her notes.

"At first, I was embarrassed that the world heard me crying, but anyone would've. What happened was scary." Tracy clenched her small fists and narrowed her eyes. "Ms. Olympia was murdered to scare us. Not just us, but all Americans. I think Officer Graham's actions scared them instead. They tried to murder our spirit. But we're stronger than that. Killing us, or our schools, won't make us weaker. We won't cower in fear or bow to the demands of killers and bad men. The students of Olympus have learned a hard lesson; one we won't forget. We'll never run in fear— we'll fight. With our bare hands if we have to.

"My parents let me listen to the special report last night. Ms. Denali, our teacher, saved us. The television show didn't tell you how kind she was to us. How worried and brave. Her example is one the students of Olympus hope to emulate. Observe, plan, act." Tracy emphasized her words with a small fist hitting the podium.

"One of the very first things she taught us was to respect others personal space, that touching someone without their permission is the act of an animal, that to be a true human being we must master our animal impulses. Honestly, I didn't understand what she meant till last week. Those men broke into the school like a pack of wild dogs, with no humanity at all. They killed as animals do, savagely.

Tears trailed down Tracy's cheeks. "We're small and unable to fight grown men. Like animals, they picked weak prey. But we won't always be small and weak. Thanks to our teacher, we'll grow and be strong. Using the lessons taught at Olympus, we'll learn. And someday, when we're big and have learned enough, we'll know how to stop these animals disguised as men. Al-Jadr has strengthened us, not weakened us. Terrorist everywhere can see that Americans won't go meekly to their doom, that fear won't lead us to bad decisions.

"The other students and I hope Olympus reopens, bigger and better on the same hill to show the world we're not afraid." Tracy gathered her notes and turned to her mother who stood behind her.

Tears streamed down Mrs. Aim's face as she took her daughter's hand. She stepped forward to the microphone.

"I'm so sorry for the families and friends of those of you who lost loved ones. I'm so proud of the students they taught and the example they set. God bless you all."

Denali smiled at Tracy who sadly smiled back.

"What an amazing child," Neil murmured.

"She deserves a great education, the best America can offer," Denali whispered back.

Neil nodded thoughtfully. The defeated slouch left his shoulders as he stared after Tracy.

Mourners lined the street for the trip to the cemetery, waving American flags and carrying flowers, their sad, angry faces stared at the tinted windows of the limousines as they passed.

"The entire world is outraged," Mr. Bachman said and laid his age-spotted hand against his son's.

"It doesn't bring her back. All our anger, our misery — it means nothing. She'll never laugh or love again." Neil covered his face with his hands.

Ryan leaned forward and hugged him, whispering something too low to hear. Neil nodded and straightened.

"I'm so sorry," Ryan said and handed him a tissue.

The funeral procession split in different directions, each casket going to different cemeteries. Hester had arranged for receptions at three different venues for the families and friends of the deceased. Only close friends and family had been invited back to the Rubenstein-Wong estate.

Overhead, an overcast sky forecasted more snow. A brisk wind gusted intermittently, rustling the flowers and greenery around the casket set above the hole in the earth waiting to receive her sister. Denali scanned the grounds, hoping to see her sister Anne.

Iggy and Bee clutched each other crying. Meteora and Anya crouched beside them, trying to offer comfort. Shiloh knelt in the fresh dirt, unmindful of his suit and whispered Navaho prayers.

Tianzi held his crying wife and glared down at the hole waiting to receive Olympia. Lee held Iaia's hand. She laid her forehead against his chest, and Zane rested his hand on her shaking shoulder. It was clear she cried although she did so quietly. Simon and Sensei stood together, holding hands before Gui. He rested a hand on each of his small son's shoulders. Danxia held Hester's arm and Dai hovered as if unsure of who to comfort first.

Denali's gaze traveled the stark, tear-stained faces

of her family. It didn't seem real. The cold and sadness felt removed from her. She wondered if she'd broken something inside her soul that she could stand here and instead of grieving wish to sleep.

More than anything she wanted to close her eyes and sleep. Maybe when she woke, the sadness on their faces would be less. She wished, like Rip-Van-Winkle, she could sleep for years and wake into a new life.

Ryan stepped behind her and pressed against her back; his body blocking the wind. But it was the warmth of his love that warmed her soul. Always, without being asked, he knew what she needed. Life and love remained, lessened with the loss of Olympia, but there and deep.

She straightened, leaning on his warmth. She could sleep later. Now, she needed to remain alert. Dai had warned of threats that the FBI took seriously enough to set guards on the proceedings and their home. She'd talk with her parents later today about leaving soon. They wouldn't be safe until Al-Jadr was handled.

She shivered and pressed closer to Ryan, wishing now she hadn't agreed to be bait. It was one thing to risk herself, but she risked everyone she loved by remaining.

TWENTY-ONE

Frenemies

Denali glanced up as Ryan entered their bedroom. "Your parents left?"

Ryan hugged her, resting his chin on her head before answering. "Yep, they appreciated the visit, it was nice of your parents to put them up like this for the weekend, and I know they enjoyed getting to know your family. Zane is taking them home. Agent Bowen has a detail on their house, but so far, no threats have been made against them, just us. I'll feel better when we're out of here. I hate to think we bring trouble to your family."

"Our family, but I agree. Lee offered to drive us to Boston tonight. He can catch a flight back to California from there. Or, we could take the train, and Tianzi will pick us up."

"I can go alone if you want to stay with your parents."

"No, I'm coming. They'll be safer with me gone. We'll be back in a few days. I really hope you get this job, but don't accept it if you don't like it."

Ryan tweaked her hair. "I'm grateful Commissioner Westfall arranged the interview. I thought I'd have to commute a long time."

She pushed back to see his face. "I still have to finish out this term. Neil will be reopening the school, and I promised to help with that too, so if they do offer you a job, a later starting date would be good."

"Tracy convinced him, huh?"

"That and the number of donations pouring in. He plans to expand and build Olympia's dream school. Olympus will once again sit on the hillside."

"You sound sad."

"Worried that the school becomes a symbol to terrorists."

Ryan kissed her forehead and was quiet a moment before he spoke. "I suppose there'll always be bad men who see children as prey. Tracy is right, we can't give in to them. We rebuild bigger and better. Not as a dare, but a statement that we won't cower. If Olympus isn't rebuilt, they'd target another school. At least Olympus will be prepared."

"True." Denali laughed softly. "Mr. Fredrick called and wants Neil to offer firearms training to the teachers. He apologized to Sensei for not being better prepared."

"Will you design the security for the new school?"

"No." A shudder traveled her. "I'll go over it and offer suggestions, but it's too much responsibility." The reminder of her failure saddened her.

"You have nothing to be sorry for."

She nodded against his shoulder. His heavy sigh ruffled her hair, making her wince. She couldn't help feeling responsible. In hindsight, it was foolish letting the security rest in one person's hands, but it had never occurred to her someone on the inside would intentionally let gunmen into the building. She'd always considered being smart was enough, but this had taught her you needed wisdom, not just intelligence. An experience security designer would've known to not let it rest in one person's hands. Being able to design a system didn't make her qualified to use it.

She straightened and pasted a false smile on her face. "Will your mom come visit?"

Ryan frowned and rubbed his thumb over her smile.

She let it fade.

"That's better. Always truth between us, even hard truth. No polite lies." He kissed her before going to the closet to remove his duffel bag. "Mom loved your house; she's a bit jealous, and a bit awed, but I'm sure she'd come again if we invite her here. I didn't invite her to Boston yet. I want us settled first."

"That sounds amazing. I want us settled too. I can't wait to leave here."

Ryan snorted and grabbed her bag. "This is hardly confinement. Even in Boston no running for you until the ribs are one hundred percent."

Denali texted her brother accepting his offer of a ride.

"I hate all the gawkers," she said as she proceeded him from the bedroom.

"Well, there'll probably be some in Boston too."

"Yeah, but not as many and there won't be any parents or relatives."

Ryan stopped and turned to her. "Are you still getting yelled at?"

"No." Denali passed him and stabbed the elevator button with a finger. "I'm getting thanked, and that's worse. It's embarrassing, and I never know what to say. And they always say how sorry they are and ask if I'm handling it okay. What am I supposed to say to that? That I never lose a wink of sleep over those men?"

"Yep, that's what I say. " Ryan stepped into the elevator and let the bags fall to his feet. She sighed heavily and followed.

Officer Ortega waited in the foyer.

"Jeff! Good to see you, man. I've been meaning to call. I'm glad you stopped by." Ryan dropped the bags again and hugged his partner. Denali twisted her hands together and hoped Lee showed soon.

"Meet my fiancé. Denali, this is my partner, Jeff.

"Yeah, we've met." Denali pasted a fake smile on her face and hesitantly offered her hand.

Ryan's eyes narrowed, and he stepped to her side.

Jeff ignored the proffered hand. "I came to see Denali and apologize." He ran a hand through his thinning hair.

"What?" Ryan stepped between them, his glare deepening.

"I was an ass, and I'm sorry. I really had no idea you'd been injured." A red flush climbed Jeff's cheeks. "I mean more. I knew you were injured in the fight, which just makes me more of an ass. Maria screamed at me for an hour, calling me a sexist pig, and it got me thinking. If Ryan had acted alone, I wouldn't have thought he was a hot head or a glory hound or crazy. I would've assumed he had a good reason. My wife might be right about me judging you differently because you're a woman. I'm sorry."

"Forget it," Denali said, feeling sick. She didn't want Ryan to know his co-workers didn't like her. Somehow it felt like making him choose sides, and she didn't want him to have too.

"What the hell did you do?"

Denali winced. Ryan had sounded really angry.

"I let your ex in the room. I heard the fight and thought Denali was faking when she came out." Jeff thrust his hands in his pants pockets. "Marie showed up with Cally, and I left her hurt on the floor."

"You left her hurt on the floor?" Ryan repeated as if he couldn't believe it.

Denali said, "No, I sat on the floor to wait for Gail to leave. He didn't know I was hurt because I didn't realize how bad it was." She grabbed Ryan's arm as he tensed.

Jeff sighed. "I knew she was hurt, not physically, but I thought the tears were for what I said."

"You made her cry? What the fuck, Jeff!"

Jeff winced.

Denali grasped Ryan's arm. "Please, stop. He's sorry, and I'm okay. Don't let me ruin your friendship."

Ryan put his arm around her and pulled her close. "A friend wouldn't make you cry or leave you hurt."

Jeff winced. "You're right. I thought I was helping, but I should've spoken to you. I'm sorry. You don't need to leave the force, I can transfer or, hell— quit. I didn't know you were staying with her here. I'd planned to come talk to you after I'd apologized to her."

"Just stop!" Denali stepped between them with her hands outheld. "This is all a misunderstanding. You thought you were looking out for him, keep doing that. Forgive your friend for an honest mistake. Ryan isn't quitting. He wants to move closer to me. My home is in Boston."

"Everything okay here?" Lee asked. One hand rested on the back of his waistband.

"Everything's fine, just a misunderstanding," Denali said.

Ryan ran his hands through his hair and stared at her a moment before slumping and offering his hand to Jeff.

"Denali will be my wife. Tell the guys if they give her any shit at all, they answer to me. I had no idea the squad has a problem with her."

"They don't anymore." Jeff rubbed his balding head with both hands. "They did at first, but once they found out she knew what was planned…" The red in his cheeks darkened. "I hate to ask for a favor when I've been such a dick, but if you could call my wife and assure her you have no hard feelings, it would get me out of the dog house."

Denali nodded.

"Your sister Anya has met with Cally, and you're right, she isn't autistic. She has an extreme case of Meniere's disease."

"Can they treat it? Ryan asked

"Cally is scheduled for surgery tomorrow." He offered Denali a sickly smile. "A specialist your brother recommended. They'll drain the fluid in her ears and insert a drainage tube. She might need a mastoidectomy or vestibular nerve section, but they won't know until they see the damage. She wasn't having 'fits,' she was falling from vertigo. Anya says her misdiagnosis is incompetent, and we should sue, but I'm so glad she can be helped. You have no idea…"

"Will she be deaf?" Ryan laid a hand on Jeff's shoulder.

"Maybe, Anya wasn't sure. But she assures me deaf will be better than the pain and disorientation

Cally suffers right now. She can hear very loud noises. The headbanging – that was to hear us, it jiggles the fluid allowing sound to penetrate. Loud rhythmic noises come through better."

Jeff threw his hands in the air. "Maybe we should sue. We took her to so many doctors and a sick girl on the floor sees it wasn't autism without even examining her."

"I do have experience with autistics. And Cally did present as typical. She never had moments of clarity?"

"When she was a baby, she was fine, perfectly normal. It didn't start until she was two and it started slowly. The first doctors told us children progress at different levels and not to worry that Cally didn't speak or walk well. Then, overnight, she changed, becoming cranky, hitting her head, screaming. She had good days where she played and walked. Maria could feed her or get her to try to speak, but it was hard to get her attention. Anya says it would be like living on the bottom of a pool, then being thrown on land. Noise would be overwhelming, sights, sounds, and tastes, clearer. On her bad days, when she cried all day and night, the ears hurt. She wasn't rocking for attention or banging her head in anger but to relieve the pressure. For a year she suffered…"

Jeff stepped forward and hugged Denali. "Even if she is deaf after this, she won't be in pain, and for that I sincerely thank you."

Ryan said, "Jeff, that's great news. Damn, I wish I

could stay and support you, but I can't blow this off interview."

"No, go. We'll be fine." Jeff stepped back. "I'm sorry to bother you at home."

"I'll call Maria," Denali said.

Ryan grabbed the bags and headed toward the door. "Let me know how the surgery goes."

"I will and thank you again, Denali."

Denali nodded and hurried to the car. A groan escaped her as she slid into the back seat.

"Fool, take stairs easier," Lee snapped as he sat in the driver's seat.

"Don't you start." Denali glared at him as he peered in the mirror.

Jeff waved as he drove his squad car away. Ryan turned to the back seat, a frown narrowing his blue eyes.

"You should've told me."

"Honestly, it slipped my mind. But even if it hadn't, I wouldn't have mentioned your partner hated me."

"He doesn't hate you."

Denali shrugged. "He doesn't now. I wasn't going to take a chance you'd change your mind about us. He was certain I was a bad choice for you."

"I'll never change my mind."

"Me either."

"Eww, knock it off, you're grossing me out," Lee said.

Ryan laughed. Denali glared.

"She needs French fries; she hasn't had any all week." Lee laughed when Denali grunted. "A tip from your brother-in-law on marital bliss with Denali. Feed her French fries and she'll be much easier to get along with. Take her for long runs; she gets cranky if she's cooped up. Never ask her to go shopping. If she's staring off into space with a puzzled expression, don't disturb her."

Denali snorted, then laughed.

"If you want to distract her, a shiny gadget or tool will work."

"I can distract her," Ryan assured him and grinned at Denali.

Denali giggled, the giggle changing to an outright laugh as Lee pretended to vomit.

*　*　*

"Well, here we are." Denali gestured at the houseboat moored between a seventy-foot yacht and a forty-foot sailboat.

"Nice." Ryan stepped aboard the teak decking on the main floor. Two blue deck chairs sat on the small deck. Above them, an edge of a navy-blue umbrella peeked over the upper deck rail.

"I refinished all the floors myself. The kitchen is all new. None of the original was worth saving."

A gray marble countertop covered the bottom, white cabinets in the small galley-style kitchen.

Stainless-steel appliances matched the stainless-steel sink. Most of the room was taken up by overstuffed dark gray furniture covered in colorful pillows. A small round table with four white leather chairs on a colorful rug separated the galley from the living space.

Windows lined the walls framed in gauzy white curtains. Steep stairs led to the lower and upper deck.

"There's a grill on the top deck and another small refrigerator and sink. This is a half-bath." She opened a white door and let him peek into the small bathroom beside the stairs. "The other door is the pantry slash toolbox. Right now, it has more tools than food.

"Downstairs we have a full bath." She led the way down the stairs and pointed out the closets hidden in the white paneling lining the walls. "The engine room is in here with the water heater and pumps. I can go about six weeks on my water tanks, so, with both of us, that's probably three weeks, but here at the dock I can hook up to sewer and water."

She opened the door beside the engine room. "All walls below deck are soundproof and fire resistant. This is our guest room. I put in the larger window as a fire escape. The twin beds can slide and latch together to be one, but most of my friends and family are single, so two was better for me. The couch upstairs pulls out too. If your parents come, we can easily convert this room for them." She gestured through the window. "The guy who owns the yacht almost never takes it out, but he does host parties. The sailboat comes and goes. If the yacht bothers you, we can move, but it can take a while to find a big enough slip."

"This seems like a great location."

"It is. We get two parking spots and can use the clubhouse. And I can bike to school. You need a pass to enter even visitor parking, so it's pretty secure."

Ryan chuckled. "Not really, anyone could take a boat to our back door."

"True." Denali bit her lip.

"Don't worry about it, we'll figure something out. "Show me the bedroom."

"Mmm," she mumbled as she kissed his chest unable to stand on tiptoe to kiss his lips.

He cooperated and leaned down as she dropped her hands to his waistband.

"You're going to like our room. The cabinets on the side of the bed pull out to form tables you can use in bed, and there are power strips hidden inside to plug your phone and stuff in. I spent a lot of time customizing and modernizing, everything works off voice commands from the lights to the window shades." As she spoke, she stepped backward, pulling him with her, removing his belt and dropping it on the floor. The buckle clanked against the hardwood flooring. Her shirt followed. They left a trail of clothing to the bedroom.

Two hours later, dim gray light filtered through the white gauzy curtains over the rectangular windows high on the wall of the bedroom.

"You're right I like our bedroom. Show me the cabinets."

Denali murmured sleepily and pulled the blanket over her head.

"I like our house. It's much bigger and nicer than I'd imagined." He smoothed her hair back, gathering it to the side and kissing her neck. "Tired?"

She opened one eye to peer at him, making him laugh.

"How are you not exhausted?"

"You need to build your stamina back up." He pulled the blanket down slowly, kissing the skin revealed.

Denali stared down her body at him. His tousled brown hair and bright blue eyes were beyond beguiling as he kissed his way across her skin.

"Sleep can wait."

He chuckled.

She woke to noonday sun and a note on her pillow and sat to stretch carefully. Only a little sore, one spot still gave her a sharp twinge if she moved too fast. She frowned at the floor-length mirror in the bathroom. The bruises were mostly faded yellow splotches, the scars red lines. "I'm still a mess," she said to the empty room.

In the kitchen, she opened the empty refrigerator. "This is weird." She stared around her familiar home feeling like a stranger. "How long until I feel normal again?" Only silence answered her.

TWENTY-TWO

Cally

Ryan returned carrying a paper grocery bag under one arm and two, big, fast food bags in the other. The smell of French fries made her smile. He laughed when she kissed his cheek and grabbed the bag, opening it eagerly.

"I bought extra fries. What did you do all day?"

"First, tell me about the interview." Denali spread the food on the glass-topped table while Ryan put the groceries in the refrigerator.

"It went well, I think. I've been asked to return in three days for a follow-up interview anyway, which I think is a good sign."

"Did you like them?"

"Sure, what I saw of them. I only met a few of the

officers."

"Is the job the same?"

"Basically, they'll let me try for their ERT team, but I have to restart. Their training is a bit different."

Denali frowned and set her hamburger down.

"It's nothing to worry about. I don't mind more training." He handed her a bottled water and sat beside her in one of the white leather dining room chairs. "I'll miss my friends, but I'll make new ones. This will be good for us, a fresh start. Most everyone I met treated me normally. I hadn't realized how tense I was at home." He yawned and stretched, then leaned over to kiss her temple. "I could sleep for a week."

"Ha, you're tired cause you were up all night." She giggled and ate a fry when he rolled his eyes.

So, what did you do today?" he asked.

"Called the lab and asked if I could come in. I had an idea for Cally."

"Any word on that?"

"Not yet. Anya will call me as soon as she knows anything. She's following the case closely. When do you have to be back for work?"

"Eight more days."

"Good, Me too. Neil is arranging temporary accommodations for the school kids. Actually, I think it'll be awesome. He's spreading us out and sending us to other schools. Two teachers and two classes. We're reorganizing the students a bit. I'll have two classes of older kids to finish the term. He's trying to keep them age appropriate for the schools we'll be in."

"That does sound interesting. The other teachers can see what you do, and your students can mingle with children unaffected by the tragedy."

"No one will be unaffected, but I get what you mean. Neil hopes the other children will have a calming effect. The counselors all urge us to get them out in big groups right away before fear of strangers really has a chance to set in." Denali smiled sadly. "This is helping Neil, being so busy organizing. His nights must be hell though."

"I can't even imagine it." Ryan placed his half-eaten burger on the table. "Denali, if I lost you…" He took a deep breath and picked up his burger but didn't eat. "Us, together like we are…" he placed the burger on the table again and rubbed his eyes before turning to her. "Every day— every single second of every day— I grow closer to you. I need you more. I want you more. He's had years to grow closer to his wife, I can't imagine the pain of that separation. I don't want to imagine it. To lose her so suddenly and violently, for no reason like that… God, I would be so angry. I think I'd go crazy. That isn't something you recover from."

Denali hugged him, resting her face against the light stubble on his cheek. "You're a gift from God. To be able to love you with my whole heart with such perfect trust is amazing. Everyone thinks we're crazy, that it's a temporary infatuation brought on by stress, but it isn't." She pushed back to see his face. "I saw the real you and know I can trust that man. I can love you without fear of being hurt or betrayed. I saw how strong you are, how willing to do the right thing no matter what it costs, and I know you'll do that with me."

His blue eyes searched her face with such a loving expression her eyes filled with tears.

She kissed his lips lightly and spoke softly. "Time will only make us closer. Each memory we make, full of love and laughter, eases my heart, pushing that dark day away."

"I forget what good recall you have." He ran his hand over her hair as if he could smooth the memory away. "It must be hard, seeing it so clearly in your mind's eye."

"It makes me angry. The deaths hurt. I'm glad I didn't see any of them. You help. In every way, you make my life better." She closed her eyes and traced a finger over her collarbone to her breast. "I can see you so clearly, kissing me. Warm breath misting on my skin, the sound of your skin on mine, I remember it perfectly." Her eyes opened as he slid his chair back.

Dark blue eyes stared at her hungrily. "I want to remember it as clearly, but my memory isn't as good as yours; we'll have to repeat it a few times. Did I kiss you here?" He lowered his lips to the edge of her collarbone where it peeked from her T-shirt.

"Mmm."

"Or was it here?" He moved his lips an inch over,

cupping her breast through her shirt.

His voice lowered as he trailed his thumb across her nipple. "Or was it here?"

"Kiss me everywhere," she breathed.

Dinner forgotten on the tabletop, he complied.

He was breathing hard, relaxed against her with his head resting on her naked breast when the Ride of the Valkyries shrilled from her cell phone.

"My sister Anya. I better take it," she murmured.

He groaned and reached for her jeans, which had gotten kicked under the table.

Balanced on an elbow, she accepted the phone and had to look away from the light in his eyes as he gazed at her body.

"Hi." It came out all scratchy, and she had to clear her throat and try again. "Hi, what's up?"

"Did I catch you at a bad time?"

"No. We were just finishing dinner."

Ryan snickered and began kissing her leg.

"I thought you'd want to know, Cally is in recovery and the prognosis is good."

"Will she hear?"

Ryan straightened and reached for his pants.

"I'm putting you on speaker so Ryan can hear too."

"She hears; testing will need to wait until she's recovered from surgery, but she heard."

"Will the fluid return?" Ryan asked.

"Likely, but now that we know, we can monitor for it."

"Can they put in drains?"

"Yes, there are options. Time will tell what further procedures she needs. Our priority right now is easing her pain and teaching her to communicate. I got your email, and it's a fantastic idea. How soon can you get her a tablet?"

"Within a day for a quick, simple one. Give me — say — two weeks, for a more permanent one."

"Why so long?"

"I'm so busy. The programming, while not complex, will be time-consuming because of the amount. I want Cally to learn basic sign language as she learns to speak. If she does lose her hearing, she'll be prepared. I also want the program age-appropriate to interest a small child. Iggy can help me with that. I was thinking two devices, one tablet size, one pocket size."

"What will they do?" Ryan asked.

"A few things. She'll be able to tap on a picture to hear how the word is pronounced and see the sign. The screen will light if she does it correctly, but the real benefit is for us. With it, we can monitor her learning curve. If she experiences problems, needing more volume or less we'll know right away. Anya and I can interact with her remotely to help her while she teaches us."

"She can teach you?"

"Definitely. We can learn a lot from her. She's too young to skew the results. Older children will try to please adults by telling them what they think they want to hear. We'll know right away if she's frustrated or understands; she's too young to hide those things."

"Maria has agreed to all my requests to study her," Anya said. "Cally can really help us develop tools for other deaf children. My hope is when she learns to communicate, she can tell us what helped her most. Maybe we can apply that to real autistic children to help them."

"She wasn't autistic though," Ryan said, sounding confused.

"No, but she was living in a confusing, painful, world. Anything that helped her might be helpful to others stuck in their own confusing worlds."

"Man, those poor kids."

"Yeah, we'll help them." Denali laid a hand on his arm.

"Maria asked me to send along her thanks again. She and Jeff are considering having more children now."

"That's great," Ryan said.

Denali said nothing.

"I know what you're thinking," Anya said.

Denali snorted.

"What?" Ryan rose an eyebrow and examined her. "You don't think they should?"

"I don't think they should if the reason they didn't was because they thought Cally was damaged."

"I knew you'd think that." Anya sounded smug. "Marie and Jeff are thinking of adopting. She'll have time to care for a special needs child if Cally progresses like I think she will. There's no hurry though, they have plenty of time to decide."

"That's great," Denali said relieved. "I just hate to think of autistic children being treated as less than or not worthy. Different doesn't mean bad."

"Preaching to the choir, sister."

Denali laughed. "Actually, I had another idea. If Maria wouldn't mind, Iggy could use someone to care for. The loss of the baby really hurt her. She was really looking forward to being an older sister. Someone like Cally, who needs so much help, help Iggy could give, would be great for her."

"That's an awesome idea. Both girls would benefit; you really are a genius."

"Pfft."

Ryan laughed and lightly pulled her hair.

"So, FedEx me a temporary tablet and leave yourself access to upgrade it. Put in an auto record function for us when she speaks."

Ryan stood and pulled his pants up as Denali and Anya began talking about the programming. "I'm going to go shower," he whispered.

Denali nodded and waved. Smiling he left the room.

TWENTY-THREE

Do You See Me Now?

Denali absently tucked a strand of hair behind her ear and stared at the blank screen before her. Her life had completely changed, and not just with the death of her sister Olympia. Her friends here at school treated her with a mixture of disbelief and awe. She hoped in time they'd revert to normal.

Everyone in the lab avoided her glance, going about their business as if she weren't present. That would be fine except for the sidelong stares as if they expected her to pull an Uzi from her sweatshirt and start firing. And she almost wished she had one. Her once safe lab no longer seemed secure. She eyed the entrances and windows and considered how to better secure them, but the students who randomly entered and exited made the task complex. She'd need more time to design something. Marion had taught her a hard lesson and now she saw everyone as a potential security leak. She tried to tell herself she was being paranoid but found herself questioning everyone's motives for being in the room.

She sighed in relief when her friend Mary entered and dropped her book bag on the table, dragging Denali's dark thoughts into the present. Mary still treated her normally — mostly, and she trusted her implicitly.

Mary said, "I programmed those patterns you asked for. This is an amazing opportunity. We're going to learn so much. I'm sorry for the little girl, but what we learn could help so many. Thanks for thinking of me."

Denali smiled and nodded toward the laptop set up on the table. "Check my program while I finish these last connections. It's crude but temporary. We can work on a better one, but Anya wants Cally to start right away."

"What are you doing there?" Mary gestured to the tablet with its back off and innards spread across the table.

"Cally is too little to plug things in or turn them on. I'm putting in wireless charging and replacing the ACSI chip. This one will leave it always connected with no encryption. When I have time, I'll redo it, but we need to hear everything as is without the encryption and computer-boosted clarity of a cell phone connection."

"Great idea. It shouldn't be hard for Cally to learn to place it on the charging pad." Mary snickered. "Make sure you tell her parents it's always on."

Denali glanced at Mary with laughing blue eyes. "Maria assures us she'll make sure this" -Denali tapped the tablet cover— "and the auxiliary speakers will be left on all the time. Every room of their house will have one except their bedroom. She's promised to bring the tablet with them when they go out so we don't miss anything."

"It's awesome for them to do this— lose their privacy like that."

"It'll only be a couple months, a year tops. Which is why we need to get this tablet to Cally ASAP. This is the crucial learning period. To observe now is key. Can you FedEx the tablet tonight?"

Mary rose an eyebrow. "Sure."

"I'd do it myself, but I have a date."

"Your police officer?"

Mary laughed at her bright smile.

'I can't believe how much I love him already. We're so happy together. For the first time in my life, I feel like the most important person to someone."

A thoughtful expression crossed Mary's face as she sat on the edge of the table. "I never consider that before. The drawbacks to a large family, I mean. You always had to share everything. It must be a relief to have someone who's all yours." She bit her lip and glanced away, then straightened and faced Denali.

"Are you sure though? That he feels the same, I mean? What you two went through was intense. Could it be clouding your judgment?"

"It isn't clouded. We got to know each other really well, really fast because we had to. I know Ryan. I'm still learning the superficial stuff, but I know the deep down, real him."

Mary jumped up and kissed her cheek. "If anyone deserves happiness it's you."

Jerome, another of the graduate students who worked in the lab, approached and laid his computer bag on the table. "I agree; Denali should get everything she deserves. The television footage was terrifying. I can't imagine how scary it must've been in real life."

Denali and Mary exchanged annoyed glances. Jerome had a habit of butting into private conversations with coeds. Chubby, with bad acne, he followed the girls in the lab around with slavish devotion, always willing to lend a hand with the tedious programming. Some of the girls took advantage of him shamelessly.

Denali tried to be kind without leading him on. That was harder to do than it sounded when he took any kindness as a sign of interest. She never accepted his offers of help, and he never stopped offering. Whenever she invited the computer team to her house, she included him, but he always lingered after the others left until she had to ask him to leave. She hoped now that she was engaged he'd move on to someone else.

"It was scary," she said shortly. Then held up her left hand for Mary to admire her engagement ring. "Ryan and I are officially engaged."

Mary exclaimed in delight; Jerome frowned, then pasted on a fake smile.

"Is he living with you now?" he asked.

"Now and forever."

Jerome turned away, and Denali couldn't decipher his expression; it was a cross between anger, dismay and something she didn't have a name for.

"Ryan can't wait to meet my friends here. You guys will like him." Ryan would be kind to him, and maybe that's all Jerome needed, a male friend to shore up his self-esteem.

Jerome sat in the chair beside Mary and stared at the computer screen, feigning great interest. She and Mary exchange small shrugs.

"Hope I'm invited to the wedding," Mary said.

"About that, Ryan and I might elope. We don't want to wait."

Mary giggled.

"You're going away?" Jerome glanced up, scowling. "On a honeymoon?"

"I hope so." Denali laughed lightly. "Our schedules are hectic right now. We're only here a few days before we go back to Washington. Both of us have work commitments there. But we're thinking of going away to marry and honeymoon, and we're not telling anyone where."

Mary grinned at her. "I don't blame you, the media must be driving you crazy."

"A bit— "

"Hey, Pete," Jerome called and jumped to his feet. "Catch you two later. Pete, got a minute to talk about that design idea?"

Jerome ran off, the short run making him sweat and pant.

Mary frowned at him. "He needs to get a life. The entire time you've been in Washington, he's been bugging me to let him work on our project." She shrugged. "Maybe now he'll give up. How he thinks he has a chance with you... Stop being nice to him; it confuses his weak male mind."

Denali laughed. "What about you and Craig, any news?"

"No, we aren't in any rush. Why don't you and Ryan come over to our place tomorrow?"

"Sounds good. I'll ask him. Pass me the soldering iron."

Denali straightened and massaged her neck, trying to relieve the crick. "Last test."

Mary ran a final diagnostic and held up her hand. The two women high-fived. "Perfect."

"Awesome." Denali glanced at her watch. "I got to run. See ya tomorrow."

Mary waved absently, already packing the tablet

into a shipping box.

Outside, campus lights illuminated the dirty snow. Dusk had fallen early, and cold weather kept the students tucked in their dorms. Only a few walked the sidewalks, and those kept their heads down and walked briskly. Her bike sat alone in the bike rack. It was too cold for biking, but she hadn't replaced her car yet, and Ryan had their rental.

For a moment she debated calling a cab. The bike was hard on her ribs, but the ride wasn't that long. She knelt in the snow to unlock it.

"Denali!" Jerome ran up puffing, his face red from cold. "Did you hear they're moving our lab to the Maria Stata building?"

Denali straightened. "No. I thought that building was still being remodeled."

"It is, although why they bother when they just did it six years ago…"

Denali laughed as she stepped away leading her bike. "I forgot you were here then too."

Jerome rubbed his hands, then stuffed them into the pockets of his blue parka. "Let me buy you a coffee, and we can walk by to check it out. Rumor has it we can request our office space, and I want to get a good one."

Denali glanced at her watch again. "Okay, but I can't take too long." She pushed her bike to the deserted coffee cart and accepted the coffee Jerome handed her with a nod of thanks.

He walked on the other side of her bike with one

hand on the handlebars, helping to balance it. "My car is parked in the lot behind the science building. I can give you a ride if you want to leave the bike here tonight."

"That would be awesome. My ribs are still pretty sore." She handed Jerome her coffee and locked the bike in the next bike stand they passed.

"How's your programming coming? Have you and Mary made any progress on the new computer language?"

"Quite a bit actually. We've been working on it after hours whenever we get a chance."

"Did you like teaching?"

"Yes, but I like research better. What about you? How long will you stay in the lab?"

Denali was surprised when he sneered.

"You mean how long until I get a real job."

"No, that isn't what I meant at all. The lab is a real job."

"I know you all think I'm not smart enough to make my own designs, but that isn't true. No one here really sees me at all."

"You're mistaken; about me at least. I thought you worked here because you liked it. Like me. I love the energy of this place, the new thoughts and ideas."

"You love being the star."

Denali stopped walking and stared at him, shocked by his angry tone.

"Sorry, that came out harsher than I intended," Jerome said sheepishly. "But it's hard always being in someone else's shadow. No one even remembers I exist. Hell, you forgot I attended this school with you six years ago. But others think I'm important and give me important work to do. Someday, the world will recognize my genius."

"Sorry." She sipped her coffee and grimaced. Bitter and growing cold but it gave her something to do while thinking of a reply that wouldn't hurt his feelings. "I didn't forget; I mean, I remember you attended…" she trailed off uncomfortably.

"I get it. I'm the fat guy who's always around and always unwanted, boring and predictable. But that isn't the real me."

Denali yawned and waved an apologetic hand. "Sorry. I'm not bored just tired."

Jerome took her coffee cup, peered into it and smiled before handing it back.

"Sit for a minute and rest."

"No, I have to get going."

"I said sit." He yanked her arm and pulled her toward a nearby snow-covered bench. "You're in such a hurry to go home and fuck a stranger. I get it, he's handsome and athletic and gets you all hot and bothered, that's just the surface though. I was hoping you'd see past that, but you never do. None of you ever do. Your eyes pass right over me without seeing me at all. You never see my potential. To you, I'm a second-rate hack."

Shocked, she yanked her arm back and staggered. Her gaze flew to the coffee cup in her hand. "What did you do?" She dropped the cup and reached for her phone. The night grew darker. The buildings wavered before her eyes as if a heat mirage passed over them.

Jerome laughed and took the phone from her hand as she slipped to her knees. She wanted to stand, to run away screaming, and couldn't manage to even raise her head.

"Do you see me now?" His wide, hard-eyed stare was the last thing she saw before darkness took her.

TWENTY-FOUR

If They Wanted Her Dead, She'd Be Dead

Her face scrunched in pain, Denali pried her eyes open. Her eyelids felt weighted. Nausea roiled in her stomach and vomit burned her throat. She tried to take slow even breaths through her nose. The gag on her mouth would choke her if she vomited.

A dim, dank room met her eyes. Somewhere water dripped and men spoke, but the sound was muffled by thick rock walls.

A basement, she thought. *And likely not strapped to a bomb if men were above her.* Her shoulders relaxed from the tense position she hadn't realized she'd taken. The bonds holding her were likely just that and not connected to levels that would explode if she moved.

The last thing she remembered was walking from the science lab. Jerome Kensky had hailed her. She closed her eyes and gritted her teeth. He'd done this, and likely thought he'd get away with it too. Who would suspect him? She certainly hadn't. *What makes people do these crazy despicable things to each other,* she pondered as she flexed her wrists and ankles. The nausea doubled as she pulled at her bonds. She wasn't getting out of this without help.

She tried to calm her racing heart by telling herself if they wanted her dead, she'd be dead already. They'd kept her, so therefore they wanted something. It didn't really help. The memory of what they'd planned for the teachers was too fresh.

She stopped struggling, saving her strength. To tie her to a cross to burn they'd have to release her. She'd fight then. Darkness pressed on her, and she let herself sink back into sleep. One corner of her mind noted she'd been drugged and likely wasn't thinking straight. *Please, God, let Ryan and my family be okay. Please, God, let Lee or Dai find me.*

Rough hands woke her, pulling strands of hair away with the gag. Someone slapped her face. The single light bulb swinging over her head glared like the sun and sent crazy shadows over the room. The men before her seemed distorted, shrinking and growing oddly, and she realized she'd been drugged again. Dust sifted from above her as booted feet clomped across the floor. Her eyes caught on the sparkling motes drifting in the harsh light and she couldn't pull her attention back.

Someone slapped her again. She realized her head was pulled back by her hair, but the effort to care was too much, and the dust was so pretty. She didn't respond to the slap, content to stare at the glittering motes.

"You fucking gave her too much! What the fuck good is she if she's a drooling idiot? Get an IV in her, and no more fucking sedative. Keep her quiet the old-fashioned way."

"I still say we kill her and be done with her. She's too dangerous—"

"Fucking coward. She's a woman and not even a big one. Without a gun, she's helpless. Abdul is paying us a lot of money to finish Greer's work." He slapped her face again, rocking it to the side.

She made no response, letting them think the drug had her fully although she was now able to tear her gaze from the dancing motes.

"Finish his fucking work and make yourself useful and maybe you get to live."

"What the fuck?" the other man said sounding as though being denied a treat.

"I've been thinking, why waste her? Think of the son's she could make."

Horror covered her body in goosebumps, and she vomited.

"Fuck— clean her up. If you fucking killed her with your drugs, I'm going to be pissed."

She let herself flop to the ground when her bonds were cut, landing in her own vomit. Tingles cramped her feet and hands. The men exclaimed in disgust and complained about who'd have to clean her. It occurred to her all of them except one spoke perfect, unaccented English. Then it occurred to her she'd seen none of them, and she realized she wasn't as lucid or aware as she'd thought.

Wavering black shadows impaired her vision, and she wasn't sure if it were drugs or the lights. Six inches from her face a workboot covered by blue jeans became her focus. The man wore an ankle holster, and her hands were free, but she couldn't get them to move. *Please don't let this be my only chance,* she thought as the booted foot moved away. She closed her eyes and unwittingly sank into darkness again. She woke again an indeterminate time later when someone sprayed her with water. At first warm, the water soon grew ice-cold.

She tried to remain still and passive under it but couldn't help the shivers that wracked her.

"I think she's coming around."

This man had an accent, she noted. She peeked through slitted eyes. Long, wet hair covered her face. Dirty, cracked, white subway tile and what was once a transparent plastic shower curtain, but now was ripped and yellowed with age, met her gaze. She was in a bathroom. Two men stood beside the tub. One held a shower wand, which he played over her; the other she couldn't see much of except his jean-clad leg. She was happy to note she was still dressed.

She must've faded for a minute because suddenly the men had changed position and she hadn't seen it happen.

"—Seizes and shit so she'll be okay."

Denali gave her best impression of an autistic seizure and had to bite back her smile as the two men exclaimed in dismay.

"Fuck, she's going to fucking die, and we need her."

"Meh, there's more computer geeks; we can take another one." He lifted her from the tub and placed her on the cracked linoleum floor while he spoke. "Even dead we can burn her ass, make her an example."

She couldn't help the tremble his words caused.

"Get her warm and the IV in. I want to be able to tell Jahir we did everything possible." Muttering under his breath, he began stripping her wet clothes.

Before Denali could panic, the other man said, "Put the sweats on her and cover her with the blanket.

An IV was placed in her arm, and she was carried to another room and laid on a bare mattress. Her captor stapled the IV bag to the wall above her head. Twice, the room swirled, and she lost minutes.

Hope surged when they left her in the room untied and locked the door behind them. She opened her eyes and examined the room, looking for cameras or guards. Seeing neither, she sat and swung her arms, being careful not to dislodge the IV. They thought the IV would help counteract the drugs and she wanted to be clearheaded. The sharp tang of vomit burned her throat, and her thoughts felt scattered.

The room spun before her eyes. She continued to swing her arms, stretch her legs, and flex her feet, hoping circulation would hurry the drugs through her system. The dizziness lessened, and she opened her eyes again to examine her prison. A small ten-by-ten room with no other furniture except the bed she sat on met her muddled gaze. Wooden slats covered the room's only window. Water had formed a large, rotted circle beneath the window, leaving gaping holes in the floor through which light shone.

On her hands and knees, she crawled to the rotted section of flooring and peered through a hole. Beneath her, a light shone, but she saw nothing except more wood flooring and the edge of a plaid couch. Tentatively, she pressed on the wood beneath the window, finding it spongy. Talking men approached. She crawled back to the bed and pulled the blanket up to her chin.

The men paused outside the door to her room, the door muffled their conversation to unrecognizable sound. They spoke for a moment before moving away.

She lay and debated her options— try to break through the floor and escape; or wait. Waiting held risk but also reward. Everything she learned could help lead to this band of murderous thugs and a safer opportunity might present itself. But, if she missed her chance to escape, she'd die horribly or worse, live horribly. Her thoughts flittered to her coworkers who'd be at risk if she escaped. She could warn them, surely the FBI would protect them?

Ryan must be frantic. The door creaked open right as she grabbed the covers to throw them back. She tried to make her body as limp as she could. Through her eyelashes, she watched a man approach her bed. He wore jeans and a Yankees shirt and would blend into any crowd. She committed his face to memory.

"Steve?" someone called from the hallway, and the man turned towards the door.

"Yo."

"The boss wants us all downstairs and bring the pic." The speaker entered the room, half closing the door behind him and lowered his voice. "I heard Amir say Iri Saba offered double. Split between all of us that's still crap, but split between our guys..."

Steve took her picture with a digital camera. "Yeah, I was thinking the same thing. We weren't paid enough to start a fucking war, and I don't like how Jahir is looking at us, but we need to be smart. If word gets out we crossed him..."

Still whispering together, the two men left the room.

A new idea formed. If they were just paid mercenaries, her family had a lot of money, maybe she could buy her way out. That they took her picture filled her with hope. Maybe they planned to ransom her. She rose to examine the window again. The thick slats were freshly nailed. Tug as hard as she could, she couldn't loosen them.

Stapled to the wall above the bed the IV bag didn't allow much slack. By keeping her arm outstretched to the bed, she could reach the rotted hole but no further. The door remained out of reach. The light from below barely illuminated her room. She knelt and pressed her face to the floor, peering through the largest hole.

A man sat on the couch now with his booted foot crossed on his leg. The angle of the couch hid his face. Snatches of conversation tantalized her, but only the man on the couch was clear.

"Three days," he said.

Someone said something, the sound muffled by distance. The smell of frying bread came to her, making her stomach rumble. People spoke and moved, casting shadows.

"A million?" he sounded disgusted.

An angry voice retorted, the words unintelligible, but the tone clear.

"I'll do it for fucking free."

Laughter met that. Someone passed beneath her carrying a tray.

The man on the couch leaned forward to take a slice of bread from the tray, and her heart pounded. Raul's partner. Not Matt, the one who'd entered her hospital room. The hospital room someone had almost killed her in. *He must've let the fake nurse in.*

"The components are perfectly safe where they are. No one except Spiderman could reach them without going through us. Besides, they're worthless without the knowledge to put them together." He quieted, listening to someone she couldn't understand, then said, "We have no idea how they work. That's the point, we make her figure it out. Once she assembles it, she can break the encryption; I'm sure of that. Then it's just a matter of reverse engineering it."

Someone said something, of which, she only caught the words worth and time.

"Fuck yes, it's worth our time. You think being able to subvert their missiles isn't worth a little trouble?"

Another man approached the couch. Black, booted feet came into view followed by familiar black armor. "We need them to send missiles in the time and place of our choosing to subvert. My brother almost died trying to get hostages to ensure it."

"Sorry, Jahir, but your brother jumped the gun and got greedy. I get it, trying to kill three birds with one stone, but is all we need is one. One missile will prove we can do it and make all their missiles obsolete. We'll fucking own the world."

"Can't they just change the code?" the man with the tray said as he appeared beside the two men.

"That's the beauty, once inside it can read the

code, any code," Raul's partner said.

"Sounds like bullshit to me. If it were so easy…"

"It's fucking hard, which is why we need specialists to finish the work. I can't do it even with all my training. I bet there's fewer than a hundred people on Earth who understand the math." Raul's partner sat back on the couch.

You're sure she can do it?"

"What's it hurt to let her try?"

The other two men walked away, and Denali caught the word recoup. She listened for another two hours, but they spoke of nothing else interesting within her hearing. She counted sixteen men. Apparently, the room below her was used for everything because they rolled out bedrolls and settled in for the night. She returned to her bed. To break through the floor required time, she'd need to wait until morning, when hopefully, they left the room unattended.

To her surprise, she fell asleep and woke when someone opened the door to her room. Mr. Mercenary, the one who'd spoken to Steve about the double cross, brought a tray with orange juice and toast and set it on the floor, then slapped her cheeks.

She opened her eyes.

"Good, you aren't dead." He removed the empty IV and pulled her from the room. "Give me any shit and I'll hurt you." He pushed her into the bathroom and pointed at the toilet.

A red flush climbed her cheeks as she lowered her

sweatpants and sat.

He smirked.

She closed her eyes and tried to pretend she was alone. He let her wash her hands and face before pulling her back to her room and locking her in. She was just finishing the toast when the door opened again. Sweat beaded on her brow. Mahir Alfarsi stood before her. He should've been securely locked up. Her panicked gaze skittered to the man who accompanied him. Raul's partner. The wild beating of her heart drowned out his first words.

"— Jahir, no problem.

A brother, not him, Denali thought, and her heart slowed.

"Take her up and get her to work. She doesn't look that dangerous. I'll fucking guard her if you're men are afraid."

Jahir glared. "I'm in charge here," he said in English. Then, "insolent dog," in Urdu.

Raul's partner shrugged and stepped back. "As long as I get paid. I want out of this shithole; the quicker she finishes, the faster I can confirm it works and get the hell out."

"You'll be paid, and paid well." Jahir held out a hand and beckoned to Denali. "Come!"

She went meekly, ducking her head and staring at the floor. Her thoughts whirled. Raul's partner had acted as if they'd never met.

Raul's partner grabbed her shoulder and pushed her in front of him. "Cooperate, and you won't be hurt. There's no other access to the attic. If you open this door, you'll be shot. Two men will be here around the clock. The windows are boarded and alarmed. Don't waste your time trying them. We know you climb like a monkey, but there's no access to the outside." He shook her and thrust her at the chair before a desk made of planks. His eyes darted to the chimney and back to her, then he stared at the chimney as he repeated, "There's no access to the roof."

The wild thudding of her pulse slowed.

"What we need to know is how this works, if it even does." He glanced from the computer components on the makeshift desk to the chimney again.

"What's it do?" she asked, not trying to hide the tremble in her voice.

"None of your business," Jahir, snapped.

Raul's partner sighed heavily and rolled his eyes. "How can she make it work if she doesn't know what it's supposed to do?" He grabbed a beat-up notebook from the desk and dropped it in front of her. "Greer's notes. He's incommunicado in Gitmo. We can't get operatives to him, so you get to finish his work. You took the same classes and should be able to do it with incentive."

"Another day of life is your incentive." Jahir reached down and fingered her hair. "Please me, and you can have more days."

Denali lowered her eyes and clasped her hands in

her lap.

"Read the notes." Raul's partner grasped her shoulder and squeezed. "We need to know all about this. I realize it'll take you a week or so to catch up but take too long and we'll get another geek." Raul's partner stared so hard his gaze practically scorched her as he said, "We don't have all the time in the world. The FBI is searching for our nuke." He turned away and spoke to Jahil, but Denali was sure the words were meant for her. "Let's not be hasty, give her time to figure this out."

"What are you waiting for?" Jahir barked.

Denali opened the notebook

TWENTY-FIVE

Bait and Switch

The two men returned to the door where Jahir ordered the guard to bring him a chair. Raul's partner gave her one last glance, his gaze traveling to the chimney, then the notebook before he left the room.

Furious anger swept her. The FBI knew where she was and risked her life. *Did Ryan know? Did her parents think she was dead or a hostage?*

"They could've fucking asked," she mumbled under her breath as she opened the book.

Her gaze narrowed. This was her computer language. "Fucking Jerome," she muttered.

She flipped the pages, scanning quickly then went back and stared at each one, committing them to memory. Someone placed a sandwich and soda beside her elbow. She ate absently as she read. Before she knew it, darkness had again fallen. Her guard dozed against the wall. She glanced at the chimney and hesitated. She could go now, kill the guard and escape the house with the book, or she could trust Raul's partner wouldn't let her be killed and give the FBI time to search. The nuclear weapon decided her. If the FBI needed time to find it, she'd do her best to supply that time. She straightened her shoulders and let Raul's partner lead her back to the bedroom downstairs.

"Go soon," he whispered in her ear as he pushed her through the doorway. She peered over her shoulder. Jahir stood in the doorway backlit by the hall light, giving his face a sinister cast. Raul's partner brushed past him and glanced over his head from Jahir to her bed, then strode away.

Her skin crawled, his meaning crystal clear. She sagged in relief when Jahir closed the door.

On her bed, she stared at the stained ceiling. "So, the FBI wants me to escape and take the book with me," she whispered to herself. *I suppose he wants to keep his cover, but why not have the FBI come in, rescue me, take the book, and arrest these men?"*

She fell asleep pondering the question.

In the morning she had a plan. "I'll need a laptop, some tools and supplies," she said to the man who brought her breakfast.

He made no answer just pulled her by the arm to the bathroom.

Denali blushed as she lowered her pants to use the toilet. The man turned red and spun away, acting as if he were the one embarrassed.

The blush on her cheeks deepened when she noticed the blood on her underwear.

"Um…"

"Supplies will be brought, make do," he snapped in Urdu.

She almost giggled as he avoided touching her after she'd washed her hands and face. He left her locked in her room with her toast and orange juice. Raul and Jahir showed up fifteen minutes later. Raul's partner handed her a brown paper bag. The blush returned to her cheeks when she saw the feminine hygiene products.

"These should last a few days," Raul's partner said, giving Jahir a meaningful glance.

Denali's shoulders relaxed. Jahir wouldn't touch her while she menstruated.

"Make me a list of parts you need." Jahir handed her a paper and stub of a pencil. Letting them fall into her hands without touching her. She bit back the smile that wanted to form. He was afraid of her. Afraid to give her a pen. She wrote her list and gave it to him, acting as meek as she could, keeping her eyes down and face averted.

Two hours later another man escorted her to the attic where her requested supplies waited.

"What are you doing?" Jahir asked. He peered over her shoulder from a foot away.

"To understand the connections, I need to redo them one-by-one." She tapped the notebook. "This is a theory of code, not the actual code. The actual code will be inside this box here." She tapped the box and glanced at Raul's partner who nodded slightly.

"To access it, I need to be sure of the connections. A standard safety protocol is to wipe the hard drive if too many wrong attempts are made to open the file. Did Greer use that?"

Jahir shrugged.

"I'll need to proceed slowly if I don't want to destroy the information on the drive. Did Greer work with a partner?"

"None of your business."

"It would help me determine his passwords. Most people use familiar dates or information important and personal to them. Not their names, but if you could give me a list of any phone numbers, house addresses, birth dates, things like that, I can use that to figure out codes."

Jahir nodded, a thoughtful expression on his face.

"It'll take me a few days to map these connections, and I'll need better lighting and plastic sheeting to form a clean room. Or as clean as I can get it here..." Her gaze traveled the dusty attic doubtfully.

"Just tent the desk," Raul's partner said quickly. "Get her clean clothes and elastics or something for her hair. Lay a strip of carpet on the floor to trap dust and keep movement up here to a minimum to keep the dust down. That should be good enough."

The next day plastic sheeting was stapled to the floor and ceiling and surrounded the desk. Another piece of plastic covered the desk. An industrial strength wet-dry vacuum was attached to a fan taped to the side of the plastic and plugged into a power strip outside the plastic. Jahir left her alone with Raul's partner.

"Your family is safe. And no, we didn't plan this, just took advantage," he whispered as soon as the door closed. The fake nurse was trying to drug you too. We knew they wanted you. How did they get you?"

"Jerome Kensky handed me over."

"I'll get agents on him."

"Is Ryan okay?"

"Yes, but incredibly angry and causing a huge stink."

"What is the FBI waiting for?"

"The CIA. Right now, Jahir is negotiating with two different groups, both of whom are willing to pay big dollars to be able to subvert our missiles. We have reason to believe they have a nuclear weapon they plan to use in the United States and agents are frantically searching. Can you give us time? Will Greer's device work?"

"No. It isn't possible, not more than once, and then only if we're taken by surprise. Get this notebook to any of my teachers and they could fix the leak. I could fix the leak without the notebook."

"Could you make them think it is... We're tracking the money changing hands and have located two sleeper cells already. That was brilliant by the way, getting him to tell you who helped Greer, not to mention the—"

He cut off as the door opened.

Denali pointed to the computer chip under the magnifying glass. "I can connect the power, but it runs a risk of shorting. See here? This soldering is shoddy, a spark could leap." Jahir entered the plastic tent and leaned over the magnifying glass.

"That tiny speck?"

"That tiny speck can cause big problems. It might be easier for me to start completely from scratch."

Jahir straightened and examined her with narrowed eyes. The slap shocked her, jerking her head back and making tears fill her eyes.

"If you're stalling…"

She frantically shook her head. "I can do both, try this and make my own, but I'll need more parts."

"Frank?" Jahir turned to Raul's partner.

Frank rubbed his chin as if considering. "Let her try. The speck is a problem and could wipe the board. Removing it won't be easy. Ignoring it might be our best bet, but if it surges, we lose everything. I say we let her try to reproduce the hardware before powering the original."

"Fine, let her work on it." Jahir turned his cold eyes on Denali and smiled. "The police are searching for your dead body. We'll send the media pictures tomorrow. The world will know no one crosses us lightly. One way or another, you'll be of use to us."

One of the mercenaries entered, carrying a bottled

water and an apple.

"Feed her, then take her to the bathroom." Jahir gestured to Frank, and the two men left, talking quietly.

The new man handed her the food and examined the desktop as she ate.

"My family will pay a lot for my return."

He smiled and shrugged as if she'd offered him a drink when he wasn't thirsty. "Not as much as we're getting for killing you."

A chill traveled her at his calm indifference.

"Are you sure? My parents are wealthy. What could it hurt to ask?"

The man laughed. "If Jahir thought I was trying to cross him, he'd make an example of me." His eyes narrowed. "Are you trying to get me killed?"

She shook her head, the apple sticking in her suddenly dry throat. "No. Just trying to live."

He nodded and smiled and gestured her to the stairs. On trembling legs, she passed him. The two guards by the bottom of the stairs turned their back on her.

The mercenary snorted as he thrust her into the bathroom. He leaned on the doorjamb and watched her pee. "Woman on the rag gross them out. Me, I don't care. Blood doesn't bother me."

Denali let her hair swing forward to hide her hot cheeks. She was both grateful and embarrassed to get her period now. Grateful because it kept Jahir away, but having strangers stare as she performed intimate tasks was humiliating.

"Nighty-night," the man said as he locked her in her room.

She spent a few hours removing splinters of rotted from around her window and sticking them inside the thin mattress on the bed. A few bigger chunks broke off easily, and she set them aside to place over the hole. Soon she reached denser, stronger wood. She'd need a tool to break it. The hole she'd made wasn't big enough to slip through. She eyed the remaining pieces doubtfully, not sure there was enough rotted wood to break away even if she could sneak a tool into her room from the attic. Below her, men snored in the dim room. She replaced the loose pieces and went to bed. Tomorrow she'd try to smuggle a screwdriver downstairs. *Maybe she could pry the boards loose from the windows with the right tool.*

The next day, she began working on the code, entering it into the laptop in small chunks interspersed with nonsense code. She wanted it ready in case she needed it but illegible if they tried to use it without her.

Denali glanced at her guard speculatively, a different mercenary than last night. "My family—"

"One more fucking word and I'll break your fucking jaw," the man said.

Denali swallowed hard and nodded, returning to her work. He sat in the chair beside the door and glared. Another man brought up sandwiches and water and took her down to the bathroom. He turned his back, for which she was grateful.

At dusk, Jahir had a guard bring her downstairs to the basement. Frank stepped aside to let them pass. Two middle-eastern men waited before a camera with Steve and Jahir. The screwdriver she'd slipped beneath the waistband of her jeans mocked her. Even if she grabbed for it, she couldn't defeat four armed men. She scanned the room, hoping to spot Frank enter.

Maybe, he went for help, she thought, not really believing it but needing the comfort of the thought. Jahir's expression, a cross between a leer and a glower, terrified her. Her pulse pounded as they handcuffed her to chains in the wall.

"We need some blood," Jahir said as he stepped back and eyed her critically. "And skin; strip her."

The cameramen exchanged angry glances.

Steve laughed and ripped her T-shirt off, then used his knife to cut off her bra.

Denali kicked out. He punched her in the face, knocking her head into the wall.

"Don't damage her too badly," Jahir warned. He grabbed Steve's arm and pulled him back. "That's good enough; take your pictures.

Blood dripped from Denali's nose across her chin. Tied as she was, she couldn't staunch it or cover herself. She shook her head, making her hair fall around her naked breasts. Jahir leaned forward and licked his lips.

Angry tears filled Denali's eyes. She glared at

him, tempted to call him the coward he was, but not wanting to escalate the situation.

"Slap that expression off her face."

Steve laughed and hit her again, this time with his open hand. "Want her terrified? I can hurt her real good," he offered. He stepped forward and used his body to press her against the wall.

He didn't need to do anything else, she was already terrified.

"Please…" her soft begging excited him. Pressed so hard against her it was obvious. She snapped her mouth closed and gritted her teeth.

Jahir said, "Step back. Let us get the pictures."

She couldn't help the tears that leaked from her eyes.

"Perfect." Jahir rubbed his hands together. "Take her to the bathroom and clean her up. And, Steve, she's mine."

Steve grunted and released the handcuffs.

Denali stumbled up the steps before Steve. His hand tangled in her hair, the hard grip on her shoulder was sure to leave a bruise. She kept her eyes downcast, and both arms crossed over her naked breasts.

"Shower, or I'll do it for you…"

He laughed as she stepped into the tub and turned her back to remove her clothing. The aged, yellowed shower curtain didn't provide much privacy. Warm water quickly became cold, and she shivered as she rinsed the soap from her skin. Steve snickered and offered suggestions as she washed.

Her hand trembled in a mix of anger and humiliation as she grasped the ragged gray towel from him. She gratefully snatched the white sweat clothes and put them on. Her wet jeans, underwear, socks, and sneakers sat in the bottom of the tub.

"Leave them," he snapped when she bent to gather them up.

She ignored him, the screwdriver was hidden in the folds, and she needed it.

"I said leave it!"

She fell to the floor crying, clutching the clothing. She rose a hand as if she feared a blow, and fumbled with her free hand, searching for the screwdriver. It was in her grasp as Jahir entered.

"What's going on?"

"She won't leave her damn clothes."

"Get to your room."

Denali leaped to her feet and ran by the men, her wet clothes soaking the front of her sweatshirt. In her room, she spread the jeans over the rusty iron headboard, hiding the screwdriver in the crack between the headboard and the mattress as she straightened the pant legs.

She grabbed the thin blanket and wrapped it around herself before turning to the door. Jahir watched her with a satisfied expression on his face.

"See, you can learn obedience and be a proper woman."

Denali said nothing.

Jahir closed and locked the door.

She sank to the bed and hid her face in her hands. Frank had let this happen and done nothing to help her. She'd passed him twice in the hallway.

"What could he do?" she whispered. She didn't like her answer. He could do nothing except call in reinforcements, and they might arrive too late, but he would do nothing if he thought letting her be raped, beaten, or murdered would lead him to a nuclear bomb. Or was he really one of them and playing her? A shiver wracked her. She needed to save herself. The screwdriver clutched in her hand, she crawled to the window and began gouging out chunks of half rotted wood.

All day she worked on the programming. Greer had devised a way to intercept and change a radio signal. While ingenious, it could easily be blocked. It might work once though if the sender of the signal remained unaware of it. Neither Frank nor Jahir showed up during the day just a constantly changing guard from their hired mercenaries.

"I need more supplies," Denali said when Jahir showed up the next evening.

"Make me a list." Jahir pulled her by the arm to her room downstairs and pushed her in. "Get out," he snapped at Frank.

Frank hesitated.

Denali stared with wide eyes. Her gaze flitted from Frank to Jahir. Even if he helped, there were too many men to fight. She straightened her shoulders and gazed defiantly at Jahir. "If you touch me, I'll kill myself, and you'll have nothing."

"Will you kill your sister too? We have her. Anger me, and she'll pay."

Denali's gaze darted to Frank. He hesitated then shook his head minutely.

"Yes, I'll kill her too. I'd rather she be dead than at your mercy. You'll hurt her no matter what I do. Lay one finger on me, and I won't fix your computer."

Frank leaned forward and whispered in Jahir's ear. After another long appraisal of Denali, Jahir nodded and strode out. Frank closed the door behind them. Denali sank to her bed shaking. *What if she were wrong to trust Frank? What if he were manipulating her to work on the computer for them.* She had no proof, just her assumptions. *Dear God, what if they did have one of her sisters?*

Curled on her bed, she clutched her sore ribs and cried. What proof could he offer? A note or message could be faked. She needed a phone to hear for herself her family was well. A thoughtful frown on her face, she stared at the dark ceiling.

It wouldn't be that hard to make a phone with a few parts. Frank might realize what she was doing. If he stopped her or turned her in, she'd know he wasn't to be trusted. She debated asking him for a phone, then she debated who to call.

Thoughts of the chimney escape kept her awake another hour. Dare she trust it? Dare she not? Frank was either a master manipulator, saying exactly the right thing to get her to stay and work for them, dangling escape, or telling the truth and she could escape from the chimney at the first opportunity.

Not willing to put her complete trust in Frank's plan, she again scrapped at floorboards half the night, gouging at the rotted wood with the screwdriver, being careful to gather the sawdust with her fingertips. The occasional flake that drifted down she hoped went unnoticed in the filthy house.

"Can you bring me a phone?" she whispered as Frank escorted her to the bathroom the next morning.

"We're searched entering and exiting."

"Can you bring me an ACIS chip? It's less than a square inch, you could hide it in a steel-toed boot."

"As soon as I can, but I can't ask to guard you or leave. I have to wait to be sent out."

She nodded and used the bathroom. Upstairs in the attic, she assembled the components she'd need to turn the chip into a phone under the watchful gaze of a guard who had no idea what she was doing. Then she worked on programming. Again, a simple process of sending a double signal, code hidden within code. These men were monkeys playing with lights, they had no idea how these things worked.

She copied the code Greer had made to grab and switch a radio signal. Tomorrow, she could test it.

Then she'd write a program that lied and gave a false reading. The frequency didn't need to actually change, just appear too. She worked late into the night, eating what was offered and using the bathroom when brought there. Frank hadn't appeared all day. She didn't know if that meant he'd lied, was caught, or hadn't had an opportunity. She eyed the chimney and then the dozing guard. She could kill him with her screwdriver.

Every chance she let slip by felt like a betrayal. Her family would be frantic. She hoped the FBI had told them she was safe and cooperating with them. The thought of a nuclear weapon on American soil kept her in the seat and working, maybe as Frank had intended.

The next day, Jahir loomed over her shoulder as she tested her code on a radio brought up for that purpose. He beamed at her when the monitor picked up the signal. Frank leaned closer as if staring at the screen and slipped a small computer chip under her hand.

TWENTY-SIX

Progress

Her heart pounded as she palmed the chip.

"You make good progress," Jahir said in Urdu.

Her hands trembled in a combination of fear and relief as she opened the notebook and pointed at the pages of code. "I'm copying straight from this."

She rifled the pages, showing him the dense text. While he glanced at it, she began moving computer parts, casually laying the chip among them. "This next part is harder. I don't quite understand where he was going. I'll follow along and note where I have problems."

Jahir said, "Two days or your sister pays."

"Can I see her?"

Jahir pursed his lips and nodded. "If you

complete this early, you may see her. If not, you can see her punished."

The two men left her working. Frank left without acknowledging her in any way. The chimney mocked her with its possibility for escape. Fear strummed along her nerves, making her hands sweat. She had to wipe them continually on her baggy, white sweatpants. Another guard sat beside the door, this one more alert.

Her gaze drifted to the chip Frank had supplied. Her heart sank.

The chip Frank had given her didn't contain the encryption necessary to interface with a cell phone. Whether he'd done it purposefully or not, she didn't know.

She tapped the chip lightly with her fingernail and bit her lip. She could still use it. But she wished she knew if Frank was playing her. If she fixed the receiver, it would work until the signal was blocked. The process to block it was simple once you knew it needed to be done. But did the government know? She might be playing right into the terrorist's hands.

If she didn't get away to tell what was done, they could use the receiver to steal a missile. She needed to talk to someone she trusted. With trembling fingers, she removed the audio wire from the radio and inserted it into her makeshift phone then crossed her fingers and attached the chip Frank had given her.

Using the keyboard on her desk, she typed in Cally's number. She should be hacked into Cally's tablet, assuming she wasn't miles away over the ocean. *Please, God let me be within range.* Cally's tablet had no security, the only device she could think of her crude phone could connect to.

Cell phones required security certificates, which she didn't have. Cally's tablet didn't, she'd made it fast and simple with no encryption of any sort. It was meant to reproduce and record sound and be accessible by her or Anya from home so they could work with Cally remotely. The tablet was her only shot.

'*Help, get daddy,*' she typed and waited.

Her screen remained dark. She copied the code and her advice to circumvent it, hoping Anya would see and pass it on to the authorities. Hope withered as time passed. The attic darkened as night descended and she reluctantly disconnected her device and returned meekly to her room with the guard.

Men spoke and laughed loudly beneath her, apparently celebrating her progress. She gouged the wood beside the window as quietly as she could as she attempted to listen to them speaking. The voices beneath her were muffled and indistinct unless she lay with her ear on the floor and it seemed to her it was wiser to spend her time trying to escape then listen as she hadn't yet heard anything worth reporting.

As the room below her quieted, the men settling into sleep for the night, she worked on making the hole in the floor bigger until fatigue made her clumsy. She settled on her lumpy bed. Doubt haunted her, making her sleep restless. She still wasn't sure if Frank was helping her or playing her, saying exactly the right things to keep her working. The thought of a nuclear weapon in the hands of these madmen on American soil made her feel sick. When she drifted to sleep, she jerked awake from nightmares of bombs and burning school children.

Blurry with fatigue, she rose when Steve entered and followed him to the bathroom. He let her wash her hands and face and offered a comb and new elastics for her hair, all without speaking. Steve left her with a new guard, this one middle eastern. Upstairs, she connected the wires again. Her guard ate a banana and leaned back in the chair, reading a newspaper. Denali worked quietly on her programming.

Every thirty minutes she sent a new message. The day passed with glacial slowness. Each spate of letters flowing across her screen made her shoulders tighten. Cally spoke somewhere in her home but apparently at the remote receivers. No one seemed to notice her messages.

It would take her another night or two to break through the floor. Or, she could trust Frank and go through the chimney, but that might be a trap. To use the chimney, she'd have to kill her guard, and if she did that, and they caught her, her life was forfeit. And if she tried it, Frank would realize she knew all there was to know about the code.

While she debated what to do, a string of nonsense letters appeared on her screen. Cally was speaking, hopefully to the screen with her mom or dad nearby.

Denali peered over her shoulder at the guard who sat with his head leaning back on the wall and his arms crossed, his silenced pistol resting on his knees.

She typed with trembling fingers. 'Help! Get me Ryan or my father, please. This is Denali. I don't know how long I can use this to connect. Speak slowly and as clearly as you can.'

'*Denly*,' appeared on her screen and she sobbed, pressing her hand over her mouth and glancing at the guard who glanced up but returned to his paper.

'Yes, please help me. Can you get Ryan?'

'Onhsway.'

The jumbled letters filled her with hope. Relief made her lightheaded. Ryan would make sure the information she passed on got to the right people. Even if she didn't escape, America was safe.

'Wr r u.'

'I don't know. The FBI knows though, I think. I'm safe at the moment. Jahir has me working on Greer's device. Tell Dai the process will work unless they shield the lines. The range would be small, within a mile of launch. Is my family safe?'

'Ys.'

She slumped. She'd been sure Jahir had lied, but the thought of leaving a sister in his hands chilled her.

She was in the middle of explaining how to stop the signal when Ryan arrived.

'Dnle, its Ryn s it rely u?'

Tears filled her eyes.

'I think you do great in the romance department. Is my family well?'

'Ys, God wr r u?"

'Safe now. An agent is inside. I'm unsure I can trust him.'

'They fucking know where you are?'

She cringed, every word came through so clearly she knew he was yelling.

'Limited time. Need one to two more days. I'm so sorry.'

'You're staying on purpose? "Did you fucking know you were going to disappear?'

'No. I think I can get—.

She stabbed the button to erase her screen and pulled the wires apart as the guard approached. He stood behind her as she pretended to read the notebook. Her heart beat so hard she was afraid he could hear it. He stood staring a few minutes, then gestured to the door. "Time for bed." His gaze traveled her body, lingering on her breasts, and he leered. "Want some company?"

She didn't answer, just scurried past him and into her room where she clutched a blanket to her face to muffle her sobs. Ryan was angry and rightfully so. She should escape, or at least try to. *He'll understand,* she told herself. *I didn't choose to come here but now that I am, if I can help stop these men permanently... He'll understand. Please let him forgive me.* She cried herself to sleep, knowing she was needlessly worrying but unable to stop, and woke with a raging headache.

Jahir watched her all day and laughed in delight as her copy intercepted and changed a radio signal. With her fingers crossed, she handed him the box.

"The range isn't good, but it will work. Can I see my sister now?"

"Can you improve the range?"

"With parts and time. I'll need antennas set up at varying distances and one here to test where I lose range." She handed him a list of parts needed. He handed it to the guard beside the door who left the room at a run.

"Keep working. Can you make more?"

"With parts."

"You can see your sister when I have three more. Because you've been good, we'll feed her today." Jahir laughed when she glared. He left the room whistling with the box in his hand.

Denali went to work on her program. The guard paced restlessly. She badly wanted to call Ryan. The police could follow the antennas to her if she were in the city, but she couldn't take the chance of calling with that man pacing behind her.

"Can you sit? I'm afraid you'll kick up dust."

"No woman tells me what to do," he said in Urdu. He paced faster, stamping his feet, a furious glower on his face. His movements were spastic and agitated. She was already standing, moving away from the entrance, when he rushed the plastic tent.

She screamed as loudly as she could and ducked backward from his grabbing hand. Spittle flew from his lips from the insults he yelled as he fumbled with the flaps of plastic. She continued to scream for help.

"Hurry up!" she screamed and kicked the man's feet out from under him. Not willing to hurt him seriously for fear of retaliation she climbed over the desk to keep away from him.

"You should fucking pay for what you did!" He pushed the desk into her legs, trapping her against the plastic wall. On his hands and knees, he crawled over the desk and grabbed her by the neck. The plastic ripped, tumbling them both to the ground with him on top of her. He was stronger than her and demented with rage. Both his hands were squeezing her neck. Cursing herself for not grabbing a screwdriver, she slapped her hands on his ears.

Two men rushed into the room and pulled him away.

"Whore! Filthy dog." He continued to yell as he was dragged down the stairs.

"What did you do?" Jahir shouted as he ran into the room.

Denali sat and rubbed her neck, taking short hard breaths. "Nothing, he went crazy."

Jahir glanced over his shoulder at the man behind him, then snapped his fingers at her. "Come here."

A tremble she couldn't control shook her. Her gaze darted to the screwdriver on the floor beside the desk.

Jahir snapped again and narrowed his eyes.

She approached slowly with her head down. Without being told she sank to her knees before him.

He laughed. "Give me any more trouble, and you'll be sorry. Did the parts arrive?"

She shook her head.

"What are you working on?"

"Range. I have to calculate—"

He slapped her. She jerked back, putting a hand on her cheek.

He grinned, showing his teeth and slapped her again. She covered her face with her arms as his open hand closed and he began to punch her.

Frank entered and cleared his throat. "The box worked. We done with her then?"

Breathing hard, Jahir pulled away. "No, she's making more." He pulled her up by her hair and pushed her toward the plastic tent. "Go make more."

She moved the chair so she could see the door and almost wished she hadn't, Jahir's eyes on her disconcerted her. Twice, she had to erase and redo work. She couldn't stop her eyes from tearing when he snapped his fingers again.

"Bed, now."

Almost hyperventilating, she passed him and returned to her room. He closed the bedroom door; the soft click of the lock sounded like a reprieve, and she burst into tears. Outside her door, men laughed. She curled on her bed. She was pushing her luck. Any minute Jahir would snap, his thin façade of civility falling away to reveal the animal within.

The next chance she got, she'd take whether her programming was finished or not. As if to mock her, she hit solid wood with her screwdriver chisel. The hole in the floor would take weeks to carve through at this slow pace. The screwdriver gauged deep into the wood of the windowsill as she tried to pry a board loose. The boards were firmly nailed down. It would be impossible to pry them loose without her guards noticing. Nothing short of a hammer would release them within a realistic time. Like it or not, she'd have to attempt the chimney.

Below her, Jahir spoke with one of his men in Urdu. She stopped gouging to lower her ear to the floor to hear better.

"— the next school."

"This time we'll kill them when we enter. No messing around," Jahir said.

"We still need a few to torture. If we want the United States to launch a nuclear bomb, it's going to take more than a few murders."

"We have time to incite them. If we kill enough children, they'll attack," Jahir sat on the couch, only his booted feet visible.

"And the girl?"

"I haven't decided. While killing her would provoke them, wasting her genes seems like a real shame. Imagine the sons she'd have. There are plenty of women we can mutilate and burn, but not many have her breeding potential."

The man replied too low for Denali to hear.

"Uses could be found for them." Jahir sounded indifferent.

A chill traveled her spine. The callousness of these men scared her to her soul. His cold indifference to her as a woman was matched by his hatred of everything he didn't control.

Again, the man said something she couldn't hear.

"We cause enough damage, and the United States will attack, and when they do, we'll steal their missiles and turn them back on them. It's the perfect plan."

Someone else came in carrying a pizza, and Jahir rose, his voice becoming indistinct with distance.

Denali sat back on her heels and rubbed her eyes. They didn't have a nuke, they planned to steal one. How they'd planned to get one launched, sickened her. She had to tell Frank if he didn't already know.

Her doubts made her stomach turn. If Frank was working with them, talking to him was the worst thing she could do, but if he wasn't, telling him could prevent a nuclear attack.

TWENTY-SEVEN

Consequences of Her Actions

Below her men spoke, and to her surprise, a woman's laughter floated to her. Her heart began to beat hard, and it took a minute to stop the panicked breaths. None of her sisters would laugh with these men, it was one of their own women.

She dropped to the floor and peered through the hole. Her skin crawled with horror. Anne, they had Anne. Or did Anne have them? She walked the room freely and sat on the arm of the chair beside Steve. From the small portion of her face Denali could see, Anne smiled.

"Whatever you say, lover," Anne said and stood. She removed a thin, silk scarf from her pocket and covered her head.

Denali sat back on her heels and wiped her eyes

hard. How could she leave Anne here with them? She couldn't know her danger, that they'd hurt her to make Denali help them.

She leaned forward again, crying quietly.

The men below spoke too low to hear.

Steve stood and kissed Anne. "You'll be the last, and it will all come to you."

Anne laughed, and the two walked off together.

Denali cried herself to sleep. She spent the next day working feverishly. The parts arrived at noon. She assembled them and input her program. The man guarding her stood a foot away with his rifle pointed at her chest as she tested the scanner, flicking through channels and changing them. His gaze stayed on the small screen, hers flicked to the computer, and she hid her triumphant grin. It worked as she'd intended. She packed up the scanner and began assembling another. The guard returned to his seat and discarded magazine.

Trying to act casual, she connected the leads to her computer and typed a quick note to Cally. 'Scanner complete. It will work, and they don't have their own nuke but plan to hijack one of ours. Will attempt escape at earliest oppertunity. I love you.' Men entered and exited her room all day bringing parts or food. She had no chance to attempt the chimney. Every moment that passed brought her closer to panic. With her 'job' finished Jahir had no reason to spare her. Death or worse awaited her. Anne's presence gnawed at her. To attempt to rescue her would doom them both. She told herself they wouldn't kill Anne outright until they were certain they had no use for her but knew she lied to herself. She was afraid to go for her sister and have her sister refuse to come with her or worse turn her over to them.

Frank brought her dinner and a surge of hope.

"You lied, they do have my sister." She massaged her temples. The worse stress headache of her life throbbed to her heartbeat. She didn't think she could live with herself if she abandoned her sister from cowardice.

"He showed you, huh?" Frank shrugged, looking sad. "I'd hoped to spare you that. Anne is here willingly.

"Liar." She had to close her eyes against the surge of pain that accompanied his words.

"I'm sorry, but it's true. She's been talking to Zane and Anya, trying to get house codes. We warned your family. Jahir has it worked out with her. He'll kill the entire family, leaving her the sole heir. I admit it's a great plan. Everyone will believe terrorists killed them in retaliation. She'd get away with it if we didn't know."

"She'd never…" Denali trailed off. Frank's story sounded plausible. How would Frank know Anne hated them unless she'd said she did. Or he was lying… The uncertainty was killing her. "There must be another reason. Maybe she came to help me?"

"I'm sorry, but she didn't. If it makes you feel any

better, it was Jahir's idea. And frankly, she's a fool if she thinks he's going to settle for a third. I'm pretty sure she and her boyfriend Steve are working on a double cross, but so is Jahir. He's canny."

Denali pressed the heels of her hands against her eyes to stop the tears. "No, knowing my sister is okay with killing her entire family doesn't make me feel better."

Frank straightened as the door opened, admitting another guard.

"Jahir wants you downstairs; I'll watch the prisoner."

Frank sighed. His gaze traveled the chimney in clear advice before he turned and left.

Her new guard, Mr. Mercenary, stood solidly before the door with his gun pointed at her.

Denali fussed uselessly with the computer components on her desk. She reconnected the wires and hesitated. Vomit burned her throat as she typed with a shaking hand. 'Anne is here and working with them." Her fingers shook so badly she had to stop typing. The strain of holding back her tears was too much, she turned and vomited in the small wastebasket beside her desk.

The guard stood but sat again as she wiped her mouth.

She forced herself to tap out the message that would sever Anne from them forever. 'She plans to kill you all.' Not knowing how to soften that blow, or what else she could say, she disconnected the leads.

Tears trickled from the corner of her eyes, which she dashed away with the back of her hand. Ryan was likely on the other end calling to her, and she didn't dare put the jack in to read his words.

Tears again fell as she considered the last words he'd spoken to her were angry ones. She might die tonight, and he'd believe she'd agreed to this without speaking to him, that she'd hurt and abandon him.

She was sick again. The guard again rose. This time he nudged her shoulder with his gun.

"Get it together. Finish your work if you want to live." He dropped a water bottle on her desk and stood over her while she sipped it.

She did need to get it to together, she thought bitterly. Crying helped no one. Observe – Plan— Act. One by one she picked up every tool at her disposal and considered what could be done with it. With fresh determination, she resumed assembling the scanners.

Jahir returned at dusk. With a shaking hand, she handed him a black box. A small keypad and screen on the front lit with a soft green glow.

"How's it work?"

"Point in the direction of the object you wish to subvert. The radio frequency will be displayed here on the screen. Press enter, then the frequency you want it on, and press enter again." She demonstrated with an AM radio station. The station changed.

"It didn't do anything except change the station. I have remotes that can do that." Jahir sounded annoyed.

"It doesn't do anything except change the radio signal. What makes it special is it can identify signals and reroute them. In effect, hijacking them and taking control from the user. If you had a remote-control plane, and I a remote, I could steal your plane, hijack your frequency and superimpose my own and use my remote."

"I see, yes, that makes sense." His eyes lit with excitement. "Range?"

"I'm not really sure, but I think less than a mile, maybe much closer, and it could potentially take a long time to sort the frequencies depending on how many were present. Greer was working on the programing to automatically cull the common frequencies for telephones and radio stations but hadn't finished it. But even finished, there could be unknown number of frequencies from toys and machinery in any given area."

"Tonight, you can see your sister. Work on the range until I return. Can the programming be copied?"

She nodded, trying to hide her disgust. How Jahir thought she'd help him when he so obviously wouldn't keep his word, boggled her.

Jahir called for a guard. "I'll be back in an hour or so." He grinned and slapped the man's back. "It won't be long now." He turned back to her in the doorway. "You and your sister have a lot to talk about." He left the room grinning.

She had an hour. She plugged the soldering iron in.

Jahir's attitude supported Frank's version, but she was sure he'd be equally happy to confront her with a terrified sibling.

"Stop trying to excuse her, open your eyes and see," Denali whispered to herself. A wry smile crossed her face, Jerome's words were all too true. Anne's own words convicted her. Years of actions showed her contempt for her family. Denali wanted so badly for Anne to become a good person, a true sister — that she never would, hurt. That she'd try to kill her family infuriated her.

"You made your bed," she mumbled.

She straightened, dismissing Anne from her mind. Anne would have to accept the consequences of her actions. Denali couldn't save her. No one could except Anne, and Anne had given up a long time ago, happier in her life of crime than sharing the love of her parents.

Her narrowed eyes settled on her guard, Mr. Mercenary as she'd taken to calling him in her mind. He stood with one foot braced against the wall, his rifle held loosely by his side. He carried a knife and a sidearm, both holstered on his hip. There was no way she could cross the room to him; he'd have to come to her.

She turned back to her desk and unrolled a spool of thin wire. Pretending great diligence, she clumsily attempted to attach one end of the wire to the voltage meter while holding the other taut, dropping it and swearing repeatedly. In her head, a vision of herself waving a banana at a monkey almost made her laugh. She pasted the best fake expression of absent-minded frustration on her face she could manage and turned.

"Could you hold the other end a second while I attach this?" She waved the roll of wire and turned back, pretending to try to attach it again while holding the wire out flat. It curled back up, and she swore.

Mr. Mercenary snickered and sauntered over. He grabbed the wire roll she handed him.

"Great, thanks." She connected the wire to the box. Trying to neither tense nor telegraph her moves she dropped the screwdriver at his feet.

He leaned over, keeping the wire taut in one hand to grab the screwdriver.

She struck, slamming the hot soldering iron into the side of his neck with one hand while reaching for his face with the other. Her foot kicked his ankles, making him stumble forward. She released the iron and used both hands to push his face hard into the desk. The smell of burnt meat filled the air. Hot blood steamed on contact with the iron.

"Bi — his words cut off with a gurgling moan. Blood spurted from his mouth, covering the desk.

Denali glanced at the door. She was using her weight to press him into her desk, but he made no resistance. She wasn't taking any chances. Still leaning hard on his back, she grabbed his sheathed knife and slit his throat.

The coppery odor of fresh blood filled the room, covering the smell of burnt meat. Denali snatched up the wire from the spreading pool of blood. Slick with blood, her hands slipped from the metal latch of the small door used to empty ash and clean the chimney. To open the door, she had to wrap her hands in her sweatshirt.

The door opened with a loud squeal, making her heart pound hard. She'd bet the chimney would fit her, Frank might assume she'd check if she got the chance and if it didn't fit, his lies would be betrayed, if they were lies, she was still undecided.

A sigh of relief escaped her when she stuck her head inside. She ran back to her desk and grabbed the wire cutters and the screwdriver from the floor. The laptop cord in hand, she grabbed Mr. Mercenary's gun and threaded it on the cord then knotted the ends and put it around her neck. She kicked off her sneakers and tied the laces, stuffing her socks and tools inside them and placed them around her neck, then returned to the small metal door.

The bolt on the outside of the door ratcheted back. Denali fumbled for the knife she'd dropped, certain she wouldn't make the door before the man there entered.

Blood coated her shirt and face, never mind the corpse at her feet. He'd know instantly she'd killed one of them.

Her frantic gaze darted to the chimney as the door began to swing open.

Police sirens approached in the street. The door stayed half open. She hesitated. Go to the door and tie it closed, or go for escape? Running footsteps heading away decided her. Booted feet thudded down the attic stairs. She ran to the door. Low voices came to her through the thin crack of the open door.

"— The neighbors but get outside and watch the back. If it looks like they're coming for us, we'll waste the bitch and get the hell out."

"We should take her with us," Steve hissed. "She got that shit working in no time. Imagine what she could do with enough incentive."

The two men continued to argue over killing her as she eased the door closed and tied it, wiping her sweating brow on her sleeve.

Outside the sirens continued to blare but at a distance. Whatever was happening wasn't happening here. Hope surged. If she could get outside or even attract attention, the police were close.

She dragged the extension cord in which the soldering iron was plugged to the small boarded up vent under the eaves and jammed the iron beneath it. Given enough time, the wood would catch. Hopefully, the smoke that ensued would bring the police here. Even if she were trapped in the chimney, she'd have a chance of living through a house fire.

A chance was better than staying here for a sure to be horrid fate.

For a minute, she didn't think she could force her shoulders through the small, metal door of the chimney. Adrenaline made her hands shake. Light, eddies of smoke drifted to her. Fear made her breath come in hard pants, and she had to fight not to cough.

She squirmed headfirst through the tight opening, having to hunch her shoulders and hold her breath. The flue was wider than the opening, a shaft that reached from the basement to the roof. Light streamed in below her from the fireplace there. Above her, only a dark patch of sky showed. If she fell, she'd be hurt if not killed outright.

Her ribs protested the hunched position with sharp stabs of pain. With her toes, she swung the door closed. She couldn't close it all the way or latch it, but hopefully, her absence baffled them for a few minutes if they entered soon. Every minute they delayed allowed her to get further away. She braced her back against the wall and pushed herself upward with her legs.

Press, slide her feet up, release the pressure on her back, and slide her body up. Press, slide, release, she inched her way up. Soot coated her hands and feet and turned her white clothing black. The smell of rotted, burnt wood surrounded her, overlaying the scent of blood from her hands. Cold water oozed down the left side of the chimney, soaking her shirt and making her shiver. Her sneakers flopped against her chest with the gun.

Above her, a slice of brighter darkness grew

closer with maddening slowness. With relief, she grasped the edge and pulled herself out. She'd thought there might be a trap or sensor here or even a bomb, but there was nothing. Brick crumbled and trickled onto the roof. A few pieces fell inside, tumbling along the interior of the chimney. She hoped they landed in the basement, not the main floor.

A light dusting of snow covered the roof. She sat and put on her sneakers, using the wire cutters to cut a strip from her sweat-shirt to tie the tools to before crawling to the edge and peering over. Large holes gaped in the shingles, revealing half-rotted plywood. She was afraid to step on it and fall through.

Overhead, the moon gave enough light to show another house in similar condition just feet away. Beyond the house lay an empty weed-covered lot and beyond that a low cement building. None had lights on. To her left, an apartment complex towered over the back of the house. Lights lit windows and distant music filtered to where she crouched.

A dark street before the house connected to a better lit one about a quarter of a mile away in either direction. Lights flickered in the windows of the house to the right. Another smaller, dark house stood next to it. Dilapidated housing lined the opposite side of the street. Some had lights, some not. Trash and litter were caught in broken down fences. Old cars sat in driveways or before the houses.

Five houses away, across the street, loud music

played, the deep bass thump traveling to where she crouched, felt more than heard. Two expensive cars were parked in front, and bright light lit the yard. A dog laid on the stoop chained to a cable that crossed the yard. A police car was parked in front of a red Camaro. The siren was off now, but the roof lights lit the yard in red and blue swirls. Another police cruiser approached with its lights off. The four officers conferred.

No one walked the dark street. She didn't know if the late hour or rough neighborhood dissuaded them.

On her stomach, she peered over the edge of the house into the yard. Two men carrying Uzis and wearing black armor crouched behind a half-filled dumpster on the edge of the driveway.

If she signaled, the police would be killed before they even realized they were in danger.

She crawled to the other edge and peered over to search the backyard. A rickety privacy fence bordered by overgrown hedge lined the entire back. She saw no one, but someone could easily be on the back steps and hidden from her view by the overhang.

A slight whiff of smoke reached her. Crouched, she ran across the roof, staying on the ridgeline to avoid the weaker rotting patches where the roofing had blown off and never been replaced. Back on her stomach, she peered up and down the street. Behind the police car, someone dressed all in black, including a face mask ran between two houses kitty-corner from where she lay. She didn't know if it were related to the police or the terrorists.

The police car pulled her like a magnet, but it was too dangerous to call to them. The two men with guns waited. She eased backward, testing each step as she backed up to be sure it could bear her weight before stepping on it. She took two deep breaths and sprinted forward, jumping the five-foot gap and landing on the roof of the house next door. Again, testing each section first, she crossed the roof, pausing to examine the ground below her for armed men in hiding.

Smoke billowed from the attic now. Any minute the men in the house were sure to notice. She wished now she hadn't lit the fire. If the police noticed first and approached, they'd be killed before they had a chance to explain their presence. She needed a phone to warn them off. A muffled, ironic laugh escaped her. Here she was worried about them while she was stuck on a rooftop and being hunted by terrorists.

An aluminum drain pipe connected to the back of the house with rusty screws and angled brackets. It rattled when she shook it but seemed solid enough. Every moment she expected men to erupt from the house she'd just escaped from, but it remained quiet. She hung from the roof with her hands and put her legs on the pipe, squeezed with her knees, released the roof, and began shimmying down the pipe, using the brackets to grip with her feet.

With a grinding screech, the pipe broke free from the wall. Denali grasped the rotted wood siding with both hands, letting herself slide down the pipe, ignoring the rough splinters cutting her hands. Beneath her, the pipe buckled with a metallic crunch. She peered over her shoulder then pushed off hard and rode the pipe to the ground ten feet away. The ease with which she'd escaped the house convinced her Frank had been telling the truth.

A dog barked, and a man yelled for it too quiet as she crashed to the ground, landing on her back in the weed-covered field. She winced as she pushed herself up. Thick weeds had cushioned her fall, but the brush was sharp. Swearing under her breath, she worked her way from the overgrown yard, leaving a trail a two-year-old could follow.

She debated knocking on a door but didn't know who was involved and more importantly wanted to give the FBI time to do whatever it was going to. In the shadow of a rusty Impala, she crouched and examined the road. Her gaze returned to the Impala, she could hotwire it if she could break open the dash. A car this old wouldn't have electronic locks and likely no alarm.

She wondered why no agents hid in the shadows ready for her. Surely, they monitored the house somehow. Maybe they were afraid their presence would scare her and hinder her escape. It wasn't like they could walk the street wearing jackets emblazoned with FBI to reassure her. Thoughtfully, she turned back to where she'd seen the person in black. Maybe that had been an agent. She shrugged;

she really didn't care; she could get herself away.

The lack of agents made her doubt Frank again though. Maybe he thought she'd trust him to get her out and stay. Or maybe he thought Anne's presence would keep her there despite Anne's intentions. She growled and shook her head; it didn't matter what Frank thought, what mattered was escaping. The whoop-whoop of a siren startled her. On her hands and knees, she slunk to the edge of the car and hunkered beside the tire to peek down the street. The first police car peeled away. At the intersection, he hit his siren and pulled into traffic. Apparently, they'd received another call.

"Go," she murmured, willing the other officer to follow. While she watched, a man dressed in a white, wife-beater T-shirt and baggy jeans exited the house and got into the Camaro. The police officer let him leave without approaching him. From where she crouched, she couldn't see the side of the house where she'd left the iron going, but no thick trails of smoke marred the night sky.

They must've found it and her gone by now. It must be killing them to be confined in the house by a single police car.

"Don't get cocky," she murmured to herself. They were likely outside searching for her. While she worried over the officers, she gave them time to find her.

She returned to the yard, scouring the ground for a rock she could use to break the car window.

TWENTY-EIGHT

Yes

"Denali?"

The soft whisper whipped her around. She dropped to a crouch and raised her hands as her ribs protested then sighed in relief and relaxed her tense shoulders.

"Lee."

She stopped speaking and crouched even lower when he gestured for silence. His presence reassured her. If he were here, she was safe.

On the corner of a house across from her, her brother stared in the direction of the house she'd come from. He wore black camouflage with a bulletproof vest and carried a forty-five with a silencer on the end. A pushed-up face mask revealed his worried expression. He tapped the radio on his shoulder with his chin and spoke too softly for her to hear.

She startled and swung when someone touched her arm.

"Shh— it's just me," Shiloh said and hugged her. "What the hell were you thinking?" Without waiting for her to answer, he pulled her down the street.

A black van approached from the far end of the street. Shiloh glanced both ways, then ran toward it, dragging her. Her brother Danxia opened the door and offered her a hand to enter. Shiloh followed, sliding the door closed. Her mother drove them down the street.

Denali knelt and peered out the mirrored back window. Two houses passed the one she'd escaped from, a black-clad man ran into the street. Denali's breath caught. Ryan.

Hester pulled the van over, parking before a dilapidated house with lights on in the upstairs window and a blue flicker of television in the front window downstairs.

"There are two armed men in the yard and more in the house," Denali said in rising panic. She scrambled to the front and peered out, but Lee had vanished. "Can you call them off?" Heart pounding, she reached for Shiloh's radio.

Shiloh held up a hand blocking her and pressed his headset closer. "Lee sees them."

Denali rushed to the back window in time to see Ryan leap to the top of the dumpster. The red light from the police car illuminated his furious expression for the brief second he remained in sight.

Danxia grabbed her shoulder and yanked her back when she reached for the door handle.

Two men ran from the house two doors down. She recognized Raul. Her father appeared from between two houses and intercepted the men. He wore his black silk training clothing with his jian sheathed on his back. A twenty-two snub-nosed revolver was clutched in the hand he wasn't using to push Raul back. Too far to make out what they said, the heated nature of the conversation was clear by body language.

All three men turned towards the dumpster. Gui began running, surprising graceful for a man of his advanced years.

"Da," Denali moaned as he disappeared behind a falling down fence. Only Shiloh's firm grip on her arm kept her in the car.

"They're fine. Stay right here," Danxia said.

Denali glanced at the police car. The officer surely couldn't miss all these armed men darting about. The car remained stationary, the sirens silent with the light going. Lights reflected off the closed windows making it impossible to see what, if anything, the officer was doing.

Ryan rolled into the street, struggling with one of the armored men, Gui followed and hit the man with the hilt of his sword. He and Ryan dragged the man behind the dumpster again but this time on the opposite side from the house. Both men turned towards the house.

Raul and his partner flashed their badges. Gui smacked Raul's hand away and ran back down the street. Ryan loped towards the van

She opened the back door and pulled him inside, falling to her knees and crying.

"I'm so sorry. Please don't be mad."

"You should be sorry. How could you do that to me?" He kissed her cheek, then her lips, running his hand through her dirty hair. "You scared us to death."

"I didn't know they were going to take me. I wouldn't have let them."

Danxia knelt beside her with a bag of medical supplies. "Are you hurt? Is any of this blood yours?" he pulled her from Ryan's arms and shone a flashlight over her.

"Just scrapes and bruises." She wiggled away from her brother, needing to feel Ryan and know he forgave her.

Ryan pulled her into his lap and clutched her to his chest. He nudged the radio on his shoulder with his chin. "Break off."

The police car parked before the home pulled away from the curve, following them.

"What happened?" he smoothed her hair as she cried.

To her dismay, she cried harder until she was sobbing on his shoulder.

"We're together now, it's okay," he murmured,

burying his fingers in her hair and pressing his cheek against hers.

"Anya will pick up your father and Zane," Hester said.

Denali cried harder. Her family had come for her, afraid to trust the authorities, they'd come themselves.

"Is everyone safe?" She forced out between sobs.

"Meteora has taken the younger kids into hiding with Clare," Hester said. "None of us know where. Can you tell us what's going on?"

"They have Anne," Denali gasped out through her tears.

"No. Anne went to them." Hester said, sounding angry and grim. "Agent Bowden contacted us and played us a recording of Anne speaking with her boyfriend, planning our murders and laughing. She's going to spend a long time in jail if those men don't kill her first." Her mother peered at her in the rear-view mirror. "All her choice, Daughter. She'd rather be the center of attention for a bad man then share the love of good people. Let her go and good riddance."

Denali cried on Ryan's shoulder, her mother's words not comforting her.

Hester sighed. "Anne was a poor choice right from the beginning. I thought like Danxia, we could help her despite her rough start, but I was wrong because unlike Danxia, she didn't want help. She liked being bad, the attention, the false power of it and was too lazy to try to change. I wish we'd found

her when she was a baby to teach her better, but…
Nine was too old to change her ways. Dad and I
couldn't love her enough to overcome her anger no
matter how hard we tried."

Denali wiped her face on her filthy sleeve and
breathed deeply, trying to stop the tears. Ryan took a
cloth from Danxia and wiped her face. His tenderness
made her tear up again, and she clutched him,
burying her face in his neck.

"I need you." The words emerged mumbled,
barely audible. How he'd become so important to her
in so short of time remained a mystery. The guilty,
sick feeling of betrayal made her shake.

"I know. I need you too. I came as soon as I could.
Together forever, Denali." The wild beating of her
heart slowed as Ryan rocked her. He forgave her. She
hadn't broken them with her choices. Her shaking
eased, soothed by his continuing love.

"What happened?" he murmured.

"I don't really know." She sat and wiped her face
again, forgetting her shirt was soot-covered and
smearing black across her damp cheeks. "Jerome
Kensky bought us coffee from the vendor by the
science building and slipped something in mine. We
were walking to Maria Stata when I felt sick, and he
started talking all crazy. Before I could do anything,
he grabbed my phone. The next thing I knew, I was
tied in a basement somewhere."

Ryan pressed her harder against him, the contact
comforting despite her sore ribs.

"We saw the pictures. God, I was terrified for you."

Pain and fear were clear in his voice. Denali kissed his cheek, comforting him steadying her. "Raul's partner was there when I woke again. Not Matt, the other one. They call him Frank; I have no idea what his real name is. He told me I could escape using the chimney." Her breath hitched and her head lowered. "He asked me to help them."

"Help them do what?" Ryan sounded angry again.

"Find out if Greer's invention worked. It does, but not well. He asked me to lie and make a fake so they could track the buyers. The CIA asked them to leave me there to give them time."

"Dai knew?" Shiloh sounded sick.

"I don't know."

"Supposedly Dai is on assignment. He won't lie to his mother; I'll ask him. I don't think he knew. To let his family suffer like that..." Hester trailed off.

"I didn't know if Frank was telling me the truth or if it was a trick to get me to work on the receiver. He told me the terrorists had a nuclear weapon and the FBI needed time to find it and smuggled the chip in for me. I'm sorry I didn't go the first chance I got, but if we could catch them all, we'll all be safer."

"How long, Denali?"

The cold question sent chills up her spine and made her sweat.

"The day I got there he told me about the chimney," she said in a small voice.

"Days. You let me think you were dead or worse for days."

His hurt disbelief was a lance in her chest. "I'm very sorry."

"Would you do it again?"

"Ryan…" She pulled back and searched his face.

He stared at her impassively.

Tears filled her eyes and trailed across her cheeks again. "Please? I hated hurting you. I hate the thought I'll do something you can't forgive, but how could I not try to stop them?"

He sighed and smiled sadly. "You couldn't." His anger fled, leaving him looking heartbroken. He rested his forehead on hers, his breath misting her face, cool on her tears. "I understand and forgive you, but it hurt so bad."

"It hurt me too," she whispered.

Ryan shuddered and tucked her face against his shoulder, brushing her temple with his lips. "So, now what?"

"I don't know."

"Lee has to get back to his unit. I'll go with him," Shiloh said

"Is he AWOL?" Denali turned to Shiloh.

"Yes, but not long. It shouldn't be more than a slap on the wrist." As Shiloh spoke, he took his phone from his pocket and began typing. "I'll get us on the next flight back to California and contact his CO. Your kidnapping made the news. His boss should cut him some slack for that."

"How did you find me?"

Ryan grunted, clearly still angry over the need to search for her. "We followed Raul and Matt. They led us right to you. They're parked nice and cozy three houses away."

Ryan fished his phone from a pocket and hit a speed dial. "I've got her, Dad. You can stand down. And thanks. He hit another button. I've got her, Jeff. Tell the guys thank you and send them home." He kissed Denali's brow. "We had backup waiting. I'm glad we didn't need them."

"Me too," Denali said in a small voice.

A shudder traveled her. Her family would've broken into that house to get her back. They might've all been killed. By risking herself, she risked them all. Tears again trailed down her cheeks as her breath caught on a choking sob.

"Everyone is fine. And we wouldn't have rushed in like savages," Hester said.

Ryan laughed quietly, his chest rumbling under her cheek. She relaxed against him, letting him comfort her with his presence. She woke when the van reached her house and was surprised she'd fallen asleep. Ryan lay on the floor of the van beneath her. A rough wool blanket covered them.

"Lee," Hester said in a mixture of pride and exacerbation, waking Denali.

"My team, Mom," Lee said with laughter in his voice.

"I figured as much," Hester said.

Denali knelt to stare from the window. Two men waited on the front steps. Another joined them as Denali watched. All three wore jeans and black sweatshirts.

Lee exited before Denali and greeted the three men who waited with fist bumps.

"Idiot, don't ever do that again," the big black man said and punched Lee's shoulder.

The smaller blond man pulled him away.

"Your sister is safe?" He peered into the back of the van and his lips tightened.

Denali brushed futilely at her filthy clothing. "I'm fine. Thank you for coming," she said as she exited.

"Dan Barstow." The blond man extended his hand. He jerked a thumb at the black man." This is Tom, and that's Keith. We're your brother's partners."

Keith nodded in acknowledgment, but pulled a cell phone from his pocket and turned away to speak quietly.

Lee said, "Where's Ronny? He didn't come?"

"In Boston with JT, Squirrel, and Cameron." We came here to make sure your family was safe while they went to look for Denali. I'm glad you found her."

"Stupid to come without us," Tom muttered but offered his hand to Denali, then her family.

"They're my family, man," Lee said.

"We're your family too, stupid." Tom punched his shoulder again, then sighed hard and gave him a quick hug.

"All in; all the time," Keith said and slapped

Tom's back.

Denali glanced at Ryan who grinned and shook the proffered hands.

"Thanks. I'm glad we didn't need the help, but I appreciate you coming."

Denali linked her arm with his and nodded.

"I'll arrange a plane," Hester said as she offered her hand. "I'm so glad my son has such good friends. I'll call and speak to your commander personally."

She glided up the stairs and through the door Wilma Collins, the housekeeper, held open.

A flush covered Denali's cheeks as she turned back to her brother's teammates. "I hope I don't get you into trouble."

"Nothing we can't handle," Tom said as Dan smiled and shrugged.

Keith rose an eyebrow at Dan. "If you'll excuse us, we have some things to take care of."

Dan nodded slightly.

"I'll call and arrange a meet," Lee said and slung an arm around Denali's shoulder.

The three men headed, not to the street, but behind the house.

"Let them go," Lee whispered when Denali opened her mouth. "They must have weapons somewhere... It's better not to ask."

She snapped her lips closed and smiled tightly.

"And you're all going to catch shit when you return." Shiloh shook his head but grinned at Lee. "I'll take you all back. Shower, shave, and put on a clean uniform," he added as he took the front steps two at a time. "We catch a plane in thirty-five minutes.

Lee kissed her cheek and ran after his brother. "Call me; I want to hear everything. I love you."

"I will. I love you too," Denali called after his retreating back.

❋ ❋ ❋

Two nights later, the family was gathered in the media room for the five o'clock news. Denali flopped on the couch and closed her eyes. Ryan sat beside her and took her hand. The police had questioned her for hours followed by the FBI and agents from the CIA. She was exhausted.

She'd just gotten home and had barely had time to eat and shower. Again, the news logo played with the words special report flashing in bold print across the screen.

"Good evening, this is Ronald Hill, bringing you a special report," the man on the screen said. "Late last night, the FBI rounded up a group of men in connection with the bombing of Olympus."

Behind Ronald, footage played of men wearing FBI emblazoned vests bursting in the doors of the home where Denali had been kept. SWAT surrounded the home and helicopters hovered overhead. Police cars and black vans lined the streets.

Police sirens and helicopters hovering overhead almost muffled the sounds of gunfire from inside the house as SWAT swarmed it.

Ronald let the footage play without commentary, then rewound it and played it again without volume as he did his commentary.

"Eighteen men were apprehended and are expected to be charged with the kidnapping of Delilah Rubenstein-Wong who escaped and led police to the house. Plans were found in the house leading to the arrest of five other men in Pennsylvania in possession of explosives and the blueprints of a school in Connecticut. The arrests haven't ended in America. The Pakistan government has arrested three hundred and fourteen men, and more arrests are expected.

"Three explosions have destroyed what has been described as terrorist training camps, two in the north of Pakistan, and one in western Afghanistan. The death toll has not been confirmed, but pictures show a number of dead bodies.

The picture behind Ronald changed to a long-distance aerial view. "As you can see, satellites show a large crater. Careful examination will show casualties in the burning wreckage. Experts agree the missile that destroyed them was their own. Satellites tracked a launch, the missiles turned at a mile out and returned to the launch position.

Denali slapped a hand over her mouth and giggled.

Ryan rose an eyebrow.

"Monkeys with light switches," she said muffled by her hand.

Hester laughed.

"What did you do?" Zane asked.

"They never really checked the program, just what the screens said. I wrote the program to show whatever frequency was programmed was accepted, but what it really did was target the sender. I wasn't sure it would work; I never got the chance to test it."

"Can they use that to hijack missiles if they fix your programming?" Gui asked in concern.

"Now that we know how it works, no. It's a simple programming change to block access. Al-Jadr was trying to get us to send a nuke at them to hijack and use it against us. What they'd planned for those children was horrifying. And not just those children. Their goal was World War Three, to cause such fear and anger the United States would attack in a fury so they could steal our bombs and turn them back at us before we changed the code."

"Jesus," Zane breathed, staring at the screen in horror.

Ronald Hill gestured at the screen, which showed mug shots of the captured terrorists. Anne's picture flickered on the screen. Soon the press would realize her connection, but as of right now, she was an unidentified terrorist. The press was sure to hound them mercilessly when the truth became known. Denali winced and squeezed her mother's hand.

She'd lost two daughters irretrievably.

Her mother patted her hand. "Anne was lost to us long ago." Her glance swung to Gui. "The recording hurt. We'd harbored hope that time would bring her back to us. Now… she's killed our love. In my heart, Anne is no longer my daughter but a stranger." Hester's voice roughened, and tears filled her eyes. "We mourn the little girl we had such hopes for."

Denali kissed her mother's cheek and turned to Zane who listened with a horrified expression as Ronald Hill told America what Al-Jadr had planned for them.

"They know it doesn't work now, Zane. There'd be no point to inciting us if they can't hijack a nuke. They never had their own, they planned to use ours against us. A brilliant plan if they hadn't botched it."

"You're sure it won't work?"

"Positive." Denali tapped her forehead. "It's all up here."

Zane turned back to the television, a hard smile on his face.

On the screen behind Ronald Hill, the camera panned over the crater, which was all that remained of the terrorist training camp in Afghanistan.

"You sure did put a dent in them," Zane said.

Ryan snickered.

Zane glanced at him and laughed.

Denali rolled her eyes.

"They'll be all torn up over this," Ryan said.

Denali groaned. "Don't encourage him."

Ryan winked at Denali.

A smirk on his face, Zane leaned back in his seat. "They'll be piecing together what happened for a long time."

Ryan laughed as Gui stood and offered a hand to Hester.

"We can all sleep sounder tonight," Gui said. "There will always be bad men, but this group got what it deserved."

On screen, Ronald added six more names to the list of people arrested in the United States.

"I'm sick of this," Ryan said and stood. "I want to get married."

"Now?" Denali stared at him in shock. He seemed serious.

"Yes. I know a judge who owes us a favor." His brilliant blue eyes met hers hopefully.

She grinned and offered him her hand.

"Yes."

THE END

About the Author

C. M. Conney lives and works on the family farm in New England alongside her husband and two grown children. She loves animals and owns more than she'd like to admit. Most days, when she isn't baking or planting, she spends her time writing. An avid reader since childhood, she appreciates work in all genres and likes to mix it up a bit in her own work.

You can find out more about C. M. Conney and her
writing on her
Amazon Author Page or at acelyonbooks.com